PROPHECY:

THE DREAMLANDS

PROPHECY:

THE DREAMLANDS

Book two of the Brotherhood of the Star trilogy.

By Andrew Lawrenson

Published by Pyrian Publishing

Prophecy: The Dreamlands

ISBN 978-1-910980-03-3 (Kindle)
ISBN 978-1-910980-04-0 (Paperback)
ISBN 978-1-910980-05-7 (Hardback)

Published by Pyrian Publishing
info@pyrian.co.uk

2 4 6 8 10 9 7 5 3 1

For Carol and Ian

"Men of broader intellect know that there is no sharp distinction betwixt the real and the unreal; that all things appear as they do only by virtue of the delicate individual physical and mental media through which we are made conscious of them"

    — H.P. Lovecraft, "The Tomb"

Prologue.

A man dressed in thick black robes glided silently along the unlit corridor, stepping quickly into the open doorway. His name was Aloysius and he had waited for this moment for a long time; he would be denied no longer.

The room he found himself in was cold, silent and empty. He looked quickly over his shoulder and then strode hastily across the room, his black robe making him almost invisible in the dim light. When he reached the plain brick wall on the far side, he stopped. Slowly, he ran his hands up and down over the bricks, feeling the rough surface under his fingertips, scanning from left to right until he found what he was after – a small piece of stone unlike the others, smooth and cold to the touch. He pressed down hard on the stone, pushing it into the wall until it slid to one side behind the others revealing a small metal lever; he grasped it in one hand and twisted it firmly.

For a moment nothing happened, but then a low rumbling noise started to grow. The wall to his left slid to the side with a grating noise, opening to reveal a hidden room. As he stepped inside, a wide smile spread across his face; finally he had found what he had been searching for all these years.

An obsidian altar sat in the shadows beneath a huge black painting on the wall: a crude depiction of a goat's head surrounded by a forest of trees.

A tall statue carved from jet-black stone stood atop the altar, the figure of a hideous goddess with the head and legs of a goat, horns curling from her head like tentacles. Before her lay two metal orbs, each resting on a recess built into the stone.

He stepped nervously into the room and stopped before the altar; he was not surprised to find himself sweating with fear and apprehension, even on this cold night. He looked down at the jet-black surface and could see a circular band of inscriptions etched into its surface around each of the orbs. They were written in an ancient language, thought by many to be extinct and known only to a select few.

He nervously reached forwards, running his fingers over the inscriptions. He was one of the few who could understand these words, surely carved into this altar when the world was a much younger place. He smiled as he read the secrets revealed beneath his fingertips – these were indeed what he was after.

He extended his hand towards the first of the orbs. It was about three inches in diameter, its surface etched with minute engravings of signs and sigils, the shapes interlocking to form a cohesive pattern that covered the entire surface. He ran his fingertips over the cold metal and felt an almost primal surge of energy coursing through his body. *They were too weak to use these properly*, he thought to himself, too scared of their power and too ignorant of their true potential, but he would show them. Under his rule, the order would be great again; there would be nothing they could not achieve.

He muttered a low prayer to the dark goddess under his breath before reverentially lifting the two orbs from their resting places, taking one in each hand. Then he stepped backwards again, giving a brief bow before the altar and to the statue standing upon it. His head lowered, he took another step back into the doorway and turned, only to stop in his tracks.

Standing before him were a dozen men, the two at the front brandishing long scimitars. They parted to reveal the high priest standing behind them, dressed in his ceremonial green robes.

'I have suspected your treachery for some time, but now your betrayal is clear for all to see,' he pronounced in a booming voice for all to hear. 'Seize him!'

Two muscular men stepped forwards to grab him. Aloysius tried to duck backwards as they reached for him, but they grasped him by the arms, pulling him forwards and forcing him to his knees. As he dropped to the floor, one of the armed men placed the tip of his sword at his throat. The high priest bent forwards, carefully taking the metal orbs from the man's hands and stepping into the hidden chamber, reverentially resting them back in their rightful places on the altar.

'Take him to the temple and restrain him,' he called softly, not looking back. He knelt on the floor before the altar, bowing his head low. 'I will deal with him momentarily.'

The high priest stood on the dais at the rear of the temple, his head bowed and his hands clasped together before him.

Hanging in front of him, attached to two tall wooden stakes by a sturdy set of chains and manacles, was Aloysius. His long hair was matted to his face by sweat and he had been stripped to the waist. There were deep red cuts up and down the length of his back, still bleeding from where he had been savagely whipped.

'Your betrayal of our order has been witnessed by all,' the high priest spat at him, before turning to face the congregation kneeling before him. These men were all dressed in similar dark green robes, although not as grand as the high priest's; they uttered a low chant in hushed tones as they prostrated themselves on the floor before him. 'For your sins, you are to be forever cast out from this place, never to return.'

He picked up the two metal orbs that sat upon the altar, brought forth from their resting place for this ritual, and held them high in the air, in supplication to his dark goddess. He held them high above his head for all his followers to see and then started to chant, his voice low and sepulchral. As he began to recite the ancient words, a breeze picked up within the confines of the temple, the air swirling around the priest and Aloysius. Sparks jumped between the two orbs as he held them aloft.

The strength of the wind started to increase, and the congregation intensified their own chanting to match. The priest's shouts grew louder, struggling to be heard over the violent rush of air as he called forth to the heavens. As his voice reached a crescendo, two bolts of electricity leapt from the orbs, merging into one and striking Aloysius in the chest. His body jerked with brief but violent spasms before collapsing, hanging limp from the chains.

All at once, the wind disappeared, leaving only dust hanging in the air and a faint smell of ozone. One by one, the priest's followers stopped their chanting and looked up at the priest and Aloysius.

'The banishment is complete,' the high priest called to his congregation. He stepped forwards, looking down at Aloysius with scorn on his face. 'You will tell me everything about your duplicity and all of those who have acted alongside you,' he said. 'Once you have revealed all your secrets to me, your body here will be destroyed. If you do not resist, I will at least make it a swift death for you.'

'I will tell you nothing,' muttered Aloysius as he hung from the chains before he spat on the floor by the priest's feet.

The priest knelt down next to him. 'You will have no choice in the matter,' he whispered in his ear, bringing the two metal orbs to either side of Aloysius's forehead. As they made contact, his body jerked as if being electrocuted, his muscles straining against the restraints. 'You will tell me who revealed our secrets – exactly who has betrayed us – and the names of all those who stand alongside you.'

Aloysius's body twisted, his muscles straining as his body was wracked with pain, but he was powerless to resist as the power of the orbs flowed through his head.

'It... was... Eunan,' he groaned between clenched teeth.

A cruel smile spread across the high priest's face, but was immediately replaced by an expression of alarm as the wooden doors of the temple burst open with a crash, a mob of men in black robes and hoods swarming through the door. The worshippers who knelt on the floor started to get to their feet but the intruders were coming in too fast. Crossbow bolts were unleashed towards the first two men to stand. They fell backwards as the bolts hit them, crimson circles spreading out around the wooden shafts that now protruded from their chests. Other intruders charged forwards through the doorway wielding swords. They swept them through the air with the grace of those well practised in the art of war, their foes falling to the floor at their feet.

The high priest stepped backwards, grasping the metal orbs tightly in his hands, when a crossbow bolt sunk itself into his left shoulder. The orb in his hand fell from his grasp, dropping to the floor with a thud and rolling away. Panic on his face, he looked down at the orb and then turned to see a second intruder readying a loaded crossbow at him. He had no time to make a decision. He closed his eyes, a look of grim determination on his face; with barely a sound, he winked out of existence just as the bolt shot forth from the bow, flying through the space he had occupied just moments earlier and burying itself in the wall.

Another of the attackers darted across the room, sweeping the orb from the floor as he headed towards Aloysius. He drew to a halt before the limp body that hung from the chains. His hands moved fast, releasing the shackles that bound him, and Aloysius collapsed to the floor with a thump.

'Awake, master Aloysius,' he said, slapping the man gently on the cheeks. 'We have come to rescue you.'

In another time and another place, Aloysius jerked awake, sitting bolt upright. He was sitting on a straw mattress on the castle floor, drenched in sweat.

'It is too late,' he muttered to himself. 'I have failed.'

Chapter 1.

December 14th, 2012. Glasgow, Scotland.

Jack Knight was sitting with his head in his hands when the door opened. He had barely been in the interview room long enough to get comfortable, but was already glad of the change of scenery; apart from the first couple of interviews when he arrived, he'd spent most of the last twenty-four hours in a cold and cramped police cell.

He looked up to see a middle-aged man with short dark hair and a crumpled grey suit step in through the door. He pulled up a chair on the opposite side of the table, the metal legs of the chair making an irritating screech as they were dragged across the floor.

He sat down, dropping a beige folder thick with papers onto the table; the thud rang out in the small room. 'I'm Detective Inspector Watts,' said the man in a thick Glaswegian accent. 'You've made me quite a busy man tonight, Mr Knight.'

'What's happened to Detective Inspector Cross then?' asked Jack.

'She's no longer in charge of this case – I am,' replied Watts, 'although she's still assisting me. You'll be interested to know that she's corroborated at least *some* of your story.'

'Swell. She's put in a good word for me then?'

Watts smiled politely back at him and then looked down and rifled through his papers, before pulling one out and looking at it closely; from where he sat, Jack couldn't see what was on it. 'Why don't you tell me what happened last night? What you can remember of it.'

'For crying out loud,' said Jack with a sigh. 'You lot grilled me for hours. Surely you must have it all written out for you somewhere in that folder.'

'Just humour me. Go through it one last time.' He looked Jack firmly in the eyes. 'Why don't you start from the very beginning?'

Jack held the stare, looking back into the cold grey eyes of the detective, not letting his eyes wander. 'As I told your colleagues, it all started when I inherited my family house, and someone broke in looking for something. He was the first one of the cultists we ran into, but not the last – not by a long shot.'

'Do you know what he was looking for?'

'No,' lied Jack. 'We never found out. He was packing heat and Jennifer was trying to get away when there was a struggle. He ended up going over the banisters and broke his back – but she was only ever acting in self-defence. That was when we called the cops and Detective Inspector Cross first got involved. What we didn't know at the time was that the stiff was part of a cult. Not long afterwards, we contacted a historian, Ian Williams, to look into my family history. When he started investigating, he must have found out something that the cult didn't want anyone to know, and they bumped him off. We went to Ian's place to look for him and the hatchet man tried to snatch us too.'

'The *who*?'

Jack closed his eyes and took a deep breath; he was still having trouble readjusting to modern language, although it was slowly all coming back to him again. 'The killer.' he clarified. 'Presumably the same one who killed Ian. We managed to escape, but only through sheer dumb luck.'

Watts shuffled through his papers, pulling out another sheet and looking at it. 'That was the road accident in Oxford?' Jack nodded. 'Messy business,' he said, returning the sheet to his folder. 'Continue.'

'We tried to hide from them, but they kept coming after us. We decided to beat it, but even when we hooked it abroad to America, the cultists kept on coming – eventually kidnapping Jennifer and taking her back here to the Necropolis, where they were planning to kill her.'

He could see Watts roll his eyes whenever he used the word 'cultists', but he continued with his version of the events, trying to be consistent with his earlier statements. 'Through Ian Williams, I'd got in touch with a private dick, Peter White, who had helped him with his historical research and that kind of thing. He helped us try and find out what they were after – but not with much success. When Jennifer was taken, he offered to help me try to find her. We caught a lucky break when I remembered something and we both travelled back here.'

'What was it you remembered?'

'One of the cultists had mentioned the Necropolis,' lied Jack. He didn't think Watts would believe that he had seen it during a lucid dream. 'It meant nothing to me, but Peter correctly guessed it meant the graveyard here in Glasgow. We were trying to find Jennifer when they attacked us – that was when Peter was stabbed. They would have dropped me too if Detective Inspector Cross hadn't stepped in – you should give her a medal, by the way. I went down into the catacombs to try and find Jennifer and... Well, I can't remember what happened to me down there.' He'd told the lie so many times in the last twenty-four hours that he was almost starting to believe it himself. 'The last thing I remember was talking to Detective Inspector Cross.'

'Very convenient for you, I'm sure,' shrugged the detective.

'I'm being on the level with you here – I'd like to know as much as you,' replied Jack, sounding exasperated. 'I haven't gone *completely* crackers – something happened to me down there, God damn it. Hell, just *look* at me!'

Watts shrugged again. 'D.I. Cross concurs. She confirms the...' He paused as he considered what to say. '...the change in your physical condition.'

'You mean the fact that I went in a man in my early forties and came out looking like I'm in my fifties?' There had certainly been some confusion when Jack had returned to the surface, a decade older and sporting a thick beard. Detective Inspector Cross had even gone as far as taking his finger-prints to make sure he really was Jack and not some older relative. It was ironic, he had thought, considering the oil painting hanging above his stairs. With everything else that had been going on, he didn't know whether she'd noticed that he'd also come out wearing different clothes – something he'd decided not to point out.

Watts looked at him closely. Normally, he'd consider himself a good judge of character, but he was having trouble reading this particular suspect;

it was something about the way he spoke and acted. He kept using old-fashioned language – it was almost normal now, but the transcripts of his first
interviews read like a Raymond Chandler novel. 'Yes,' he finally replied. 'She
also confirmed that one of the men attacked you without provocation and
would have killed you if she hadn't stepped in. She seems to be willing to go
out on a limb to back you up. If you feel indebted to her, you should do her
the courtesy of telling us everything you know.'

Jack smiled and gave an almost imperceptible shake of his head as he
considered it. If he told them everything he knew about the Brotherhood of
the Star's plans to bring back their ancient gods and his own personal
journey, they'd think him insane. He should know; he'd had first-hand experience of being committed. No, they currently thought he was hiding
something, but that was better than them believing he was mad. Asylums
would be significantly better now than they had been a century ago, but he
still had no intention of returning to one.

'Look,' pleaded Jack. 'I've told you everything I know. If anything else
comes back to me, I promise I'll spill everything, but...'

Watts let out a small sardonic laugh and shook his head. 'You're even
less help than the other guy we captured.'

'What? You captured one of the cultists?'

'We captured one of the *men* who were involved. At the moment, we've
got no evidence of any cult.'

'Then why did they kidnap Jennifer?'

'Well, if he ever starts talking, I'll be sure to ask him.'

'How did you catch him? What happened?'

'You should remember – you were there. D.I. Cross apprehended the
man that attacked Peter White and was about to attack you.'

Jack nodded, remembering back to that night; by his internal calendar,
that had happened almost ten years ago. 'Of course,' he said. 'As I mentioned, my memory is a little hazy.' He thought for a moment. 'So no one
else came out of the tunnels before me?'

Watts eyed him curiously. 'Several men did come up out of the tunnels a
couple of minutes before you, just before the whole place started to collapse.
They rushed D.I. Cross, taking her by surprise, and there was a bit of a
scuffle. They managed to get away, but they didn't manage to take the prisoner with them. We've got him in a cell right now.'

'Is she okay?'

'Cross? She'll be fine. Just a few scrapes and bruises. Her ego took the biggest beating – she thinks she ought to have arrested a few more of them.'

'So, what about the cultist she *did* arrest? What's he had to say to explain himself?'

Watts seemed to ignore the use of the word this time. 'He refuses to talk – he hasn't said a single word since we arrested him, not even to ask for a lawyer.'

'Then he can't explain what happened either?'

'Can't or won't.' He looked Jack firmly in the eye. 'Something I'm getting a lot of.'

Jack ignored the insinuation. 'Do you know who he is?'

'He's got no ID, and his fingerprints aren't in the system. We're running his picture and DNA to see if we get a match, but... well, I'm not hopeful.' He pulled a photograph out of the folder and slid it across the table to Jack. It was a mug shot showing a man in his thirties with short black hair. Jack could recognize him as the man who had stabbed Peter White but no more. 'I don't suppose *you* can tell me who he is?'

Jack shook his head. 'Sorry.'

Silence hung over the pair of men and Jack slid the photograph back across the table. Detective Watts was eyeing him closely.

'So... what's the rap?'

'What?' Watts replied, a look of confusion on his face.

'What are you charging me with?'

'We've got a lot of options, but we're not sure any of them would stick. After that whole place collapsed, there's precious little physical evidence left behind, and as I said – no one's talking.' Watts picked up the photograph and placed it back in the folder, before letting out a long sigh. 'Look... while I'm convinced you broke the law along the way, I'm also fairly sure that you and your partner were ultimately the victims here. If it ever went before a jury, I'm sure you'd be found innocent in the court of public opinion. We've got you bang to rights on trespassing in the Necropolis, but well... in the grander scheme of things, that doesn't really seem worth it, does it?'

'What are you trying to tell me?'

'We're not pressing charges – *at the moment.*'

'So can I leave?'

Watts pulled back the sleeve of his jacket to look at his watch. 'We can only hold you for twenty-four hours without charging you, and that expired five minutes ago. You're free to go.'

Jack started to pull his chair back.

'But Mr Knight...'

'Yes?'

'We're going to want to talk to you again.' He smiled at Jack. 'I'd advise you to stay in the country this time if you don't want to harm your case. Consider yourself warned.'

Jack nodded and stood up. 'What about Jennifer?'

'She was also released a short while ago. I think she's waiting for you in reception.'

'And the cultist?'

'As to our *suspect* – with D.I. Cross's testimony, we've got him on attempted murder and can probably implicate him in the kidnapping of your partner... He's not going anywhere for a long while.' He stood up and walked over to the door. 'Come on – I'll show you out.'

Jack shuffled slowly down the corridor behind Watts and into the large reception area. He was exhausted, both mentally and physically – he had barely slept in the police cells. Hell, it must have been thirty-six hours since he last slept properly.

He felt weary, like he had an enormous weight bearing down on his shoulders, but as he stepped into the reception and saw Jennifer again, his weariness lifted and he sped up into a jog. She turned, seeing him approach across the room, and opened her arms, capturing him in a tight embrace.

'It's good to see you again,' Jack whispered in her ear as he held her tight in his arms. She had a large bandage on one cheek from where he had grazed her with a gunshot.

'You too,' said Jennifer. She kissed him and then resumed their embrace, holding each other tight. They had stood there for a good twenty seconds when they heard a cough from beside them. Jack took a step back and as he did so saw a familiar face standing next to them – Detective Inspector Cross, a wide smile on her face. She held out a hand towards Jack. He took it hesitantly and then gave it a firm shake.

'I think I owe you some thanks,' said Jack. 'I'm not sure I ever thanked you properly for saving my life back there.'

'Just doing my job. I'd like to say it's all in a day's work, but I'm not sure there's anything normal about what happened yesterday.'

'Welcome to *my* life,' Jack chuckled. 'Speaking of what happened back there, do you know how Peter's doing?'

'He's in intensive care. It looks like he's going to be okay, but it's still too early to say for sure. I think he needs some of your luck – you're one lucky son of a bitch.'

Jack looked across the room at his reflection in a window, at the grey hair and cold eyes that stared back at him. He managed a weak grin. 'From where I'm standing, it really doesn't feel that way.'

'Well, you're alive, and you've got Jennifer back.'

'I suppose that's what really matters,' he agreed.

'And you don't remember what happened to you down there?'

'No,' lied Jack. 'I remember talking to you and then going down those steps… and then the next thing I can remember is staggering out of there with Jennifer.' He looked at Jennifer as he said this, to avoid making eye-contact with Cross. Every time he told his story though, it became that much easier for him.

'And I was bound and gagged for most of the time,' added Jennifer. 'I couldn't tell what the hell was happening down there until Jack grabbed me and we got the hell out of there. We only just made it out before the whole place collapsed.'

'Well, I'm led to believe that amnesia is quite common after a severe and stressful experience,' said Cross. '*And convenient,*' she muttered under her breath, just loud enough to be heard.

Jack felt his cheeks flushing, but covered himself by giving Jennifer another hug and then kissing her.

Cross gave them a moment or two. 'Go home,' she said. 'Get some rest – you deserve it. Just don't go fleeing the country again – I'm sure someone's going to want to talk you again soon.'

'I know,' said Jack. 'Detective Inspector Watts has already warned me.'

Cross shook both their hands again. 'I know this has been a stressful situation for you both – but I've got to say... Next time, leave the heroics and vigilante justice at home.'

'Oh, trust me,' said Jennifer. 'There's not going to be a next time.'

Jack looked sheepishly at Cross. 'I don't suppose you could you do me another favour?' he asked.

Cross looked back at him with a surprised look on her face. 'What?' she asked.

'I don't suppose I can borrow some money to get home? I don't think either of us have our wallets or purses. I don't even have my car – we came up here in Peter's.'

Cross sighed. 'I can do better than that,' she said with a weak smile on her face. 'I've got to drive back to Exeter myself – I can give you a lift.'

Chapter 2.

December 14th, 2012. Dartmoor, England.

It was early in the evening when Jack and Jennifer arrived back at their house in Dartmoor, tired and exhausted. The journey back with Detective Inspector Cross had been long and uncomfortable in the back of her car. They had barely slept, and talked even less, the mood being decidedly awkward. Once they had arrived back in Exeter, she had arranged for a taxi to take them home from the police station.

Jack and Jennifer stood on the porch of their house in the evening twilight, watching the taxi disappear down the driveway. Jack put his hands into his trousers and came up empty-handed. 'Bloody hell,' he cursed. 'I forgot I didn't have any keys. I think I lost them back in France during the Great War,' he said with a little chuckle.

'Don't look at me,' exclaimed Jennifer. 'I haven't seen any of my possessions since the Brotherhood kidnapped me.'

Jack slowly walked around the house. It was shut up tight, all the doors and windows locked in place, just as they had left it.

'We could call a locksmith?' suggested Jennifer, as they stood on a patch of bare dirt behind the house.

'I don't have my mobile, and the house phone is... Well, it's in the house.'

Jack peered through the kitchen window. It was dark inside, but he could just make out that the key to the back door was in the lock.

'We could walk over to one of our neighbours,' suggested Jennifer, as Jack bent down and picked up a fist-sized rock from the floor.

'What are you doing?' she asked nervously.

Jack looked up and around at the house. 'It's changed a bit over the years since I last left here, but this is my *home*. I've travelled through space and time, faced unimaginable horrors and defeated an ancient cult. I'll be damned if I'm going to be stopped now by a locked door.' There was a loud crash as he brought the rock down onto the glass pane nearest the door handle, making Jennifer jump. He used the stone to carefully knock as many pieces of glass from the frame as he could, and then cautiously reached in through the empty space, being careful not to cut himself. With a twist of the key and a quiet click, the door unlocked. 'We can call a glazier in the morning,' he muttered, opening the door and stepping in, the broken glass crunching under his feet.

'Let me get a brush and help clean that up,' said Jennifer. '*Try* not to make any more mess than you already have.' She stepped into the pantry and returned moments later holding a dustpan and brush, which she held out to Jack.

'Do we *really* need to do this now?' he said with a sigh, but he took the dustpan and brush without waiting for an answer. He dropped to his knees, sweeping up the shards of glass while Jennifer locked the door again, removing the key from the lock and putting it in a drawer. When they had finished tidying up the mess, they slowly trudged up the stairs in unison.

Jennifer took hold of the door to the master bedroom but Jack put his hand on hers to stop her.

'If it's all the same to you, I'd rather sleep in one of the other bedrooms tonight,' he said. 'I could really do with a good night's sleep.'

'So... our bedroom's out of bounds now?'

'Only until I remove those carvings I made on the back of the head-board. It's nothing my electric sander can't deal with, just...'

'Just not tonight,' she agreed.

Jack nodded back. 'It can wait 'til the morning.'

In the main guest bedroom, they both stripped down to their underwear and climbed into the bed. Jack was asleep almost before his head hit the pillow.

Jack awoke the next day still feeling tired, his body stiff and aching all over. He rolled over and looked at the clock next to the bed. It was just past noon; he had slept for over sixteen hours. Jennifer was gone, already out of bed. With a deep groan and a large exertion of willpower, he pulled himself out of bed and stumbled into the bathroom. He stripped naked and stepped into the shower, letting the steam and hot water reinvigorate him. He stood there with his eyes shut, letting it flow over him until the hot water was exhausted and he was forced to get out.

He stood in the bathroom and wiped the condensation from the mirror, taking a long look at his reflection. With a sigh of resignation, he picked up a can of shaving foam, spraying a generous ball into the palms of his hands and applying it to his beard before picking up his razor.

When he was done, he looked at himself in the mirror. It had been a good few years since he had last been clean shaven. It wasn't the only change – a lot had happened to him over the last decade – but it was a good place to start. He had trouble remembering what he had been like so long ago, but it was gradually coming back to him. With his beard gone, he looked and felt younger, more like the man he had been when he had inherited this house. He hoped he wasn't too much of a stranger to Jennifer.

Dressed and refreshed, he headed downstairs in search of Jennifer. First, he headed for the kitchen. Finding it empty, he put the kettle on and made himself a cup of coffee. The rich taste refreshed his memories as much as his body; he hadn't had a decent cup since that fateful night. It was hard to believe that it was only two nights ago according to the calendar.

He wandered back out into the hallway with the mug in his hand and found Jennifer behind the closed door of the study, wearing her dressing gown and hunched over her laptop.

'What are you looking at?' he asked.

'There was something Silas said at the end,' she replied without looking up, 'a name.'

Jack thought for a second, and then nodded. 'Aloysius,' he muttered quietly.

'That's the one,' she said, turning to face him. 'I assume it doesn't mean anything to you?'

He shook his head. 'No. Nothing.'

'I've tried googling it, but it's useless – there are millions of hits. It's a common Latin name, and there are schools and churches using it all over the world. I was thinking about looking through the books in the basement to see if any of them mentioned it.'

'You're forgetting, baby – I've already read them all. From your point of view, they've been untouched for the best part of a century, but I only read them a year or two ago. I'm pretty sure I've never heard the name before.'

'I know you're still readjusting,' she said,' but don't call me *baby* – not unless you want me to keep referring to you as *old man.*'

'Duly noted,' he said, with a tap to his forehead.

'Oh well,' she sighed. 'With Silas dead, it looks like we'll never find out what was on his mind.' She closed the laptop and stood up, taking a better look at Jack. Without the beard, she thought he looked younger than last night, but still older than he had any right to be.

'Do you want to talk about it?' she asked, walking over and taking him by the hand. 'The time you spent there?' She thought for a second and then corrected herself. 'The time you spent...*then?*'

Jack looked her in the eyes. God, he had missed her. 'I'm not sure I'm ready just yet,' he said. 'Much of what I went through, I never want to have to deal with again. I'm sure a psychiatrist would say that's unhealthy for me, but what the hell do they know? They weren't there.' A small smile crept onto Jennifer's face as he looked at her. 'You should know something though. The one thing that kept me sane, the one thing that helped me keep my shit together... it was you.' Jennifer looked up at him. She could see he had a tear in his eye; she was misting up herself. 'I promised you I would rescue you, and I knew I couldn't let you down. I was the only one who could save you.'

Jennifer gave him a brief kiss on the lips and then wrapped her arms around him, nuzzling her cheek into his chest. 'Everything you went through... I only have a vague idea of what it was, but...' She looked him in the eyes again. 'You know I would never expect that of you. I would have forgiven you.'

'But I'm not sure I could have forgiven myself,' he whispered back to her, kissing her forehead softly.

They stood there silently for a moment before they released their embrace. Jack walked over to the window, looking out over the grounds and contemplating in silence for a moment. 'There is one possibility,' he finally said.

'I'm sorry?'

'The name Silas mentioned – Aloysius. We do have one possibility for working out who – or what – he meant.'

'What is it?'

'The cultist they arrested – he ought to know.'

'And you think he'll tell you? We didn't part on the best of terms.'

'Probably not,' he admitted with a shrug. 'But there's only one way to know for sure.' He walked back over to the desk, opened a drawer and rummaged through it until he found what he was after; the business card that Detective Inspector Cross had given them. 'Let's make a call and see what we can do.' He picked up the phone, rapidly dialling her number and then holding the phone to his ear. It rang several times before it was picked up.

'Detective Inspector Cross,' came her familiar voice.

'Hello, Detective. It's Jack Knight again.'

'My, my – I wasn't expecting to hear from you so soon. I don't suppose your memory has returned?' There was a definite edge of sarcasm in her voice.

'No, I'm afraid not,' he said apologetically.

'Then what's the call about, if you don't mind me asking?'

'Well... I was thinking about something Detective Inspector Watts said to me. About the man you arrested that night – you know who I'm talking about?'

'I am familiar with the man we have in custody, yes...' she replied. She sounded slightly sheepish. Jack wondered if she would have been blushing with embarrassment if they were holding this conversation face to face, annoyed that they only had the one of them.

'I'm sorry, of course you are,' he muttered. 'But with regards to my memory, I was thinking of something that might be helpful.'

'What would that be?'

'I'd like to speak with him. Maybe he can jog my memory.'

Jack could hear Cross exhaling a long breath on the other end of the line. 'He'll be remanded in custody somewhere by now.'

'You don't know where?'

'No, it's not really my case anymore. But I suppose I could find out.'

'That would be great –'

'I have to warn you though,' she interrupted, 'you can only visit him if he agrees to see you. He hasn't said a single word to us – what makes you think he'll want to talk to you?'

Jack thought for a moment. 'I don't know, but... well, what harm can it do – I've got nothing to lose. He can only say no.'

'It's a bit more complex than that,' replied Cross. 'Victims aren't normally allowed to meet their attackers prior to the trial. It might be possible, but I wouldn't hold my breath.' She didn't seem convinced. 'I'll find out where he's being held and enquire as to whether or not he'd be willing to see you. But even if he does agree, it's possible for the prison warden or the CPS to override the decision.'

'I see. Do you think that would happen?'

'Probably. To be honest, I think it's unlikely he'll even agree to see you in the first place. But let's just take it one step at a time, shall we?'

'That's great – I owe you one,' said Jack.

'Oh, I think you owe me more than that,' said Cross with a faint laugh as she hung up the phone.

Jack put the phone back on the desk and turned to face Jennifer.

'Well?' she said.

'She's seeing where he is and if he'll agree to see us,' said Jack. 'She doesn't sound very optimistic though.'

'Well, at least she's trying,' she said. 'My research sure isn't getting us anywhere.'

'Yeah,' said Jack. 'Beside which, you've got more important things to do... like planning our wedding.'

Chapter 3.

December 18th, 2012. Dartmoor, England.

It was four days later when Detective Inspector Cross called back.

Jennifer was in the living room, lying back on the sofa and staring at the ceiling while she chatted with a friend on the phone. It was Lauren, one of her oldest school friends, and Jennifer had asked her to be her maid of honour. Now they were trying to organize her wedding plans. She'd decided just to have a small wedding, and they were trying to arrange it as soon as they could; she'd repeatedly teased Jack about his age and how they ought to get married while he was still in control of his faculties. A local registry office had an opening in just eight weeks and now they were under pressure to get everything organized in time.

She had just said goodbye, leaving Lauren with a long list of tasks to look into, and had hung up the phone, when it rang again almost instantly.

'Hello?' she said. She could tell from the caller ID that it wasn't Lauren calling her back, but she didn't recognize the number.

'Hello there. This is Detective Inspector Cross – is Jack Knight there?'

'He's outside in the garden,' she said. 'I'll go and get him.' She put the phone down on the table and went to look out of the window; Jack was busy digging up a patch of weeds in one of the flowerbeds. She opened the window and leant out to call his name; Jack stopped digging and turned to face her, resting his spade against a tree.

'Cross!' she shouted, putting her thumb and little finger to her ear and mouth – the old-fashioned sign for a phone call.

'Why? What have I done now?' he called.

'No,' she shouted back. *'Detective Inspector Cross.'*

Jack jogged back in, not bothering to remove his boots and leaving a trail of muddy footprints across the kitchen and hallway. He snatched the phone from the table like a kid with a new toy, ignoring the tut of disapproval from Jennifer.

'Hi there. Is it good news?' he asked breathlessly.

Cross sighed. 'No. He didn't agree to see you, and I double checked – you wouldn't have been allowed to see him anyway. Not when you're a witness to Peter's assault – even if you aren't down to testify at the moment.'

Jack cursed under his breath. 'Okay,' he said, his shoulders sagging. 'Well, thanks for trying.'

'There is one bit of good news,' she added.

'What's that?' said Jack, cheering up again.

'Peter White is officially no longer in a critical state. His surgery went well, and they're expecting him to be moved back to the Cheltenham General in a few days, when his strength is better.'

'That *is* good news.'

Jack hung up the phone and turned around to see Jennifer standing in front of him holding a mop. She gave a nod of her head to indicate the muddy footprints he'd left across the clean floor. *'Now* I'm cross.'

Two days later, Jack arrived at the hospital for the early evening visiting hour. As he stepped into the ward, he could see that Peter was lying in his bed half asleep; drips, catheters and monitoring equipment were still all attached to him, quietly performing their duties.

As Jack pulled up a chair and sat down, Peter opened his eyes. A smile appeared on his face and he visibly perked up.

'You had us worried for a while there,' said Jack, 'but they tell me you're going make a full recovery.'

Peter nodded sluggishly – the nurse had warned Jack that he was still on some serious pain killers. 'So they say. I really don't recommend being stabbed, if you can possibly avoid it.'

'I'll try to bear that in mind,' replied Jack with a polite smile.

'What about you and Jennifer?'

'We're both fine. Engaged to be married in fact.'

Peter nodded. 'That's good.' He squinted, leaning forwards to take a closer look at Jack's face. 'But you… You look…?'

'It's a long story,' said Jack, holding up a hand to halt that avenue of discussion. 'But I promise I'll explain fully when you're feeling better.'

Peter lay back again and sighed, thinking for a long moment. 'And Silas?'

'He's no more.'

Peter nodded and smiled. 'It seems to have all worked out in the end then.'

Jack smiled back. 'It would appear so.'

As the visiting time drew to a close an hour later, Jack made his excuses and left, promising Peter that both he and Jennifer would visit him again soon.

It was dark and bitterly cold as he stepped out of the main hospital building, forcing him to fasten the collar of his jacket to keep himself warm. All was calm and quiet as he walked back across the street towards the multi-storey car park; there were only a few cars on the roads and almost no other pedestrians nearby. In the distance, he could see an ambulance drawing up to the rear of the hospital, its blue lights flashing but with no siren.

As he stepped past a collection of large waste bins and opened the door to the ground floor of the car park, a noise from behind him made him jump, a rattling metallic noise like an empty can being kicked along the ground. He stopped and looked over his shoulder, but the passageway behind him was deserted, just as it had been when he had passed through moments before.

With just a hint of paranoia, he picked up his pace and hurried up the stairwell towards the third floor where he had parked. The stairwell was dark, half of the lights not working, and it had the obligatory faint smell of urine. As he reached his floor, he stopped and looked back down the stairs; there was still no sign of anyone following him. He shook his head and tried to put his earlier jump to the back of his mind.

He pushed the heavy door open and stepped into the car park. This level was quite empty, but parked halfway down he could see his car, just beyond a cluster of other cars and vans. It was dark in here too. Moonlight was coming in through the open walls to the side, but all the lights along this side of the car park were out.

He stood still and listened for a moment; nothing was moving in here. All he could hear were the distant sounds of traffic on the nearby roads and a hum from one of the stairwell lights behind him.

'Let's get the hell out of here,' he muttered to himself, and hurried along the path towards his car, fishing the keys from his pocket as he went. As he drew close, he stepped past two white vans. Out of the corner of his eye, Jack spotted a man emerging from between them, but by the time he'd noticed the fist swinging towards him, it was too late to do anything about it. The man's fist connected with his stomach and Jack curled up, the wind knocked out of him. The car keys fell from his hand, skidding along the grey concrete and coming to a stop a few feet away in the middle of the road.

Jack staggered backwards a couple of steps and took a look at the man. He was dressed all in black: black leather boots, black combat fatigues and a black jacket, the hood up over his head and covering his face. This had an all too familiar ring to it.

He came in again, swinging his right fist towards Jack's face. Jack managed to clumsily side step the blow, but was hit by the man's left fist impacting on the right-hand side of his face. Jack fell backwards onto the concrete, his head spinning. He was seeing flashing pinpoints of light before his eyes.

'What do you want?' he managed to utter, as he shuffled backwards on his hands and feet.

'Revenge,' uttered the man. He took a step forwards, drawing a knife from out of his jacket.

Jack froze in shock as there was an almighty bang, echoing through the open concrete structure. As one, Jack and his assailant turned to see the source of the noise. Standing in the darkness near the stairwell, they could see a man; there was a gun in his hand, the barrel pointed up at the ceiling.

'Leave him!' shouted the man with the gun. When Jack's assailant hesitated, he repositioned the gun, aiming it at the attacker rather than the ceiling. 'Go!' he barked at the man again.

Jack's attacker stood above him, glancing down at him momentarily with a snarl on his face. 'This isn't over,' he hissed, slipping the knife back into his jacket. He took a few tentative steps backwards, retreating away from the armed man but keeping a close eye on him. Then he turned and ran, gathering pace as he headed towards the far exit.

Jack lay on the floor in shocked silence as the armed man strode quickly towards him, pausing just momentarily to pick up Jack's keys on the way. He stopped when he reached the spot where Jack's assailant had stood just moments before.

He leant forwards, offering his hand. Jack took hold of it and was pulled to his feet. 'Mr Knight?' he said. 'We need to talk.'

Chapter 4.

'We should go,' said the man, looking first at Jack and then over both shoulders in turn. 'There may be more of them around and my approach, while effective, may attract some unwanted attention.' He held out Jack's keys. 'Shall we take your car?'

'Who... Who the hell are you?' Jack managed to stammer.

The man looked over his shoulder again nervously. 'I'll explain everything to you in a moment,' he said. When Jack didn't move, he added, 'Look – if I wanted to harm you, I could have easily shot you – or just left you to him.'

Jack looked at his rescuer. He was young, probably in his mid-twenties, with short blond hair and blue eyes. He too was wearing mainly black, but Jack could see a white shirt under his coat, open and tie-less. He took his car keys back from the man in somewhat of a daze. His head was still spinning slightly. 'Where are we going?'

'Anywhere,' replied the man. 'Just somewhere away from here.'

Jack nodded, mainly to himself, and then stepped towards his car, pressing the button on his fob to unlock it. He climbed into the driver's seat, and the other man climbed in opposite him. 'So, what do I call you?' he asked, as he turned the ignition and put the car in gear.

'You can call me Sebastian,' the man replied, as the car slipped out of its parking space and along the concourse, accelerating down the ramps towards the exit.

They drove in silence for a couple of minutes, until they reached a secluded residential area away from the hospital. Jack pulled the car up onto the grass verge by the side of the road and turned off the engine. 'Okay,' he asked. 'Just who the hell are you, Sebastian?'

'Before I tell you, remember… I did just save your life.'

'What the hell's that supposed to mean?'

Sebastian sighed. 'I belong to the Brotherhood of the Star. My master sent me to keep an eye on you – he thought something like this might happen.'

'Hold on,' said Jack, a look of shock on his face. 'If *you're* a member of the Brotherhood, then who the hell was he?'

'He was one of my brothers, another member.'

The look of shock on Jack's face turned to one of confusion. 'Just what the fuck is going on here, Sebastian?'

'I'll try to explain,' said Sebastian slowly. 'I'll start at the beginning. It all goes back to the foundation of the Brotherhood. It was founded by a man called Aloysius several centuries ago.'

'Aloysius?' said Jack. 'That was the name that Silas mentioned to me. Right before I sent him straight to hell.'

'Err, quite,' said Sebastian nervously. 'Aloysius was a man blessed with the gift of prophecy. He made a great many prophecies, some vague and some very specific.'

'And they've come true, have they?' asked Jack, a mocking tone clear in his voice.

'For the most part, yes. As is the nature of this kind of thing, some prophecies are stated more clearly than others – but all the ones we understand have come true.' Jack laughed openly at this, but Sebastian continued. 'Most of the prophecies that Aloysius left us came to pass in the early days of the Brotherhood. It has been… well, quite a long time since we have witnessed any new revelations. Not within any of our lifetimes.'

'I don't understand what this has to do with me,' said Jack with a shake of his head.

'That's what I'm trying to explain. What's important for now is that not all of the Brotherhood completely believe in these prophecies. For a long time now – since before I was born – there have been two rival factions within the Brotherhood. One group has an absolute belief in the sanctity of these prophecies, and the other... well, the others are more sceptical. Even within our modest organization, we are not immune to petty political squabbling,' he chuckled quietly to himself.

'I'm still waiting to hear what relevance this has to me,' said Jack dryly.

'Patience,' said Sebastian. He took a deep breath. 'Silas was the leader of both the Brotherhood and the faction of non-believers. Following his death, there will be a power vacuum within the Brotherhood, and I fear that it will likely be filled with his supporters, others who do not fully believe in these prophecies. They are also likely to want revenge against you and your partner for the death of Silas. That is why you were attacked tonight.'

Jack thought for a moment. 'Then you're from the other faction?'

Sebastian nodded. 'Yes. That's why my master wanted me to make sure you were okay.'

'But why would he care about me?' asked Jack. He thought for a second before answering his own question. 'This Aloysius – he made a prophecy about *me*, didn't he?'

Sebastian nodded again. 'Yes – my master believes so. More than one, in fact – enough that he has a vested interest in your safety.'

'So let me get this straight – half of your cult wants to kill me, and the other half wants to keep me alive?'

Sebastian shrugged. 'Something like that.'

'I always thought you lot were insane. Now I find out you really are schizophrenic.'

A dry, polite smile spread across Sebastian's lips. 'That is, of course, your opinion.'

Jack thought for a moment. 'So... these prophecies. What do they say?'

Sebastian held up a finger. 'Not just yet.' Jack exhaled loudly in frustration, shaking his head. 'I promise, all will be revealed,' he continued in a placating tone. 'The time has not yet come for my master to reveal everything.' He looked at the annoyed expression on Jack's face. 'He will, I assure you – but first you must truly believe.'

'I don't understand.'

'No, but you *will*. You must go to Bruadar Castle in Scotland.'

Jack sighed. 'I've only just got back from Scotland!'

'Well, you must go there again. On the west coast of the Highlands, just west of Glen Toraig, you will find what remains of Bruadar Castle. Go down deep under the castle and you will find an ancient temple that lies far beneath the more modern building. Sebastian reached into his jacket and pulled out a fine, silver chain with an old iron key hanging from it. 'Here, you will need this,' he said, holding out the key towards Jack.

Jack hesitated momentarily, then reached out and took the key in his hand.

'Find that temple,' Sebastian continued, 'and then see for yourself the paintings that it contains. When you have done that, you will have begun your path to enlightenment.'

Jack gave a brief laugh with a shake of his head. 'Are you serious?'

Sebastian nodded. 'Very much so – trust me when I say that your future depends on this. But you must also be careful – the castle has been abandoned for some time, and the tunnels underneath are home now to others. The place was a kind of nexus, a weak point between worlds, and now creatures will sometimes be found lurking in the darkness beneath.'

'I thought you said you had an interest in my safety.'

'And I do – that's why I'm warning you. It may be dangerous, but this is also important. I think a man of your... *experience* should be able to handle the task.'

Jack thought for a moment. 'And if I don't go?'

'Then my master and I will speak to you no more, and you will never know.'

'Never know *what*?'

Sebastian smiled and shook his head. 'I have told you all that my master will allow for now. Go to Bruadar Castle. See for yourself, and then you will understand. I will contact you again afterwards, and we will continue this conversation.' With that, he pulled on the door handle, opening the car door. The cold night air swept into the car.

'Wait!' cried Jack. 'Just who is this master of yours you keep talking about?'

Sebastian stopped halfway out of the car and turned back to face Jack. 'A great man and one who can possibly save your life.' With that, he leapt out of the car and disappeared into the darkness.

✳ ✳ ✳

It was late when Jack arrived home, stopping the car in front of the house and climbing out into the cold night air. He glanced around; the property was dark and silent, all except for a small light he could see coming from between the curtains of their bedroom.

He groped around with his key in the darkness until he finally found the lock and managed to open the door. He let himself in quietly, unsure as to whether Jennifer would be asleep in bed or not; she would sometimes leave a light on in the bedroom for him when he came back late. He took his damp shoes off in the hallway and made his way up the stairs before stopping to poke his head through the bedroom door.

Jennifer was sitting up in bed reading a book – a novel for a change, rather than magazines about weddings.

'I was wondering when you'd get back,' she said, looking up. She put a slip of paper into the pages of her book and then rested it on the table next to the bed. 'How's Peter?'

'He's been better, but I think he'll pull through.' Jack came and sat down on the edge of the bed. 'You're not going to believe what happened to me afterwards, though,' he added.

'What?'

'Someone from the Brotherhood attacked me in the car park.'

What? Are you okay? I assumed all that shit was over.'

'I'm fine, but I almost wasn't. He had the best of me until I was saved by a Good Samaritan – and you'll *never* guess who that was.'

'The police?'

Jack shook his head. 'Try again.'

'Was it someone we know?'

'No.'

'This isn't twenty fucking questions, just tell me already!'

'Another cultist from the Brotherhood.'

'What the fuck? Are they fighting over you now?'

Jack chuckled. 'That's surprisingly accurate.' He patiently explained to Jennifer about the schism within the cult and what Sebastian had told him about the prophecy.

'But he didn't tell you what this prophecy was?' asked Jennifer.

'No. He said that first, I have to truly believe.'

'Believe what?'

'There's something I apparently need to see in Scotland, an ancient temple underneath some place called Bruadar Castle. Once I've done that, he said they would tell me more.'

Jennifer thought for a second. 'I don't trust him, Jack. You've got no idea who he is.'

'He saved my life tonight.'

'So you say. Did it ever occur to you that it could all have been staged, just to make you trust him? This could all just be a trap.'

Jack hesitated for a moment; that *hadn't* occurred to him. Ultimately though, he didn't see what difference it made. 'To what end?' he replied. 'If they wanted to capture me, they could have. If they wanted to *kill* me, they could have.'

Jennifer wasn't convinced. 'I still don't trust him. Have you forgotten what they tried to do to us? What they *did* do to me?'

'Of course not—'

'Then what Jack?' she interrupted angrily. 'Suddenly they're the good guys? Suddenly we're supposed to trust them?'

Jack hadn't expected Jennifer to react quite so aggressively. He had to remind himself that, although most of their experiences with the Brotherhood had happened a long time ago from his perspective, for her it was just a few days. He reached forward, taking one of her hands in his and squeezing it gently. 'Look, I hear what you're saying, and I can appreciate where you're coming from... And honestly, I know we can't trust them... But if this Aloysius did make a prophecy about me – or multiple prophecies – well, if you were in my place, wouldn't *you* want to know?'

Jennifer shook her head in disbelief. 'The old you would never have trusted one of them.'

'Things have changed,' he said simply.

'What's that supposed to mean?'

'I've seen things... been places... I suppose I've got a different perspective on things now. There are things out there, beings that are unimaginably old and powerful. If there's the slightest possibility that we're going to get dragged in to all of this again, I need to know as much as possible about what's going on.'

Jennifer sighed. 'It sounds to me like you've already made up your mind.'

'I have.'

'And nothing I can say will change it?'

'I don't want to sound like I don't care about what you think, because I *do*... but I need to know this, Jenn. If you were in my shoes and someone said that they knew what was going to happen to you, what would *you* do?'

'A few months ago, I suppose I would have laughed and ignored them. But now, with what we know... and especially what you've been through...' She sighed again. 'I suppose you may be right.'

Jack nodded. 'I promise I'll be careful.'

'Ahem,' she coughed. 'You think I'm going to let you go on this fool's errand on your own, with no one to look after you? I'm not letting you out of my sight.'

Chapter 5.

December 19th, 2012. Dartmoor, England.

Jennifer came down the next morning to find Jack standing in the hallway, putting on his jacket.

'You're not thinking of going without me, I hope?' she asked him, a scornful look on her face. 'I meant what I said about going with you.'

'I've got something I need to do first,' he replied. 'Thought I might try and see if I can find out who my friend from last night was.'

'How's that?'

'I've got an idea of someone who might be able to track him down.' He pulled his car keys out of his pocket and opened the front door. 'I'll be back in a few hours – we'll go to Scotland tomorrow.'

'But where are you–'

She stopped as she realized she was speaking to an empty room.

Jack walked up to the front desk of Exeter Police Station and greeted the duty sergeant sitting behind the desk.

'Hi there,' he said. 'I'm Jack Knight – here to meet Detective Inspector Cross. She should be expecting me.'

The policeman picked up the phone on the desk, consulted a sheet of paper and then dialled an internal number. Jack stood there nervously while they waited for someone to answer the phone. Eventually, someone picked it up. 'Hello, Ma'am,' said the policeman. 'I've got a Mr Knight here to see you.' He grunted a couple of times in acknowledgement and then put the phone down. 'She's busy at the moment – take a seat,' he said, gesturing towards a couple of benches against the wall. 'She'll be with you as soon as she's free.'

Jack went over and sat on the bench. It was plain wood, without any cushions, hard and unyielding. He shuffled about, trying to get comfortable without any success – it was a long ten minutes before Detective Inspector Cross finally appeared through a door on the other side of the room. He stood up, stretching his stiff back and trying to massage some feeling back into his thighs before he walked across the room to greet her, shaking her by the hand.

'You said you had something for me to do with this case,' she said gruffly. 'Is there something you've remembered?'

'Not quite,' he said. Cross gave him a look that showed a complete lack of surprise. 'But I think I might have something that could help track down the other members of this cult,' he added.

She looked at him suspiciously. 'Explain.'

Jack hesitated for a moment. He hadn't particularly thought this through. 'One of the cult members came to visit me last night.'

'Did he threaten you?'

'No. Well, one did. There were actually two of them...'

'Slow down,' she said calmly, and then paused. 'Perhaps we ought to sit down and do this properly.'

She led him back over to the door she had come though. From around her neck, she picked up a card hanging from a lanyard and swiped it through a keypad next to the door, before typing in her PIN. The door buzzed and she pulled it open, leading him through. Together, they proceeded down the corridor, Cross looking for a vacant room until she poked her head into one labelled *Interview Room C* and found it empty. She gestured for him to go in and sit down at the table.

'I'll just be two minutes. Don't go anywhere,' she said, closing the door.

Jack sat there, nervously drumming his fingers on the table. He'd been in far too many of these rooms recently. When Cross returned, she had a mug in one hand and a plastic glass of water in the other, a pad of paper under her arm. She put the water in front of Jack and the pad on the desk in front of her, before sitting down opposite him and taking a sip from her mug. She turned to a fresh page in the pad of paper, pulling a half-chewed biro from her jacket pocket. Jack looked around, taking another look at the room they were in.

'I bet you've been in a few of these rooms in the last week or so,' she said, a lighter note to her voice now.

'A few,' acknowledged Jack with a smile.

'So,' she said with a deep breath. 'In your own words, tell me what happened last night.'

'Is this being recorded?' asked Jack.

'Do you think it should be?' replied Cross.

'Err... no?' replied Jack nervously.

'You're not under arrest, and this isn't being recorded, so just relax. As I said, *in your own words...*'

'Okay,' said Jack, taking a deep breath. He should have prepared this more. 'Last night I went to see Peter Cross in the hospital. He's expected to recover fully, by the way, thanks to your help.' Cross nodded and motioned for him to continue. 'On the way back to the car, a cultist attacked me and then–'

'How do you know he was a cultist?' she interrupted.

'Well, I... He was...' Jack stopped and sighed. 'I suppose I don't for certain, but I've seen enough of their lot to recognize them.' Cross smiled. 'And he said he wanted revenge.'

'Well, okay,' said Cross. 'I'm guessing he didn't seriously hurt you.'

'No – just this bruise on the side of my head.'

'So what happened?'

'He was scared off by another cultist – at least that's what he said he was.'

'He called himself a cultist, this second man?'

'Well, not in those exact words, but he did tell me he belonged to the Brotherhood of the Star – and that the man who attacked me belonged too.'

'And they're the same bunch that took Jennifer before?' asked Cross. Jack nodded in response. 'Wait – so one cultist tried to attack you, and another tried to save you?'

'Yeah, it didn't make too much sense to me either.'

Cross laughed. 'For a change. So why did he save you? Apart from his civic duty, of course.'

'He wouldn't say.'

Cross sighed and leant back in her chair. 'So where's this going Jack? Did you want to report an assault?'

'I don't think there's much point. I didn't get a good look at the one that attacked me – it was dark and he was wearing a hood...'

'Can you tell me *anything* about him?'

'He was wearing all black and was well built. His hood was covering most of his face, but I think he had a short black beard.'

'Anything else? Anything distinctive? Did he say anything to you?'

Jack thought for a second. 'He only spoke a few words... but I think he may have had a northern accent.'

'Nothing else?'

Jack closed his eyes and tried to visualize what had happened. He thought of the man drawing his knife from his jacket. 'Wait – when he drew his knife, there was something about his hand. I think it had a scar along it.'

'His right hand?' Jack nodded. 'Okay, that's something at least.'

'I got a good look at the other one,' added Jack, 'but I can do you one better. He came in my car to get away. I think he may have left fingerprints on the door handle.'

'Okay,' sighed Cross. '*He's* left fingerprints. But he didn't actually do any-thing wrong, did he? Didn't he actually *help* you?'

Jack thought about the discharging of a firearm, but decided not to mention it. 'Yes, but if they're all part of the same cult...'

'Legally, I don't think guilt by association quite works that way.'

'I know, I know... but if you could find out who he is, couldn't that help lead you to the others, the ones that assaulted us and kidnapped Jennifer?'

Cross sighed again. 'I've got to tell you, of the others I've come across who you *allege* were part of this Brotherhood–'

'They *were*,' stressed Jack.

'Regardless, none of their fingerprints came up in our system.'

'Oh,' said Jack simply, a glum expression on his face.

Cross smiled a weak smile at him. 'They may be cold-blooded cultists, hell bent on world domination – but as far as I can tell, they also appear to be *dis-*

creet and law abiding cold-blooded cultists. Still... It's a bit of a long shot, but I suppose it wouldn't hurt to try,' she added with a weary sigh, making the expression on Jack's face lighten slightly. 'Come on,' she said. 'Is your car in the car park?' Jack nodded. Cross stood up, leading him back out of the room and towards the reception. 'I'll meet you out there in just a moment.'

She joined Jack in the car park just a few minutes later, a small black bag in her hands.

'What's that?' asked Jack.

'A fingerprint kit,' replied Cross. 'What did you expect?'

'Don't you have CSI guys for that?' he asked.

Cross chuckled. 'They're a bit busy with *actual* crime scenes.' Jack felt slightly offended, but decided not to press the point. 'Besides which, I'm not actually in charge of this investigation.' She unzipped the bag, taking out a small jar of fine black powder and small brush. 'If it turns up anything, I'll be sure to let Detective Inspector Watts know. Is this it?' she added, pointing to the passenger door on his car.

'Err, yes,' he replied. 'I don't know how good the outside handle would be, but he also used the inside handle – its metal.'

Cross opened the door and inspected the handle; it was chrome plated, smooth and clean, a perfect surface for lifting prints. She unscrewed the lid of the jar and gently brushed some of the powder onto the door handle with the brush.

'See anything?' asked Jack.

'Hold on,' muttered Cross, like a parent to a nagging child. She blew gently on the handle, brushing the area gently. 'Yes, I think I do.' She pulled out her phone, zooming in and taking several close-up photographs, before checking them on the screen. 'Looks like we've got two good prints here.' She thought for a second. 'We've already got yours, for elimination purposes.'

Jack nodded. 'So what now?'

'You let me get on with my job. If anything important turns up, I'll be sure to let you know.'

Chapter 6.

December 20th, 2012. Bruadar Castle, Glen Toraig, Scotland.

Jack and Jennifer spent the entire day driving north, first heading along the motorways towards Glasgow, before being forced to take the smaller roads as they drew closer to their destination. It was early evening and they were driving along the west coast of the Highlands when they first caught sight of Bruadar Castle.

The large stone ruins were situated on a peninsula of rock and rough grass sitting a few hundred feet above the harsh sea below. Behind it, they could see the dying red sun as it dipped below the horizon, out across the stormy ocean. The wind was howling, sweeping huge North Sea waves against the base of the rocks, the spray flying high up the sheer cliff faces.

What they could see of the castle was a plain square building built out of a uniformly dull brown-grey stone, and all that remained were its simple square walls, with no turrets or towers to be seen; any it may once have had were presumably now lost to the weather over the years, fallen into the raging sea below. The stone structure was at the far end of the peninsula, bordered on three sides by the water; at points, the cliff face looked perilously close to the castle walls. It might only be a few more years before large sections of the main building would themselves disappear beneath the waves.

From where they had stopped their car, they could just make out a narrow dirt track worn into the long grass. It curved its way along a winding path towards the castle's outer walls, where it finally stopped at a large wooden door, which stood closed.

Jack drove as far as he could up the track until their progress was blocked by two large boulders, deliberately placed on the path to stop anyone driving any closer. He turned off the engine and they both climbed out of the car; the castle stood just a few hundred feet away from them, silhouetted against the dying light as it grew dimmer before their eyes, the sun continuing to drop further below the horizon.

Jack opened the boot and lifted up the floor, revealing the spare wheel underneath; stowed inside was a bundle wrapped in red cloth. He pulled it out, unwrapping it to reveal a combat knife in a leather sheath. He slipped it into his jacket pocket and gave it a pat.

'Just in case,' he said to Jennifer with a nod.

She reached past him, taking hold of a metal torch they kept in the car in case of emergencies. 'May also come in handy,' she added, before starting down the path on foot.

As they drew closer, they could start to see the details of the castle's structure more clearly. Walls ran around the building to the left and right, encompassing what was presumably a small courtyard within. The large double doors at the front were the only visible entrance, and there were no windows at ground level; the few windows that they could see higher up were dark and empty. There were no signs of life audible above the roar of the wind and the crashing of the sea far below them.

Jennifer approached the massive wooden doors, which stood closed before them, towering above her. She braced her legs against the floor and pushed hard against them, but they didn't budge even a fraction of an inch. They were stuck fast; whether from a lock or just stuck in place she couldn't tell.

'I don't fancy our way in through the front door,' she called to Jack over the wind.

Jack nodded. 'Let's try going around,' he suggested to Jennifer. 'See if we can find another way in. Maybe we've got a chance where the stonework is crumbling.'

From the door, they turned to their right, following the stone wall until they reached the corner. Jack peered around the side, looking at the narrow dirt and stone path that ran alongside the wall. Directly in front of them, the path was several feet wide, but as it stretched away it grew narrower; in several places, it was less than two feet wide, sometimes as narrow as six inches.

Next to where they stood was a narrow valley between the peninsula and the mainland. Jack leant over the edge to look down and instantly regretted it. He wasn't particularly afraid of heights when he knew he was safe, but there was no fence or guard-rail here; one wrong move and there was a two hundred foot drop into the sea – or if they were unlucky, onto the jagged rocks below.

'What's that?' called Jennifer, tapping on Jack's shoulder and pointing along the wall. Jack turned around to look, glad to be distracted from the thought of the drop before him. Halfway down the wall, he could see a section that seemed to be crumbling, the top of the wall lower and rougher than the rest.

'I think you're right,' agreed Jack. 'That does look like something. C'mon.'

They set off cautiously down the path, trying not to get too close to the edge, but as they continued it became harder and harder. As they approached the section of crumbling wall, the ground narrowed to less than two feet wide and they were forced to turn sideways, shuffling along the ledge with their back to the wall. For twenty feet, their progress was nerve-racking, the path barely a foot wide and crumbling underfoot in places, but before long it widened out again slightly, allowing them to relax just a little bit. They shuffled along a little further until they found themselves underneath the damaged section of wall. The top of the wall was lower than the rest, but was still at least eight feet tall.

'Do you think you can make it over if I help you up?' called Jack. The noise of the crashing waves below was a constant reminder of their precarious position.

Jennifer looked at the wall and then at the narrow ledge below her feet. It was about two feet wide here. 'I think so,' she replied with a gulp.

Jack got down onto his knees, kneeling in the dirt and trying not to look over the side. He bent forwards so that he was on all fours, allowing Jennifer to stand on his back. She stood behind him and reached up, but could only just get her fingertips to the top of the wall.

'Okay, I'm going up. For God's sake, keep still,' she pleaded, a strong sense of urgency in her voice. She took one step up onto his back and then lifted the other foot, pulling herself up by her fingertips as she went, holding herself close to the wall. Jack started to wobble as she lifted her second foot off the floor, the force pushing him sideways, but he threw his weight against the wall, bracing himself against the solid mass. When they were both steady, she pulled herself up to peer over the wall into the courtyard within.

'It looks empty,' she called down to Jack. She tried to pull herself up with her arms, but failed. 'I can't quite make it,' she said. 'You're going to have to raise me slightly higher.'

Jack braced himself and then pushed up with his arms and legs, trying to lift his back higher off the floor. There was no noticeable difference. He stopped and gave a low groan. 'Have you put on any weight lately?' he hissed.

'Jack!' she spat back under her breath. 'Now is not the time!'

'Okay, okay,' he replied apologetically – at least she wasn't wearing heels. 'Hold tight, I'll try again.' He pushed up harder with his arms this time, as he also tried to raise his knees upwards. He felt the weight on his back lessen as Jennifer managed to take hold and lift herself up, the wall now starting to take her weight.

As Jack was pushing upwards with all his strength, when Jennifer's weight disappeared he lurched upwards, momentarily unbalanced. His right leg started to slip towards the edge, the loose rock crumbling underneath it. He span around trying to flatten himself against the wall, his arms flailing to find something to hold onto. One of Jennifer's legs was hanging in the air as she pulled herself over the top of the wall, and he grabbed hold of it in desperation. For a brief moment, her body stared to slide back down, pulled back by Jack's tight grasp on her leg, but then she managed to grab hold of something, arresting her retreat. Jack finally steadied himself against the wall, lessening his grip on Jennifer. He was now facing the wall, and he closed his eyes, unwilling to look down.

'What the fuck, Jack!' shouted Jennifer from up above him. 'What the hell are you playing at?'

'Don't worry about me – just trying not to die,' he panted. He could feel his heart beating, sweat running from his armpits despite the bitter cold of the night. 'See if you can find something to help me get in.' There was a quiet thud as Jennifer dropped onto the other side. Jack waited in silence, standing with his eyes shut facing the wall. 'Jennifer?' he called out quietly after a minute. He opened his eyes and looked up.

Jennifer's head was poking over the top of the wall, looking down at him. 'Hang on one moment,' she said before disappearing again.

'Don't worry about me – I'm not going anywhere!' he hissed back. The wind was starting to pick up now, gusting in from the ocean. He watched, as a length of rope was lowered down over the wall.

'I'll tie the other end to something and hold on tight – you climb up,' Jennifer called down to him.

Jack waited patiently until he heard a call from Jennifer to tell him she was ready. He prayed silently and then took hold of the rope, pulling firmly on it. Slowly and tentatively, he pulled harder, until he was putting all his weight on it. When he was confident it was going to hold, he carefully started to pull himself up, using his feet to walk up the wall. As he neared the top of the wall, Jennifer pulled on the rope with all her strength, lifting him just enough for him to grab hold.

When he was safely lying on top of the wall, he swung his legs around and dropped ungracefully to the floor, landing on the rough dirt with a louder thump than Jennifer had made.

He stood up and looked around at their surroundings. They were standing in what did indeed look like a small courtyard. The floor was bare gravel and dirt, peppered with weeds and discarded rubbish – presumably from previous visitors. To their right were some derelict wood and stone outbuildings that might once have been stables or storage areas. To their left was the main building; a single empty doorway beckoned them inside.

Chapter 7.

The inside of the castle was bare stone, a narrow corridor with an arched ceiling. From where they stood, most of the visible walls were spray painted with graffiti, none of it even vaguely artistic. On the stone that wasn't covered with paint, people had instead carved their names or initials. *Presumably local kids,* thought Jack, although he wasn't sure there was anywhere near here he'd consider local — it must be a dozen miles to the nearest village.

Jennifer unzipped her coat, pulling her torch from an inside pocket and turning it on. The beam of light illuminated the corridor, showing several open doorways on either side. 'Here,' said Jennifer, passing Jack the torch. 'You go first.'

Jack advanced slowly with Jennifer close behind him. He peered through a doorway to his left. The room was empty except for a collection of empty beer bottles and cans scattered all over the floor, along with a strong smell of urine.

'We're looking for some kind of way down,' Jennifer reminded him.

Jack grunted and came back out. 'Nothing in there,' he agreed.

The next two doorways led to similar rooms, empty apart from more remnants left behind by kids passing through. A fourth doorway showed more promise though: a spiralling stone staircase leading down. The steps were worn smooth from centuries of use, shallow puddles of water making many of the steps slippery. With great care, Jack began the descent, placing one hand against each wall to brace himself, the torchlight erratic in the darkness.

As they reached the bottom of the staircase, it opened before them into a long room with an arched ceiling. On either side were barred cells, each of them now standing open, their doors long gone; this obviously used to be a dungeon or prison. Grooves ran from each cell into a central gully down the middle of the corridor, which in turn ran into a small grill in the floor at either end.

Jack cast the torchlight back and forth, and when he saw nothing immediately dangerous, stepped inside. The air in the room was cold and damp and had a strong musky odour. Puddles of water lay on the floor. As he crept further into the room, the torchlight illuminated a metal gate on the far side, blocking any exit through a narrow corridor that continued on the other side.

'Is this it?' asked Jennifer from behind him.

'Maybe,' muttered Jack. He stepped carefully across the room until he was standing right before the gate. 'Here, take this,' he said to Jennifer, passing her the torch. She took it, shining its light on the gate and the corridor behind it.

Jack took the gate in both hands; the metal felt cold and wet, flakes of rusty metal coming off in his palms. It held fast though, barely moving as he shook it back and forth.

'Try the key,' Jennifer reminded him.

Suddenly from somewhere above them came an inhuman scream, less of a human voice than a canine howl.

'I don't think we're alone in here,' whispered Jennifer, and Jack could hear the fear in her voice. From somewhere in the darkness behind them they could hear movement, scampering footsteps echoing down the stairwell.

Jack reached into his jacket, fishing out the key on the chain. He tried to insert it into the lock, but his fingers were cold and his nerves racing. It slipped from his hands, falling to the stone floor with a small tinkle.

'Shit!' he cursed. 'Did you see where it went?' The sounds of movement were getting closer now. Jennifer frantically shone the torch across the floor. Jack saw a glint in the darkness as the light passed over the metal key, and he dove to his knees. He snatched it up, kneeling on the floor as he fumbled with the key, clumsily thrusting it into the lock.

'Come on,' muttered Jennifer under her breath. Whatever there was in the darkness, it couldn't be far away now.

'It won't turn,' cried Jack.

'Shit. Try harder!' She didn't want to voice the thought that they were both thinking; *what if this wasn't the key to this gate?*

'I am!' he cried. He stood up, twisting the key back and forth until suddenly something gave, the lock opening with a loud crack that echoed in the darkness.

As the gate opened, a terrifying sound came from the other end of the room, a deep feral growling. Jennifer turned, the light of her torch illuminating a towering humanoid creature standing at the bottom of the stairs, its large pale yellow eyes staring at them across the room. It paused, momentarily startled by her bright torchlight, and they could see it clearly: a huge muscular body covered in pale white flesh, its long arms and legs ending in intimidating claws. Its face was vaguely human but elongated and canine; when it growled at her, they could see a mouth full of sharp fangs glistening in the torchlight. It reminded them both of the beast they had seen beneath the church in Novéant-sur-Meuse, but this one had larger legs and its face bore neither nose nor forehead.

'Get the hell through,' urged Jack, as he pushed the stiff gate open. Jennifer scrambled through the gap, Jack following directly behind her. From behind them, they could hear the creature scurrying across the room on its long hind limbs, its claws scraping against the stone floor.

They turned, Jack slamming the gate shut and Jennifer raising her torch to reveal the monster mere feet away. Jack lurched towards it, reaching through the bars to grab the key from the lock, pulling it free just as the monster reached them. As he leant over, the knife slipped from his jacket pocket; he momentarily hesitated as he watched it glide through the air, and the beast lunged towards him. Its long talons made contact as he pulled his hand back through the gate, slicing through his jacket, but just missing his skin. He fell backwards onto the floor as Jennifer continued to illuminate the beast with her torch, causing it to cover its eyes with its long sinewy arms.

Up close the beast was even more terrifying; as it opened its mouth to howl in rage — apparently angry at being denied its prey — they could see saliva dripping from its mouth and smell its foul putrescent odour.

Jack clambered backwards on his hands and feet, Jennifer taking several steps back to join him. They both looked at the knife, which lay on the floor by the gate – mere feet away but easily within the reach of the monster.

'Nice going. We're going to have to leave it,' Jennifer sighed. 'We need to get going,' she added, backing along the corridor. 'I just hope we don't meet any others.'

Jack looked at the beast, at its teeth and the vicious claws on the ends of its long powerful arms. 'If it came to a fight, I'm not sure a knife would make any difference.'

'If we brought a gun next time instead, do you think you could manage not to throw it at their feet?' she retorted.

Feeling suitably admonished, Jack didn't reply but simply turned and followed her down the passage. He paused to look back over his shoulder, taking one final look at the monster, which was holding the bars of the gate in both hands and shaking them violently. 'We may need to find another way out.'

Chapter 8.

December 20th, 2012. Cheltenham, England.

Detective Inspector Cross climbed out of her car and looked across the car park at Cheltenham General Hospital. Detective Inspector Watts had tasked her with talking to Peter White, finding out what he remembered and judging whether he could be a credible witness in court, able to identify his attacker in a line-up.

She checked in at reception, where she showed her police identification, the receptionist giving her directions to the ICU ward where Peter was currently located. She thanked her and set off across the hospital.

Getting out of the lift on the second floor, she looked around for directions to the ICU ward and spotted a sign hanging from the ceiling. As she headed off down the corridor, a short beep came from within her jacket; she had a new message on her phone. She stopped, pulling it from her pocket and glancing at the screen. It was a message from her partner, Detective Sergeant Brooks: an update on one of her cases. She unlocked the phone and skimmed quickly through the message, before she decided it wasn't urgent and returned the phone to her pocket. As she raised her head again and looked back down the corridor, she saw a man standing near the entrance of the ICU. He was dressed all in black, along with black hair and a black beard.

As she watched, she saw him rub his chin, and spotted a long scar stretching down his right hand. His head turned to look towards her, and their eyes met across the busy corridor.

She took a step towards him, but he'd already made her. He bolted, running down a side corridor at full sprint.

'Stop! Police!' she shouted as she took off after him. She reached the corridor and just saw him disappearing through a set of doubled doors at the other end, pushing over a trolley behind him. Metal instruments scattered over the floor with a crash.

She sprinted after him, hurdling the stricken trolley and throwing herself through the doors. The man in black was already a long way down the corridor in front of her, heading for the staircase.

'Stop that man!' she yelled, as she resumed her sprint towards him.

A male nurse stepped forwards in front of the suspect, but he didn't even slow, barging into him and knocking him backwards into a couple of bystanders.

From a door just in front of Cross emerged an elderly man in a wheel chair who was being pushed by an orderly. She had to take avoiding action to stop herself from colliding with the man, stopping short and almost toppling over. At the other end of the corridor, she could see the man in black disappearing through the double doors to the stairwell. She cursed and resumed her sprint down the corridor after him.

'Police!' she yelled as she ran. 'Out of the way!'

She burst through the doors not more than ten seconds after her suspect, but he was already gone. She chanced that he would have gone downstairs, heading out of the hospital, and she started down the steps two at a time. As she reached the first floor, the double doors from the stairwell were still slowly closing on their hinges. Hopefully, that was from him.

She burst through the doors and looked around. Her heart was racing, her breathing rapid. There were corridors leading off directly in front of her and to her right. A fire-exit door stood open to her left.

'Which way did he go?' she shouted at some shocked patients and visitors standing in the hallway. One of them raised an arm to indicate the fire exit, her mouth hanging open in surprise.

Cross didn't wait to thank her but turned and darted through the doorway. She found herself outside, standing on a metal stairway attached to the rear of the building. In the back alley below her, she could see the man in black sprinting away in the dim light.

She ran down the stairs as fast as she could, the metal steps clanging beneath her as she went. As she reached the bottom, she turned towards the alleyway where she had last seen the man, but he was gone. She sprinted to where he had been, stopping at a crossroads where the narrow road peeled off in four directions, each of the roads cluttered with vehicles, bins and other hiding places. The man was nowhere to be seen.

'Damn it!' she shouted into the night. Taking deep gulps of the cold wintry air to try and get her breath back, she span around, looking down each road in turn, but he was gone.

Cross slowly returned to the ICU, stopping at a water cooler on the way for several glasses of water. She asked each of the ICU nurses whether they had spoken to the man or seen him up to anything unusual; none of them had.

Frustrated, she instead turned her attention to Peter White.

'How can I help you detective?' he asked in a wheezy voice as she pulled up a chair and sat down next to his bed.

'How are you feeling?' she asked. 'The doctors tell me you're going to make a full recovery.'

'Yes,' he replied with a shrug. 'I'm not doing too badly – I'm very lucky, really, all things considered. But something tells me you're not here for a social visit.'

'No,' she admitted. 'I'm here on official business – here to see how much you can remember of your attack.'

'Pretty much everything,' he replied. 'Quite vividly, in fact.'

'Then you think you could identify your attacker in a line-up?'

Peter closed his eyes, trying to remember that night in his mind. 'Most definitely,' he said when he opened them again.

'And would you be willing to testify in court?'

'I would.'

'Good. It probably won't be necessary given that I'm also a witness, but it never hurts to have a preponderance of evidence.' Peter nodded back at her. 'When you're feeling better, I'd like you to come down to the station and give a formal statement. Can you do that?'

'Certainly. Anything I can do to help.'

Cross took a business card out of her jacket pocket and placed it on the cabinet next to his bed. 'That's got my details on it.' Peter nodded again in acknowledgement.

Cross stood up to go, pushing her chair back against the wall. 'Oh, just one more thing,' she said. 'You haven't seen a man dressed in black around have you? Black hair, black beard?' Peter shook his head. 'You haven't had any unexpected visitors?'

'No,' said Peter, a curious expression on his face. 'Is there something I should be worried about?'

'No, no,' replied Cross, comfortingly. 'It's nothing to be concerned about,' she said with a wide smile, while simultaneously wondering about getting someone to watch the ward. She considered whether to tell him about the assault on Jack but decided against it; he didn't need any more stress in his current condition, and there was nothing he could do about it in his state anyway. 'If there are any changes, I'll let you know.'

Chapter 9.

December 20th, 2012. Beneath Bruadar Castle, Glen Toraig, Scotland.

Jack and Jennifer started down the dark stone corridor, leaving the inhuman screams behind them.

'You know, there may be other ways through to this side of the gate,' said Jennifer as they walked.

'You're right,' replied Jack. 'Let's go faster.'

The corridor was cold and damp, with shallow puddles of fetid water on the floor, as well as moss and lichen growing on the walls. Before long, the worked stone corridor turned into a tunnel dug out of the rock with a paved floor and wooden beams supporting the ceiling; they looked damp and rotten, surely a disaster waiting to happen. As the corridor continued, twisting and turning through the rock, it remained on a constant downwards slope, until it eventually flattened out and opened into a natural stone tunnel.

The ceiling here was low, forcing them to hunch over as they shuffled along, but it soon opened up again. As they stood up, stretching their backs and looking around, they could see they were now in a natural cave; the rough rock walls were dark and dry here, with loose rubble and gravel underfoot. It didn't look like anyone had passed this way for quite some time.

There was a rough archway leading out of the cavern, and Jack took the lead, holding the torch in front of him as they stepped through the opening and into another large room. This was no longer a natural cave, the walls having been plastered and the floor covered in smooth planks of wood. On the far wall was a large mural, covering the wall from floor to ceiling with pictures and writing. In the centre of the wall, one picture in particular drew Jack towards it. Two altars stood in the centre of the room, various items resting upon them. As Jack approached, he stopped at the first altar, on which stood a candelabrum with three candles. Next to it sat an old matchbox. Jack picked it up, the box feeling damp under his fingers as he opened it; he wasn't surprised when the matches inside failed to ignite.

'Let me try,' said Jennifer, rummaging through her handbag. She pulled out a cigarette lighter. 'I thought I'd try and be more prepared this time.'

It took a couple of attempts, but before long they had the three candles alight, helping to illuminate the room with a flickering glow. Jack picked up the candelabrum, and together they continued their journey to the mural. As they drew close, they could see that it was a fresco, painted into the plaster.

'How old do you reckon that is?' asked Jack.

'Oh, a hundred years at least...' replied Jennifer, looking at the faded paint and crumbling plaster.

'And do you agree that looks a lot like...'

'Oh, yes.'

The fresco was discoloured from time, but the centre clearly showed a large swirling cloud of air, and from it, a man falling to the ground. Jack slowly ran his fingers over the picture, wiping some of the dust from the surface. The face of the man on the wall before him was clearly recognizable as his own, complete with the grey beard he had worn until recently.

Underneath the picture was an inscription, written in Latin. Jack ran his fingers along the words, mumbling to himself.

'Can you tell what it says?' asked Jennifer.

'I managed to learn some of the basics when I was away,' said Jack, concentrating hard. 'I think it says... *he will fall from the sky, returning to behead the Brotherhood.*'

Jennifer gave a low whistle. 'Wow.'

Jack nodded. 'I'm guessing this is one of Aloysius's prophecies.' He turned to look up at Jennifer. 'How could he have known?'

Jennifer just gave a shrug of her shoulders; she had no reasonable answer.

He stood up, moving the candles around to get a better look at the rest of the painting. It was a collage of many thoughts and ideas: humble priests and fearsome gods, helpless children and powerful armies. His eyes passed over the multitude of images but couldn't stop returning again and again to his own face in the centre.

Jennifer was now standing right next to the painting, inspecting it close up. 'That's definitely you. I'm no expert, but it looks ancient. I don't think it's been touched up recently, and this only happened a few days ago.' She took her phone out of her pocket and proceeded to take several pictures, close-ups of the different sections. 'You can't deny he foresaw you returning and killing Silas,' she added, as she stepped back to take some shots of the whole image.

Jack sighed. 'No, I can't. There's no way that's just a coincidence – and if he can make one correct prophecy, then why not others?'

'You more than anyone should appreciate how some people might be able to know what's going to happen in the future.'

'You think he travelled in time?' asked Jack. 'Actually witnessed these events?'

Jennifer shrugged again. 'I don't know. I just know that we can no longer discount those kinds of theories out of hand.'

Jack was about to say something, but then jumped when he heard a loud bark from above, back down the tunnels.

He looked at Jennifer, who returned his glance. 'I think they may have found that other way through.' They both looked frantically around the room. There were two other passageways out of the room, one on either side of them. 'Which way?' he called.

Jennifer grabbed him by the hand and they headed for the nearest exit, the one to their right, running as fast as they could. Their speed blew the candles out, and Jack threw the candelabrum to the floor, running now just by the light of their torch. Twice they came to a fork in the path and they blindly picked a path. The sounds behind them were getting louder now, seemingly gaining on them.

'I can see light ahead – a way out,' cried Jack, as they turned a corner in the passage. They sped up, Jack holding his torch more closely now, no longer needing it to see where they were going.

Jennifer stopped abruptly and Jack smacked into her, almost knocking her over. He looked past her and was glad he hadn't. They were standing in the mouth of a cave on the side of the peninsula that faced the mainland. A sheer drop was in front of them, steeped in shadows and disappearing into a murky gloom, although they could hear the sea splashing against the cliffs below.

'Oh *shit*,' Jennifer cursed. They could still hear sounds approaching in the tunnels behind them – canine growling and the sounds of claws on stone. 'Nowhere left to run.'

'Except down,' said Jack in a shaky voice.

'What? You want us to jump?'

Jack swallowed hard and then nodded. 'If those things catch us, we're dead. If we jump...' He looked down into the darkness again, where he could hear the waves breaking.

'Okay,' she said. 'On three. One...'

Jack looked over his shoulder. The sounds of claws scrabbling along the corridor were growing louder and then one of them burst around the corner. It paused, its tall pale face turning towards them. 'Three!' he said, grabbing her by the waist and jumping from the ledge.

Chapter 10.

They landed in the water with a splash, sinking deep beneath the surface and almost striking the bottom before they rose again, pushing back up until they burst through the waves. Jack gulped down large breaths of air, turning to check that Jennifer was okay. She flashed him a thumbs-up sign as they were both swept along by the tide, the strong current dragging them along. They managed to tread water, just about keeping their heads above the crashing waves, until the incoming tide finally washed them onto a small section of stony beach. They crawled out of the water on their hands and knees before collapsing on the stones. Exhausted, wet and freezing, they lay on their backs taking deep breaths of the cold night air.

Jennifer was the first to get up, rolling over and then crawling to her knees. 'How the hell are we going to get back the car?' she asked, looking at the dark cliffs all around them.

Jack stood up and looked around at the sombre landscape all around them, trying to get his bearings. 'I think there might be a path up the cliff over there,' he said, pointing down the beach. The moon had poked out from behind the clouds, casting dim illumination over the cliff face. Jennifer strained to see but thought she could just about discern what he was pointing to. She nodded in agreement, and they set off along the beach in silence.

When they reached the base of the path, they could clearly see the trail leading steeply up the cliff, a thin groove cut into the rock. They clambered their way up it, their journey interrupted by irregular rocks and bushes that they had to find their way around; it was obviously a long time since this had been a common route – if ever. Eventually, however, they made it to the top and looked around. The wind was stronger up here and chilled them to their bones in their soaking wet clothes.

'Over there,' said Jennifer, pointing off into the distance. Jack looked and could just make out the road where they had stopped their car, back near where the peninsula joined the mainland.

Slowly, they trudged back to where they had parked, the water squelching in their shoes and their wet clothes chaffing as they walked. As they finally reached the car, Jack pulled the key fob out of his pocket and pressed the button to unlock it; nothing happened. 'I guess it didn't like being immersed in cold salt water,' he said to himself.

'It's not the only one,' muttered Jennifer under her breath. She sighed as she remembered the phone in her pocket and pulled it out; it was quite dead. 'There go my photos,' she groaned.

Jack was forced to unlock the car with the key, setting the alarm off in the process. It shut off as soon as he inserted the key into the ignition, but it had still broadcast their position to anyone or anything nearby.

'Let's get out of here,' urged Jennifer. 'I'm ready to find somewhere warm and dry.' She had taken off her jacket and top, and wrapped herself in an old blanket that they kept in the boot.

Jack started the car and reversed back to the main road as quickly as he could. Back on the main road again, he gunned the engine, the wheels squealing on the tarmac as he rapidly accelerated away, putting some ground between themselves and the castle. As the engine started to warm, he turned on the car's heaters, setting them to maximum heat in an attempt to start drying themselves off.

When they had found their way back to the motorway, they stopped at a cheap hotel just off the junction. They received odd looks from the hotel staff, who wondered why they were so wet on a dry night, but it didn't stop them from taking their money for a room.

In their room, they each took a quick shower to warm themselves up. When Jennifer came out of the bathroom wrapped in a towel, she found Jack sitting in one of the hotel chairs, still wearing just his towel. He looked to be deep in concentration, his fingers steepled in front of his face.

'Anything I can help you with?' she offered.

'I'm just thinking back to what Sebastian told me,' he said. 'That I needed to see what was back there in order to truly believe.' He looked up at Jennifer. 'I've got to say... I'm feeling fairly convinced.'

'You do still know you can't trust him, right?'

Jack shrugged. 'I'm aware of your feelings about him.' Jennifer opened her mouth to say something, but Jack held up his palms to acknowledge her. 'I know I can't trust him. But I also need to hear what he has to say. You saw what was painted on the wall back there. What else might he know about my future? About *our* future?'

'We'll worry about that tomorrow. Come on, come to bed,' she whispered demurely. 'It's late, and I'm cold.' She let her towel drop to the floor and then slipped underneath the duvet. Jack stood up from his chair and then crawled into bed beside her, all thoughts of prophecies already out of his mind.

Chapter 11.

December 22nd, 2012. Exeter, England.

Detective Inspector Cross was sitting at her desk when her partner opened the door and stepped into her office. In one hand he was holding a CD in a clear jewel case, and in the other a mug of coffee.

'I've got that CCTV footage from the hospital,' he said.

'Good job,' said Cross, looking up from her computer.

'*And* I brought you another coffee.'

'*Great* job,' she said with a smile. She stood up, taking them from him and placing the latter on top of a pile of papers on her desk. She popped the CD out of its case and inserted it into her computer. 'Let's see what we've got, shall we?'

'What are you looking for?'

'When I was visiting Peter White at the hospital I spotted a man matching the description Jack Knight gave us of his attacker. At first I thought it could just be a coincidence, but he did a runner as soon as he saw me, so he was definitely up to *something*. I was wondering whether we might catch sight of him coming or going.'

She clicked on the first of the video files on the disk. It showed four different black and white views of the hospital car park, one in each corner on the screen. She clicked a button to put the video in fast forward, watching the people and cars dash across the screen.

'So what does he look like?'

'Huh?'

'This man. Who are we looking for?'

'Tall man, dressed all in black, black hoodie, black beard. Had a scar on his hand, but you'd never see that on these.' Dave Brooks nodded, his hands on the back of her chair as he leant over her shoulder to look at the screen.

They worked their way through three different video files until they found what they were after.

'Wait! Is that him?' asked Brooks.

Cross paused and rewound the video. The video was small and grainy, but in the corner of the car park they could see a man dressed in black hurrying into a small hatchback. Cross checked the timestamp in the corner of the video. It was just a few minutes after she had given chase to the man in the hospital. 'That's got to be him,' she said.

'It's too grainy to make out any detail though,' said Brooks with a grimace.

'Just wait a moment,' she said. They stood there in silence for a moment watching the video and waiting for something to happen, and then they saw the car pull out of the parking space, turning and driving towards the camera. As it drew closer, Cross paused the video; the car's number plate was clearly visible at the bottom of the screen. 'Bingo!' she muttered.

'We've got the bastard!' chuckled Brooks.

'Let's not celebrate just yet,' replied Cross. She scribbled the number plate down on a Post-it note. 'Can you check this against the DVLA and stolen cars, and then see if it's been spotted on any number plate cameras?'

'Will do, boss,' he replied, taking the small piece of yellow paper from her.

Chapter 12.

December 23rd, 2012. Dartmoor, England.

Jack was sitting on the sofa reading a book. They had started to put up Christmas decorations and a green pine tree now stood in the corner of the living room, a box of lights and tinsel patiently resting on the floor next to it. He wasn't feeling in any great rush to finish the decorating; he'd got quite used to a plain and sober holiday.

Jennifer stepped through the door holding the oil painting of Robert Knight from above the staircase – the painting she now knew to be an almost century-old portrait of Jack.

'Don't you like it anymore?' he asked.

'I get to see enough of you already, without you looking over my shoulder every time I go up and down the stairs,' she replied. 'Besides which, I wouldn't have thought you'd want the constant reminder of what happened to you.'

Jack gave a small grin and a shrug of his shoulders to acknowledge that she was probably correct, and turned back to his book.

No sooner had he started reading again than the phone started to ring. He sighed with annoyance at the constant interruptions and folded the corner of the page over to mark his place, putting the book down and picking the phone up from the coffee table next to him. He looked at the screen; the incoming number was simply listed as *Withheld* and he pressed the button to answer the call.

'Hello?'

'Hello, Mr Knight,' came a voice he recognized.

'Sebastian.'

'Yes,' he confirmed. 'Did you go?'

'Yes,' said Jack simply.

'And did you see? Tell me what you saw,' said Sebastian.

Jack paused for a moment to collect his thoughts. 'I saw a painting of myself... of what happened at the Well of the Worlds. There was a prophecy about me returning from the past to kill Silas.'

'And would you call that an *accurate* prophecy?'

Jack sighed. 'Stop playing games, Sebastian. You know I would.'

'It's not a vague prophecy, is it? Not something that you could apply to a multitude of events, after the fact?'

'Not with that picture, no,' said Jack grimly.

'That prophecy – as well as many others – was made by the founder of our Brotherhood, almost three hundred years ago. It's also not the only one to refer to you... or to your family.'

'What do you mean?' said Jack. 'What else did he say?'

'All in good time, Mr Knight. First, do you believe? Do you believe Aloysius actually had the gift of prophecy?'

Jack sighed again. 'If what you say is true about the age of that painting... then I can't see any other explanation. I don't know exactly how old it is, but it definitely hasn't been painted recently.'

'Good,' said Sebastian. 'Meet me by Siblyback Lake, tomorrow night at eleven. I have something to give to you. Come alone.'

Jack was about to reply when he realized that Sebastian had already hung up.

✳ ✳ ✳

The following evening, Jack climbed out of his car and into the crisp night air. Illuminated in the glow of his car's lights, he took a look around; the park was dark, the car park deserted.

He locked his car, and as the lights softly dimmed themselves away, he took a few seconds to allow his eyes to adjust to the darkness. He still couldn't see anyone moving, and could hear no sounds except for distant traffic.

He set off across the grounds towards the lake, the ground underfoot crisp and hard with frost. The sky was patchy with clouds and the moon was currently hiding behind them, the light of a few stars his only illumination as he slowly approached his destination.

The surface of the lake was still and clear as he approached, the reflection of the night sky twinkling on its surface. Before it stood a park bench, and Jack turned slightly to head towards it. He looked around, circling the bench and looking for anyone approaching. When no one came, he sat down and looked at his watch: 11:02pm. Somewhere across the lake, a lonely owl hooted in the darkness.

He sat in silence for what seemed like an eternity, the cold night air sharp on the back of his throat. He checked his watch again and was surprised to see that only two minutes had passed.

'Mr Knight?'

'Jesus!' cried Jack, startled. He stood up and turned to see Sebastian standing behind him, his back to the lake. The water was still perfectly calm; Jack had no idea how he had got there.

Jack glanced over Sebastian. He was dressed in his customary black but this time was wearing a thick winter coat. Over his left shoulder hung a leather bag – a satchel or messenger bag.

Sebastian looked up at the sky and turned his head around, admiring the heavens. 'Nice night,' he said calmly.

'Enough of the chit-chat,' said Jack. 'Why am I here?'

'Do you trust me?'

'You tried to murder my wife and bring about the end of all mankind. Of course I don't.'

'I applaud your honesty, Mr Knight, but nevertheless you *are* here... on your own, late at night.'

Jack gave a small laugh. 'You've got me there,' he admitted.

Sebastian gave a little chuckle. 'Okay... Allow me to re-phrase the question. Would you be open to a strategic alliance?'

'What – us working together?' The incredulity was obvious in his voice. 'Why on Earth would I agree to that?'

'Tell me, Mr Knight. Do you love Jennifer?'

Jack frowned, unsure about where this was heading. 'Of course I do—'

'—and are you planning to marry her?'

'Not that it's any of your business, but yes, I am.'

Sebastian looked down at the floor and took a deep breath. When he looked up, the smile on his face was gone, replaced with a serious expression. 'What if I told you that Aloysius foretold the death of your wife – a *premature* death? What would it be worth to you to know the manner of her death, Mr Knight? What if you were able to prevent her untimely demise? Exactly what price would you pay for that information?'

'You can't be serious?'

'Oh, I'm deadly serious. The real question here is not whether you can trust me but rather can you put aside your feelings of revenge and hatred towards my master and the Brotherhood in order to save your wife?'

Jack was feeling light-headed and leant against the bench for support. He hadn't known what to expect from Sebastian but had never expected this. He closed his eyes for a moment, considering the proposal. When he opened his eyes again, he looked into Sebastian's face, trying to judge what was going on in his mind; the stoic look on his face wasn't giving anything away. Then something struck him. 'So you think the future can be changed, that the prophecy isn't written in stone?'

Sebastian sighed. 'To be honest, I'm not sure. Personally, I'm a believer in fate, that we all have an intertwined destiny, but can *you* afford to take that chance? What would your wife think if she knew that you had turned down the chance to save her?'

'Are you threatening me?'

'Not at all. I'm just trying to make your options clear to you, Mr Knight.'

'Okay.' Jack realized he had been curling his hands into fists, and released them. He took a deep breath to calm himself and exhaled it slowly. 'Just say that I agree to help you. What exactly is it that you're after? What do you want from me?'

'My master would like to meet you.'

'Where?'

Sebastian smiled a broad smile. 'Somewhere far away from here.'

'I'm not supposed to leave the country. The police still have me as a *Person of Interest* after what happened up in Glasgow.'

Sebastian shook his head, the smile still on his lips. 'That won't be necessary. Not that I think you're someone who pays too much attention to what the police want, eh? No, my master would like to meet in a much more... *interesting* place.'

'You're part of an organization which repeatedly tried to kill us, not to mention trying to summon *Great Old Ones* into the world. You still haven't told me why I should trust you.'

'You haven't been paying attention, Mr Knight. My master has no ill feelings towards yourselves personally, unlike, I should add, many others in the Brotherhood. You may have trouble believing it, but we actually have an interest in keeping you alive, one that my master *could* share with the whole Brotherhood. As to their grander designs... well, your meddling has brought a halt to those proceedings for quite a few years.' He looked up at the heavens again. 'It will be a good while until the conditions are right again, possibly never. We can help each other, Mr Knight, if you would just put the past behind you.'

Jack thought in silence for a moment before responding. 'Why me?' he asked. 'There must be others? Others in the Brotherhood who could help?'

'My master has his reasons,' he replied simply. 'They will become clear over time, but for now, I shall just say that you are uniquely positioned to help him.'

Jack shook his head in disbelief. 'Okay. Let's just assume I agree to help him. What is it he wants of me? Surely not just to meet me?'

'The key to your future lies in the power of dreams, Mr Knight. I believe you are aware of the power they can hold?' Jack nodded, thinking back to the ritual he had used with Peter White to divine the location of Jennifer when the Brotherhood was holding her captive. 'There is another world that exists beyond this one, a land of dreams – like this world but different. There is an ancient rite that will allow you to cross over into this world, travelling through your dreams. That is where you and my master shall meet and then journey together to find Aloysius's true legacy, where he will reveal Aloysius's prophecies to you.'

'You want me to meet your master in my dreams?'

'Not just in *a* dream,' he said with a slight shake of his head. 'In the *land* of dreams. It is where my master spends most of his time these days. He only returns to this mortal world for matters of the utmost importance.'

Jack looked back at him, an incredulous expression on his face. 'You're being serious?'

'Absolutely. When you travel to these dreamlands, your dream self will be able to meet my master's dream self.'

'And when I'm in these lands...'

'Your mortal body will be asleep here, quite safe, I assure you.'

Jack contemplated this for a second. 'And when we find this legacy of Aloysius together, then he'll tell me the prophecies? Tell me how to save my wife?'

Sebastian smiled. 'Yes, Mr Knight. We believe Aloysius left something behind in the dream world. His true legacy, itself described in another of his prophecies. If you help my master find it, and surrender unto the Brotherhood that which is ours, then he will tell you all he knows about these prophecies. He will also convince the Brotherhood to leave you and your partner alone, if you will do the same.'

Jack thought hard. He didn't trust Sebastian and his master any more than the rest of the Brotherhood, but he needed to know. He loved Jennifer too much to let her die if there was the slightest chance he could save her. He knew what Jennifer would say, that this was a stupid idea and not worth the risk – and part of him knew she was right. But he also knew that he had gone too far and seen too much to abandon her now.

'Don't forget your attacker from the other night,' added Sebastian when Jack didn't reply. 'He was just the first of many. The Brotherhood has been around for a long time and has a very long memory. Left unchecked, you'll be looking over your shoulder for the rest of your life.'

'Okay,' said Jack with a reluctant sigh. 'So how do I travel to this dream world? Where do I find this rite?'

Sebastian took the bag off his shoulder and passed it to Jack. 'This contains an ancient tome,' said Sebastian. 'The *Liber Somniorum*. Inside you will find all the instructions you need.'

Jack undid the buckles and peered into the bag; he could see an old leather-bound book inside.

'I trust you can read Latin,' said Sebastian.

'I can muddle my way through,' replied Jack. 'I've got a good dictionary.'

Sebastian nodded. 'I've marked the page with the ritual on it with a bookmark.' Jack pulled the bag open again and looked closer, this time noticing a piece of paper sticking out between the pages of the book. He closed the bag again.

'When you arrive,' continued Sebastian, 'you should head for the town of Aladoth. My master will meet you there, in the tavern called *The Moon Cat*.'

'Okay...' said Jack cautiously. 'And what do I call this master of yours?'

'Randolph,' said Sebastian. 'His name is Randolph.'

'And do you expect me to go alone?'

'If you wish to bring your partner with you for aid and support, I'm sure that would be fine.'

Jack thought for a second. 'How am I going to explain any of this to her?'

'You may need to be... *economical* with the truth. It may not be good for her to know of her premature death.'

Jack laughed out loud. 'No shit – and she may be rather reluctant to help you.'

'Oh, of that I'm sure.'

'Hell, I'm not sure I want to help you myself yet.'

Sebastian looked at him again, a satisfied smile on his face. 'I have faith in you, Mr Knight.'

✵ ✵ ✵

Jennifer was sitting in the living room, leafing through bridal magazines, when Jack came in through the front door. She was tired, barely paying them any attention, and turned to look towards him as he entered. 'Well?' she asked, when he didn't say anything.

Jack had spent the entire journey home thinking about what to tell her, and he still hadn't decided. If he told her that he was doing this to try and save her life, he was fairly certain she would refuse. He didn't think that she would consider it worth the risk.

'There are more prophecies about me,' he eventually said. 'We need to visit someone Sebastian works for – he calls him his master – who will reveal them to me.'

'So where is he?'

'In another place.'

'What's *that* supposed to mean?'

He came over and sat down on the end of the sofa next to her. 'I've told you how I managed to have a kind of lucid dream before – well this is similar. We need to visit this other place through our dreams. That's where Randolph – his master – will meet us.' Jennifer gave him a bemused look. He opened Sebastian's bag, pulling out the old leather book. 'This tome will explain how to get there, or so I've been led to believe. He needs me to go there and help him find something – and in exchange he'll tell me about the prophecies.'

'So why does he need you?'

Jack thought for a second. 'He wouldn't explain fully. At least not yet.'

Jennifer looked at him closely. She used to think she knew him well enough to tell when he was lying, but he had just spent ten years apart from her; she was no longer sure she knew him like she used to. She was sure he was hiding *something* from her, but she couldn't tell what. She considered calling him out on it but decided against it. She didn't like it, but she ought to have faith in him; he had earned that from her. 'You know you can't trust him,' she eventually said.

'I know.'

'He'll have his own agenda. It may not be apparent to you at the moment, but you'll just be part of a larger plan.'

'I know,' he repeated, more emphatically this time. 'Look, I know he can't be trusted, but this is just something I need to do.' He took her hands in his and looked deep into her eyes. 'You may not be able to trust *him*, but you trust *me*, right?'

Jennifer looked him in the eyes. She knew she *ought* to trust him – she had agreed to marry him, after all. She just wasn't sure that she did any more. She sighed. 'Yes, I trust you,' she said, as much to reassure herself as to reassure him.

'Good,' he said, leaning over and kissing her on the cheek. 'Now, let's get to bed.'

Chapter 13.

December 27th, 2012.

The basement was dark, the only light coming from five candles that had been placed on the floor; each was positioned at the point of a pentagram, which had been crudely carved into the dirt. Lying within the symbol was a grey-haired man, stripped to the waist, his hands and feet bound to stakes by dirty strips of leather.

Standing above him was a man in a long black robe, his face hidden by the hood. In his right hand, he held a dagger, its long blade twisted and glimmering in the candlelight.

'You will tell me what I need to know,' said the hooded man. It was a statement, not a question.

'I'll tell you nothing,' spat the man from the floor in an attempt to look brave, but the look in his eyes betrayed his true emotions.

'I have waited a long time for this,' replied the hooded man. 'I have been searching for this for most of my adult life. I will not be denied when I'm so close.' He knelt down on the floor and placed his dagger on the floor next to him.

The grey-haired man stared back at him. He wondered if any help would be coming; could he hold out until it came? He had guarded these secrets his whole life. His best hope now might be to take them to the grave.

'If you're not going to capitulate, you leave me no choice,' muttered the hooded man. He stood up, walking over to a stone altar where his leather satchel lay. The grey-haired man could not see what he was doing, but when he turned back around, the hooded man was holding two small vials of liquid, one a deep purple, the other an inky black.

'What have you got there?' cried the grey-haired man, but the hooded man ignored him, walking past him and kneeling down on the floor above his head, just out of view.

The hooded man started chanting, a low murmur at first, then gathering pace and volume. The grey-haired man had never heard this language spoken aloud, but he thought he recognized scraps of it from his studies; it was an ancient language, one he had believed to be dead for centuries.

The hooded man came into focus above his head as the chant reached a fever pitch. He reached down, grabbing the grey-haired man's chin and forcing his mouth open. He poured the contents of the first bottle into his mouth, the purple liquid burning his mouth and tongue. He tried to spit it out, but the hooded man had forced his mouth shut again and was holding it closed.

When he had reluctantly swallowed the liquid, the hooded man let him open his mouth to breath and then poured in the black liquid. He was already feeling faint, able to put up less resistance as his mouth was forced shut a second time. The second liquid had a sickly metallic taste, reminding him of the taste of blood. He coughed as the liquid went down the back of his throat but was unable to stop himself swallowing.

'It's no good poisoning me,' he finally spat at the hooded man when he'd removed the hands from his mouth. 'I've sworn never to reveal my secrets to the likes of you. I'll die first.'

He heard a deep chuckle from the dark shadows of his torturer's hood.

'My dear Nathaniel,' he whispered in soothing tones. 'This is not to hurt you, but to keep you alive. If you do not tell me the location of your secrets, I will wreak upon you such terrible agony that before the night is out, you'll be begging me to just kill you.'

He stood up and walked around to the feet of his prisoner, picking up his dagger from the floor. He held the blade in front of his face, twisting it one way and then the other in the flickering light, watching the pale candle-light reflect from the cold steel.

Then he knelt down at the side of the grey-haired man and dragged the tip of the blade across his stomach, ripping a fine seam across the skin, dark red blood oozing out and running across his flesh to the floor. His prisoner gritted his teeth, a deathly grimace on his face, desperately trying not to show any fear or weakness to his captor.

'Now then,' he said calmly. 'Let us start at the beginning. You are going to tell me everything I want to know, and then maybe I will let you die a peaceful death.'

Chapter 14.

December 28th, 2012. Dartmoor, England.

Jennifer awoke late the next morning to find Jack already up. She pulled open the bedroom curtains to reveal another dull grey sky, the branches of the trees bending in a strong wind. Putting on a dressing gown, she stepped into the bathroom to freshen up. She'd taken the bandage off her cheek now and she looked at her face again in the mirror; there was a red scar along the side of her face and she wondered if it would ever truly heal. It wasn't particularly disfiguring – it could have been a lot worse – but it was a constant reminder of what she had been through every time she looked in the mirror.

Trying to put it to the back of her mind, she went down to the kitchen to make herself a cup of coffee. She eventually found Jack in the study, the *Liber Somniorum* lying open on the desk in front of him.

'Find anything interesting yet?' she yawned.

'A bit,' he said. 'I still need to work on my Latin some more.' A large Latin-to-English dictionary was sitting on the desk next to the tome. He leafed through the yellowed pages of the book, searching until he came across the one he was after. 'Here, look at this,' he said, beckoning her over.

She came close and leant over his shoulder to have a look. On the page was a series of lines and curves. When she caught sight of them in her peripheral vision, some kind of optical illusion seemed to make them dance before her eyes, gliding over the page, but whenever she focused on any particular section it seemed quite normal.

'Is that the spell?' she asked.

Jack nodded. 'It's similar to a couple I used before when I was trying to get you back.'

'But this'll actually make us travel to somewhere else?'

'Well, we won't actually go anywhere, our bodies will still be right here.'

'So it's what?' she asked. 'Clairvoyance? Astral projection? Mass hallucination?'

Jack smiled and shook his head. 'I don't know. We'll just have to try it and see.'

'And is it safe?'

'It depends what you mean by *safe*. I suppose our bodies would be secure in our beds, but our minds...'

'I don't like this, Jack. There are just too many unknowns.'

'I'll agree with you there. I'm trying to make my way through the rest of the book, to see what other information I can glean, but it's slow going. I'm not great with Latin at the best of times, and this seems to be some kind of odd dialect.'

Jennifer stood up straight again. 'Well, okay, you see what you can find out – I'll make us some food.' She wandered out, heading towards the kitchen.

'Did I tell you I'm seeing Lauren again this afternoon?' she called from the kitchen. 'We're trying to arrange a date and location for the wedding.'

Well, that'll give me some peace and quiet to concentrate on this, Jack thought to himself. 'Do you have any ideas yet?' he called back to her.

'As we're looking for something soon, we're probably limited to the registry offices – all the fancy places are booked years in advance, and we're not exactly regulars at our local church.' She thought for a second. 'I don't suppose your new-found friends in the Brotherhood are licensed to carry out weddings?' she asked sarcastically.

Jack chose to ignore her question. 'Registry office sounds good then,' he replied simply.

Chapter 15.

December 28th, 2012. Exeter, England.

Detective Inspector Cross walked back into her office with a fresh mug of coffee in her hand, only to find Detective Sergeant Brooks sitting in her chair, talking on the phone. He held up a finger to her, acknowledging her entrance.

'Yep,' he said into the phone, and scribbled something onto a pad of paper. 'Yeah, got it. Thanks.' He put the phone down and turned to Cross. 'Got some info on that number plate you asked me to look into.'

'Yeah?'

'Belongs to a Jeremiah Crane, local man.'

'Any news on the car?'

'No, no reported sightings. It's not reported stolen either.'

'Okay.'

'He's got a mobile registered to the same address as his car. I tried calling and got no response, so I sent a constable round. He said no one was in and the neighbours hadn't seen him for several days, so I took the liberty of requesting a phone trace. That was the phone company on the phone.'

'And?' she said. She walked round the side of the desk and nodded towards her chair.

'Oh, yeah, sorry boss,' he muttered, climbing out of the chair. 'It's been at roughly the same location for a couple days, somewhere in the country-side.' He handed the pad of paper to her; it had some co-ordinates written on it. 'Being out in the sticks it's a bit hard to narrow down to an exact location, but there's only a few buildings out that way – a few farmhouses, old country homes, that kind of thing. You reckon we should go take a look?'

Cross took a sip from her coffee and then looked at her watch; the afternoon was getting on, but there were still a good few hours left in the day. 'Yeah, give me five minutes, and we'll go see if Mr Crane can help us with our enquiries.'

Cross sat in the passenger seat as her partner sped their unmarked police car down the narrow country lane. She gripped the door handle as he slung the car around the tight bends. He always did drive a bit too fast on these roads for her liking.

'Are we near yet?' he asked.

Cross consulted the GPS on her phone. 'Pretty much,' she said. 'We're at the rough co-ordinates of where the phone was tracked to.'

Brooks slowed the car down, peering left and right out of the windows. 'But there's nothing out here,' he said.

Cross joined him in looking out of the window. All they could see around them were fields, with just the occasional farmhouse. 'There's not much,' she had to agree. 'We'll have to spiral out, checking the few buildings there are.' She scanned the horizon again. Silhouetted against the slate grey sky she could make out an old farmhouse standing dark and lonely on the top of a nearby hill. 'Let's try over there,' she suggested.

Brooks turned the car into a narrow dirt track leading up the hill, slowing the car to a crawl as he drove along the rutted earth. In front of them, a pair of white wooden gates stood open at the start of a driveway that led up to the farmhouse, while the dirt track continued onwards. As they neared the gates, he drew to a stop. They both scanned the area; there were no lights on, no signs of activity.

'Okay, let's try the next one,' said Cross.

Brooks put the car back into gear and was about to pull away when he stopped. Further away from the house, hidden behind a large hedge at the side of the road, was a dilapidated outbuilding. Poking out of it was the rear of a car. 'That car there,' he said, pointing to it. 'Isn't that the model we're looking for?'

Cross squinted. 'I reckon it is,' she said. 'Pull in – we'll go check it out.'

Brooks slowly drove the car through the gates, pulling over and stopping near the outbuilding. In unison they opened their car doors, stepping out and walking over to the ramshackle structure. The car looked like it had been abandoned in a small barn, which was open on one side. The barn was in a bad state of repair; the stonework was crumbling and the corrugated iron roof was rusting away with several large holes clearly visible.

Cross pulled a slim LED torch from her pocket and turned it on, passing the light over the number plate on the rear of the car. 'Bingo!' she said. 'That's our car.'

She stepped gingerly over to the side of the vehicle, casting the torchlight through the side windows. The interior was messy, covered in food wrappers and empty bottles, but contained nothing suspicious. She cast the torchlight around the interior of the building; it too appeared devoid of anything of interest.

'Shall we take a look around the grounds?' asked Brooks, drawing his own torch from his pocket.

Cross nodded, and they started towards the house. 'You go that way,' she said, pointing towards the far side of the house where a couple of stables stood. 'I'll take this side. There's a chance our suspect is still here and I don't want him getting away again.' Brooks nodded back in confirmation, and she walked towards the front of the house, stopping to look in through the window. It looked like a normal living room, nothing out of the ordinary.

From there, she walked around to the side of the house, keeping her eyes peeled for any sign of movement. As she neared the rear of the building, she could see a wooden barn standing behind the property, its large door hanging open. Raising her torch, she strode towards it, slowing as she reached the doorway, casting her light left and right through the opening. Several different types of crates and barrels were stacked against the left-hand wall, and a rusting tractor sat on large flat tyres to her right.

She was just about to turn and leave when something in the corner of the room caught her eye – a wooden trap-door, which was standing open. Cautiously, she approached it. In the quiet of the night, her footsteps were painfully loud on the stone floor. As she reached the trap-door, she peered down with the torch; a metal ladder was set in the wall of a short shaft, descending down to a passageway below.

She turned around, scanning her surroundings; nothing stirred. She contemplated getting her partner first but quickly decided against it. It was almost certainly just an old storage cellar, but she still ought to check it out.

Brooks cautiously stalked along the side of the farmhouse, moving up to the side door. Through the windows set in the door, all he could see was a dark and empty kitchen. He placed his hand on the metal door handle and gave it a tentative twist. To his surprise, the handle turned and the door swung open. Taking a deep breath to steady himself, he stepped inside.

The room he found himself in was quiet and gloomy. Two sets of dirty plates and cutlery sat on a large kitchen table. Next to them were two wine glasses, a small amount of red wine still sitting in one of them. Slowly, he stepped across the room towards an open doorway on the far side.

As he drew closer, he spotted a couple of small black rectangles sitting on a granite countertop near the door; closer inspection revealed them to be a wallet and mobile phone. He opened the wallet; inside was a small amount of cash and credit cards in the name of Jeremiah Crane. He looked at the phone, an old Nokia model, and then thought for a second. Taking out his own phone, he checked the signal; only one bar, but he did have reception. He scrolled through his call history until he found the call he placed earlier to Jeremiah Crane's number and then tapped the screen to redial it. He waited, and a few seconds later, the phone on the counter sprang to life, vibrating on the hard stone surface. He hung up; this was definitely the place.

He stepped through into the hallway and from there quickly scanned the other downstairs rooms; all appeared empty. With a deep breath, he headed up the stairs.

Cross was standing in a low tunnel leading away from the ladder. Electrical cables ran along the low ceiling, with a bare light bulb hanging every twenty feet. She thought about looking for a light switch, but if there was anyone down here with her, she didn't want to alert them to her presence.

Slowly, by the light of her torch, she started inching down the corridor. As she approached the end, she saw that the corridor opened into a wider room; she could just discern a low buzzing noise and the smell of rotten meat from ahead. She drew a telescopic metal truncheon from her jacket pocket, extending it with a flick of her wrist; it gave a sharp crack as it snapped to its full length. Nervously, she took a few more steps towards the doorway and stopped. The smell was stronger here, making her stomach churn and she felt slightly nauseous. By the light of the torch, she could see the source of the buzzing; flies skittering around the air – lots of them – momentarily illuminated in the shaft of her torchlight.

Cross covered her mouth with her arm and stepped through the door-way. What she saw made her stop in her tracks. The rotting corpse of a man was in the centre of the room, lying in a large pool of his own blood. His arms and legs were bound to stakes in the floor, four points of a pentagram, which had been carved into the floor, a burned-out candle at each point. At the far end of the room stood a crude stone altar; standing in the centre was a stone statue of some kind of goat-woman hybrid. Daubed on the rear wall, in some unidentifiable dark pigment, was a crude symbol of a goat's head, surrounded by what looked like trees.

She drew her phone out of her pocket to call Brooks and swore under her breath; the thick dirt roof and walls were blocking any reception.

'Brooks!' she yelled. 'I've got something down here!'

She stepped forwards, almost gagging from the stench now, and knelt down next to the corpse. She ran her torch over the scene before her. His fingernails were missing from both hands, and the flesh on his chest had been sliced in a cross and then peeled back, his ribcage visible. Just above his waist, his belly had been sliced open, his entrails spilling out onto the floor. Flies were buzzing all around the body; she waved her torch around to try and disperse them but this had no discernible effect.

Even with her years of experience at crime scenes, this was just too much for her. She retched, her body convulsing but only dry heaving. She turned around and took a step away, trying to take a deep breath to calm her nerves, but the foul air only made it worse.

She turned back to the body and noticed something shining in the torchlight next to his head. Cross aimed the torchlight towards it and gasped; it was a small pile of human teeth, their metal fillings glinting in the light.

She stepped towards them, doing her best to avoid stepping in the blood, and reached down towards the teeth. As she did so, her arm brushed against the side of the corpse's face and its eyes flicked open.

For the first time in her professional career, Cross screamed.

'Help me,' whispered the body in a voice as dry as desert sand.

'DAVE!' she yelled at the top of her voice. She glanced down and saw his face looking back up at her; it was paper-white, the skin dry and waxy. 'Don't worry,' she said. 'Help's here now.' She swallowed, trying not to look him in the face. 'You're going to be okay,' she said in a soothing tone, but she didn't believe a word of it.

From the darkness of the corridor came a welcome voice. 'Are you down there?' It was the voice of her partner, standing over the trap-door.

'Call for an ambulance and backup,' Cross shouted back.

'What have you found–'

'NOW!' she screamed.

She turned back to the man lying below her. She couldn't understand how he could still be alive. The amount of skill it must have taken to have done this and not kill him was unbelievable – as was the amount of pain he must have suffered at the hands of his attacker. The man looked into her eyes and mumbled something too quietly for her to hear. She knelt down, positioning her ear over the man's lips. She closed her eyes so that she didn't have to look at him, and hated herself for doing it.

'What is it?' she whispered quietly.

The man muttered something unintelligible and then a phrase she could just barely make out. *More than the mare.*

What the hell? she thought. She turned and looked into his face again; his lips had stopped moving, his eyes were still. Maybe this time he really was dead. For his sake, she hoped so.

Brooks stumbled into the room through the low doorway. He stopped as he saw the scene before him. 'Holy fuck!' he exclaimed. 'Is he…?'

Cross shone her torch into the man's open eyes; the pupils didn't react, not narrowing at all in the bright light. 'Dead? Yeah, I think he is.' She stood up, taking a few wobbly steps towards her partner. 'Let's get out of here until backup arrives. I need some fresh air.'

Chapter 16.

December 28th, 2012. Dartmoor, England.

Jack was just sitting down to eat dinner with Jennifer when his phone rang. He pulled it out of his pocket and looked at it. The calling number was again given as *Withheld*.

'Jack Knight,' he said as he accepted the call.

'Mr Knight,' came a voice he recognized. 'This is Sebastian. I'm calling to let you know you're going to have to go tonight.' His voice sounded faint and distant.

'Tonight? Why so soon? I haven't had time to fully research the incantations yet.'

'Then I suggest you get studying, Mr Knight. My master has a small window of opportunity for this to work. You're going to have to do this tonight.'

'I've been thinking about this. How am I going to find this town and then Randolph in time? We'll only be asleep for what... eight to ten hours?'

'Time works differently in your dreams, Mr Knight. Have you never had dreams that have seemed to cover days or weeks?'

'Then how long have I got?'

'It's not an exact science. But one full night's sleep should give you one to two weeks in the dream world.'

'Well, that should relieve the pressure a bit.'

'But remember, you must go tonight. Miss your chance and you will never find out.' With that, the line went dead.

Chapter 17.

December 28th, 2012. Exmoor, England.

A black Ford was cruising down the dual carriageway back to Exeter. Detective Inspector Cross was at the wheel. She'd left the scene in the hands of the forensic team over three hours ago and was now heading from the police station back to her house. It was late and she was tired; she'd had enough for one night.

She was reaching to adjust the heating in the car when her phone went. The dashboard display indicated that it was her partner, Dave Brooks calling; she pressed the button on the steering wheel to take the call hands-free.

'Dave,' she said. 'What have you got for me?'

'Some news on the vic. It looks like he was the owner of the house but not the owner of the car – we're still trying to track him down. He seems to have disappeared into thin air.'

'Do you think the owner of the car is our suspect?'

'Could be, but he's not the guy you chased at the hospital. Not according to descriptions from his neighbours.'

'So what do you reckon? Someone stole his car and he's...' She trailed off, thinking of the man she had found under the barn.

'We can't be sure, but it's sounding more likely.'

'Okay, so talk to me about our victim. Any big secrets? Any enemies or people wanting him dead?'

'That's the thing. This guy was a suspect in an investigation several years ago. Several young women went missing without a trace and he was one of the key suspects, but they could never pin it on him – there just wasn't enough evidence.'

'You're thinking he was our man and someone related to the victims wanted revenge? I've got to tell you, that doesn't tie up with the crime scene we just looked at.'

'No, that's just it. I've just had a chat with one of the investigating officers. During the investigation, they thought there was some weird cult in-volvement – they thought the women had been abducted as part of some ritualistic sacrifice. There were two main suspects they were looking at, both believed to be part of the cult, but they could never prove anything.'

'And our guy was one of these two men?'

'Yeah. The other one was someone called Morgan Lamarre.'

Cross slammed on the brakes, pulling the car to a sudden stop. The car behind was forced to swerve around her, its horn blaring. That was what the dying man had whispered to her; not *More than the mare* but *Morgan Lamarre*.

'This Morgan Lamarre – do you have a last known address for him?' she barked down the phone.

'Yes, boss,' said Brooks, reading it back to her.

Cross looked over her shoulder and then span the car around, driving over the grass verge in the centre of the road.

'Dave, I'm going to go and check him out. I'll call you back shortly.'

Chapter 18.

Detective Inspector Cross pulled off the quiet country lane and headed up the long driveway towards the house. It was situated deep in the countryside, the only building for miles around. Even before she arrived, she could tell something was wrong; a car was parked askew on the front lawn, its driver's door left wide open. In the dim illumination of the car's interior lights, the roof of the car looked horribly out of shape, the metal bent and twisted.

She pulled up a short distance from the car and turned off the engine, leaving her headlights on for illumination. As she approached and looked more closely, the cause of the damage to the car's roof was obvious – a smashed and broken corpse lay on top. She looked around in confusion. The car stood fifty feet from the house, and there was nothing any closer for a body to fall from. She checked the body for a pulse out of instinct, knowing what she would find. There were no signs of life, but the body wasn't yet cold; whatever had happened here had not occurred all that long ago.

She took a few steps towards the house and looked at it carefully for the first time. It was a large two-storey country house made of sandy-brown stone, crenels running all the way across the front roof. All the lights were out, but the front door stood ominously open, the shadowy interior inviting her to enter.

She pulled her phone from her pocket to call her partner for backup, but it simply said *No Signal* at the bottom of the screen. *Damn the countryside,* she thought to herself. She pocketed the phone and started to walk back towards the car to use the police radio but then stopped. She'd been on her way home from the station when she'd had the call from Dave; she'd come in her own car. *Damn it,* she thought to herself again, taking out her torch. *I'll have to use the phone inside instead.*

She approached the house cautiously, checking behind her before she stepped through the open doorway. Once inside, she stopped and gasped as she looked around; she didn't know what she had expected, but it wasn't this. The hallway was in disarray. Antique paintings had been knocked from the walls and now lay on the floor, their frames broken. The stair banisters had been demolished, the wood lying in a thousand pieces on the floor, as was what might have once been some kind of antique display cabinet, now only useful as firewood.

More ominous was a thick crimson smear running down the centre of the hallway and through the far doorway; the door itself was lying smashed on the floor. Someone had been dragged through this hallway bleeding – bleeding *profusely.*

As she took a step forwards, she caught sight of a neat circular hole in the wall next to her. She turned, stepping closer to get a better look, bringing her face right up to the wall and using the light of the torch. It looked like a bullet hole. If there had been a gunfight, maybe whoever had been dragged through here had been shot first? What the hell had gone on here?

She pulled her phone out of her pocket. It still read *No Signal.* She knew she shouldn't carry on alone, but if this was recent, whoever was behind it might still be here. There might be people who were hurt and in need of medical attention.

She closed her eyes and took a deep breath, willing herself some extra courage. She drew out her telescopic truncheon again, more for reassurance than anything else; she didn't think it would stop whoever had caused all this destruction.

Stepping over the remnants of the door lying on the floor and then through the doorway, she cast her torch around what must have once been an ornate dining room, complete with oil paintings and animal heads on the walls. However, the large wooden dining table lay in two pieces on the floor, split in half down the middle. Lying between the two pieces of the table was the body of a man. *Just* the body; his head was missing from the neck up, a large pool of blood congealing under him. She turned away, only to see what had caused the smear of blood along the floor: a body lay against the wall, its stomach ripped open with its innards spilling out onto its lap. From somewhere in the background, she could hear a faint sound like an alarm siren. Had someone else already called for the police?

At the rear of the room were large patio doors; most of the panes were smashed with the glass lying shattered on the floor. She stepped closer, trying to ignore the two dead bodies. *Three*, she corrected herself, as another body came into view in the rear corner, its skull smashed in, barely recognizable as a face any more. She had to get out of here. She moved swiftly to the doorway and stopped, now recognizing the sound of the alarm. A phone lay on the floor by the door, emitting a two-tone noise to indicate that it had been left off the hook. Counting her blessings, she crouched down and swept some fragments of glass from it before she picked it up, resetting it as she did so; the sound changed to a normal ring tone. She stepped out of the doorway, out of that room, onto the patio and into the calm fresh air of the winter night. She looked at the phone, rapidly dialling her partner's number.

'D.S. Brooks,' came the familiar gruff voice from the other end of the line.

'Dave,' she said in rapid hushed tones. 'It's me. I need backup urgently.'

'Where are you?'

'Lamarre's place.'

'What do you need?' he asked.

'Send everything we've got,' she replied in a deathly grim voice.

From behind her, she heard a sound like creaking leather and sensed something moving. She turned and caught a momentary brief glimpse of a large black shape sweeping over her before a blow to the head sent her falling to the floor and into unconsciousness.

Cross came to lying on the cold stone of the patio where she had fallen. Her vision was blurry, her ears ringing. *What the hell was that?* she thought to herself.

From somewhere in the darkness, she could just make out large indistinct shapes moving, and over the sound of the wind she could hear an odd animal-like noise. The sound changed in pitch and intonation and she realized it wasn't an animal at all but some kind of conversation in a language she didn't know, a language she had never even heard.

From the distance, she could now hear the sound of sirens wafting over the fields; backup was on its way. She couldn't have been unconscious for too long.

Slowly, she dragged herself to her knees, her head throbbing. Her torch was gone, fallen to the floor somewhere. She was feeling about in the darkness, trying not to cut herself on the broken glass, when her fingers ran across something metallic. She picked it up and a wave of surprise swept through her as she realized what it was – a revolver, presumably dropped during the carnage that had occurred.

Still on her knees, she turned back towards the gardens at the rear of the house and the source of the sounds. It was pitch black out here and she gradually raised herself to her feet, her legs unsteady. She started to take a couple of steps away from the house when the wind momentarily cleared the clouds from in front of the moon.

Standing fifty feet away with his back to her was a figure dressed all in black, but it was what stood behind him that took her breath away and almost made her collapse again – two black humanoid creatures towered over the man, large leathery wings protruding from their backs and long tails curled on the floor behind them. One of them appeared to be holding something in its hands, a small metallic ball, its surface shimmering in the pale moonlight.

The sirens were getting closer now, but she just stood there, mouth open, unable to take in what she was seeing. Then, as one, the two creatures flapped their wings and lifted off into the air, creating a gust of wind that wafted against her face. They moved swiftly and gracefully, disappearing almost instantly towards the woods behind the house, lost in the dark of the night.

With the creatures out of sight, her senses finally came back to her. 'Police!' she shouted. 'Turn around and put your hands up!'

The figure jerked, obviously surprised by her appearance. He turned around slowly, his hands raised in front of him.

'On your knees,' she ordered, her voice cracking slightly.

'Or what?' he replied in a low voice, only just audible over the noise of the wind. 'Are you going to shoot an unarmed and defenceless old man?'

She could hear more sirens now; *they must be close now*, she thought, possibly even in the driveway on the other side of the house.

'I don't know that you're defenceless,' she said, her voice growing stronger now. 'I just know we've got a hell of a lot of dead bodies and you're the only one still standing.' She took a few steps towards him, the gun held out before her in both hands, aiming towards the ground between them.

'Really?' he said in mock innocence. 'I wouldn't know anything about that.' He took a tentative step backwards, away from her.

'Don't tempt me,' she barked, raising the gun now to point at him. 'I'll shoot if I have to.'

'We don't even know if there are any bullets left in that gun,' he replied.

'True,' she acknowledged. 'But are you willing to take that risk? I know I am.' She took several steps closer. She could see him more closely now. His hood covered most of his face, but she could see enough in the pale moonlight to see that he was an elderly man, grey stubble on his weathered face. She took a few more steps towards him, halving the distance. They both looked at each other for a moment, staring into each other's eyes, sizing up their opponents and deciding on the best course of action.

'Inspector?' came a shout from behind her, the voice of her partner. She turned momentarily towards him, but that was all it took. The man bolted.

'Shit,' she cursed. 'Over here!' she shouted as she set off after the man. *I guess he was right*, she thought to herself as she ran. *I wouldn't shoot an unarmed man.*

He was heading for the woods at the rear of the property and moving fast for a man of his age. Cross, though, was younger and fitter. She was gaining on him, and when he lost traction on a patch of wet grass she was on him, knocking him to the ground and landing on him.

'Don't you move!' she shouted at him. She could see flashlights approaching over the grass. 'Over here!' she shouted again.

She pressed her knee into the man's back, pinning him to the ground, and drew her handcuffs from her belt. Bending one arm behind his back, she slapped the cuffs around one wrist, shortly followed by the other.

Torchlight shone in her face. She put a hand out to stop it from dazzling her and saw it was her partner, along with two uniformed policemen. Brooks was panting, obviously out of breath from the sprint across the gardens.

'Are you okay?' he asked Cross.

'I'm fine,' she replied, standing up and heaving the man off the floor by his arms. She shoved him towards the two uniformed policemen. 'Take him away,' she said. 'We're going to want to have words with him.'

Chapter 19.

December 28th, 2012. Dartmoor, England.

Jennifer peered into the study to see Jack hunched over the desk. The room was dark except for a desk lamp, the *Liber Somniorum* lying open in the pool of light. Jack was studiously copying a page of inscriptions onto a sheet of paper, muttering something in a guttural language as he did so.

She watched silently, not wanting to disturb him and break his concentration, but also mesmerized by the low rhythmic chanting. She felt herself relaxing, her eyelids growing heavy as the unknown words washed over her and she watched the pen making swirls of ink on the paper.

She jumped with a start, as Jack closed the book with a snap. She wasn't quite sure if she'd just fallen asleep standing up or not. She coughed to clear her throat. 'Are you done?' she asked in a quiet voice.

'I think so,' said Jack. 'Nothing to do now but try it.' He held the sheet of paper up to show Jennifer. The lines and curves on the page seemed to be gliding over the paper, rearranging themselves before her eyes. She blinked, with a quick shake of the head; when she looked again they were stationary, just lines of ink on a page.

'I think they'll work just fine,' she said with a faint smile.

Jack stood up and carefully put the tome onto one of the bookshelves. He looked at his watch; it was a little after eight. 'Are you ready?'

Jennifer gave a small shrug. 'It feels a little early to be going to bed.' Jack opened his mouth to say something, but she knew where he was going. 'Yes, I know you like an early night, but we've got a job to do.' She took a couple of steps backwards into the hallway and then started to walk up the stairs to their bedroom. Jack followed close behind her. 'Do you know what to expect?' she asked.

'No,' said Jack. In fact, he felt decidedly unprepared, as if he was about to take an exam he hadn't studied for. 'This is different from the rituals I used before – I really don't know how this is going to work... Just that I very much doubt it'll be like a normal dream.'

Jennifer sat at the foot of the bed and started to remove her shoes when Jack stopped her.

'Don't take them off,' he said. 'I don't know where we're going to end up, but you probably don't want to be barefoot.'

Jennifer shrugged and climbed onto the bed while Jack lifted up the pillows and placed the sheet underneath. As they both lay on the mattress facing each other, Jennifer took his hand in hers and they looked into each other's faces.

'Whatever we find there, I'm sure we can face it together,' she said to him in a calm, quiet voice.

'When I've got you by my side, I feel like I can take on anything,' he agreed with a smile, giving her a small kiss on the tip of her nose.

Together, they closed their eyes and relaxed.

They opened their eyes to find themselves standing side by side in the centre of a vast hall. The walls of the room were made from huge slabs of polished white marble; in the centre were four columns of the same stone, supporting a high domed ceiling. Burning torches were attached to the pillars, casting flickering light all around them. The illumination decreased further from the centre, the corners of the room inky black with shadows. In front of them, central in one the walls, stood an enormous arched doorway, beyond which a wide set of stone steps descended into darkness.

Jennifer turned to look at Jack. 'My God!' she exclaimed, putting her hand over her mouth.

'What? What is it?' said Jack.

'You look…'

'What?' he snapped, his eyes wide as he started to fear the worst.

'…younger.'

'Younger?'

'My God, it must be at least twenty years,' she said. Jack looked at his hands; they did look less wrinkled, smoother and less worn.

She stepped forwards, taking his head in her hands to look at the difference, and as she came closer, he too could see a difference. The effect was less pronounced with her, but she definitely appeared younger too; even the scar on her cheek was gone. 'You're the same,' he confirmed. 'Maybe ten years?'

'Were you expecting this?' asked Jennifer.

Jack scratched his head. 'I'm not sure what I was expecting. Maybe this is how we were in the prime of our lives – or is this is how we see ourselves?' He looked around the room. The only windows in the room were high up the walls and showed nothing but darkness. There were no doors; apart from the archway with the stairs leading down, there were no visible exits. 'I guess we go down,' he said.

Together, they walked to the arched doorway and looked through; they could only see fifty feet of steps down the tenebrous staircase before they disappeared completely. Jennifer walked over to the nearest column and lifted a torch out of its bracket before returning to Jack. With the torch in her hand, they could see a little further than before, but still couldn't see what was waiting for them at the bottom of the stairs.

Jack took her free hand in his, and together they started downwards. They descended silently, neither of them speaking. After a few dozen steps, Jack stopped and turned around. Although he was sure it should still have been visible, the doorway at the top was gone. There was nothing there now but darkness – just as it was below them. He was damn glad that Jennifer had thought to take a torch.

They started walking again, carefully descending deeper and deeper until they took one final step and their surroundings instantly changed. One second they were standing in darkness and the next, they were outside, on a rough stone plateau, the flat stone floor lightly dusted with sand. They were part way up a rocky mountain, with a cliff face ascending behind them and a sandy desert stretched out before them, the sand rusty red in colour. The sky above them was a perfect blue, with not a cloud in the sky. Despite the golden sun hanging overhead, the air was cool and fresh, with a stiff breeze blowing over the desert towards them. Looking over his shoulder, Jack could see a lightless cave entrance in the side of the cliff, stone steps rising upwards within.

Jennifer thrust the torch upside down into the sandy ground, extinguishing it. 'I don't think we'll need this any longer,' she said.

Jack stepped forwards, one hand shielding his eyes from the radiant sunlight while he scanned the horizon. There was nothing for miles around, only hills and mountains all around the desert, but far in the distance across the pale red sand, he could just make out a collection of buildings against the horizon. He squinted, trying to get a clearer view, but the heat haze across the desert was making the air shimmer. He couldn't be certain at this distance, but it looked like either a large village or a small town built from a gleaming white stone.

He turned back to look at Jennifer and noticed something that he hadn't spotted in the dim light inside – her clothes had changed. They were ostensibly the same, but there were subtle differences and they looked more archaic. The buttons and stitching on her top were cruder and the straps on her shoes were chunkier. His own shoes had changed too, a simpler pair than he had worn before, the thin laces replaced by leather buckles. His watch was gone from his wrist, although their jewellery remained. He reached into his pocket, bringing out a small leather purse where his wallet used to be. He opened it and saw a handful of metal coins inside.

'Where is this place?' Jack wondered aloud.

'I don't know, but we're sure as hell not in Kansas anymore,' said Jennifer. 'Where do we go from here?'

Jack pointed out over the desert towards the buildings in the distance, the only man-made feature visible. 'I guess that's our first stop.' Before them lay a path leading away from the plateau, first down the side of the mountain and then off towards the sandy desert. 'After you?' he offered.

✳ ✳ ✳

They were unsure how long the journey across the desert took them. Every so often, they would lose concentration and suddenly find they had travelled a large distance, although they were unaware of any time passing. It reminded Jack of how time sometimes appeared fragmented and disjointed in dreams, jumping from one memory to another.

As they drew closer to the settlement, they could start to make it out more clearly. A tall white stone wall ran around a large collection of buildings, and although it held a large pair of wooden gates, they lay open, as if inviting them in. Several taller buildings towered over the walls, their marble walls glistening in the bright sunlight. A small lake flanked by several trees lay before the gates, a veritable oasis in this dry and barren land. Several pack animals stood there drinking, their owners casually chatting nearby.

As Jack and Jennifer approached the lake, the nearest group of men stopped talking and turned to face them. They were dressed in loose-fitting multicoloured robes and tunics, their heads covered with turbans or hoods to shield them from the sun. They could see now that the animals drinking at the water's edge were mainly camels, although Jack was surprised to also see a couple of zebras, their backs laden with bags.

Jack strode cautiously up to the water's edge, reaching in and cupping his hands to scoop out a handful of water. He tentatively took a sip; it was cool and fresh — he hadn't realized just how thirsty he was until now. He nodded to Jennifer who squatted down next to him to take a drink and wash the dirt and sand from her face.

'Well, hello there, travellers,' called one of the men, pulling down the hood of his robes as he spoke so that they could see him more clearly. He spoke with an odd accent that Jack couldn't place; when he said *hello* it sounded more like *hall-low*. He glanced up and down at them. 'You don't look like you're from around here. Can we help you?'

Jack smiled and stood up. 'You're right, there,' he said, holding out his hand. 'We're looking for a town called Aladoth.'

The man stepped forwards and took his hand firmly, giving it a vigorous shake. 'Arun,' he said in a gruff voice.

Jack assumed that was his name. 'I'm Jack, this is Jennifer,' he said with a nod towards her.

'You're in luck,' replied another of the men in the same strange accent. He stepped forwards and pulled down his hood. 'For this is it.' He swept his hand sideways to indicate the walls of the city as he spoke.

'Would you know where we could find an inn called *The Moon Cat?*' asked Jennifer.

The first man nodded his head. 'Follow the main road to the centre of town, where you'll find the market – you can't miss it. You'll find the inn on the far side.'

Jack and Jennifer thanked them and then set off towards the open gates. They were as tall as the wall, two stories high, and looked like they were made of solid oak. They appeared strong enough to keep out most forms of trouble, but Jack guessed they had never seen any real action – like the walls they stood between, they looked almost pristine, with barely any signs of wear or use.

As they stepped inside, a wide street led away from them, paved with irregular slabs of a pale grey-green stone. The tall buildings either side were mostly made of veined white marble with thin grey tiles on the roofs. The passageways between them were narrow and shady, populated either by cats or inhabitants looking to escape the glare of the sun.

The further they walked into the town, the busier the streets around them became. Everyone they passed wore the same type of clothes as the men outside – loose light-coloured robes and tunics. Brightly coloured birds sat squawking on roof tops and in window frames, some in cages but most of them free. They appeared unconcerned by the cats that they frequently encountered prowling through the streets, mostly alone but some gathered together in a temporary alliance.

Just as the men outside had said, they had no trouble finding the market. As they progressed further, the buildings were now packed closer together, and what had started as a few people on the road was now a busy throng. They rounded a bend in the street and saw before them a large square sat in the centre of the town. It was filled with hundreds of stalls, each covered with a swathe of brightly coloured canvas. Above the stalls, they could see the top of a tall jade fountain standing in the centre of the square, water flowing gently down from the top over several circular layers.

Jack's senses were overloaded with what lay before him. Not just the vibrant colours of the stalls but an overwhelming aroma from all the foods on sale and the din of hundreds of rowdy conversations – customers arguing and bartering over their purchases and traders shouting and yelling to grab the attention of passers-by.

Jack and Jennifer stood for a moment, taking in all that lay before them; with just a quick glance, they could see stalls selling brightly coloured cloths and robes, spices and foodstuffs. Others sold books, some live animals. Jack walked over to one of the nearest stalls, which contained an impressive array of fruits. Some he recognized, but many were foreign to him – what looked like bright-red lemons and clusters of small orange berries.

'Can I help you with anything?' asked the man behind the stall. He wore a lime-green tunic with a wide-brimmed straw hat and was sucking on a long thin pipe.

'Actually, we're looking for *The Moon Cat*,' said Jack. 'Do you know where we could find it?'

The man took a deep breath from his pipe before blowing out several rings of smoke. 'The inn's over in the corner there,' he said, pointing to a large building in the far corner of the square. 'Can I interest you in something to eat?'

'Do we need to eat here, if this is all some kind of dream?' Jennifer quietly whispered to Jack.

'I don't know,' admitted Jack. 'I think there's still some kind of reality to all of this.'

'I know I'm certainly feeling hungry,' confirmed Jennifer. 'I'm just not too sure about some of that fruit. I was always warned about eating odd berries.'

Jack shook his head and thanked the man. Together they slowly made their way through the busy market towards the inn, stopping only to avoid a large swarm of cats crossing the path in front of them. As the animals moved across the street, one of them stopped and turned to face them, a look of bemused curiosity on its face. It looked at Jack, cocking its head slightly, and Jack could have sworn it was sizing him up. Eventually, it just gave a short squawk, as if to acknowledge their existence, and then raced off, catching up with the rest of its group.

Jack and Jennifer looked at each other in silent confusion and then continued through the market. The stalls in this section were mainly selling food, and the rich smell of the spices and meats cooking on open fires only served to remind them of how long it had been since they last ate.

As they approached the inn, they could see a sign hanging in front of it, confirming its name: *The Moon Cat*. Above the words there was a painting of a black cat but with wispy tentacles rather than whiskers.

'That,' whispered Jennifer, 'is creepy as hell,' as she pushed open the door and they stepped inside.

Coming in from the bright outdoors, it took their eyes a few seconds to adjust to the dark interior. A long mahogany bar stood in front of them; on the shelves behind it stood dozens of bottles in a myriad of colours and shapes. Several sturdy round tables made from a similar dark wood stood around the room, most of the patrons sitting on wooden chairs around them. Many were smoking pipes, and a haze of smoke hung in the air, masking a more subtle smell of sweet spices and making Jennifer cough slightly.

Jack took a deep breath to steady his nerves, then wished he hadn't, as he too coughed from the smoke. He strode over to the bar, where a barman was pouring another man a glass of yellow liquid from an unlabelled bottle. When he had finished, he turned to face Jack and Jennifer.

'How can I help you two?' he asked. He was a thin man with short blond hair and was wearing a white silk shirt, open to halfway down his chest. From a chain around his neck hung a silver medallion – depicting the same kind of tentacled cat as was painted on the sign outside.

'We're actually looking for a man called Randolph,' said Jennifer. 'We were told he might be here?'

The barman looked her up and down and then decided he approved. 'He's normally a regular here,' he said with a smile, 'but I haven't seen him here for... oh... a few weeks now.'

Jack and Jennifer exchanged apprehensive glances.

'Do you know where he might be?' asked Jennifer. The barman shook his head. 'What about when he might return?'

The barman shook his head again. 'He's a private fellow. Keeps to himself mainly.'

Jack couldn't help a small chuckle. 'Yeah, that sounds like him.' He turned to face Jennifer. 'Any ideas?'

'Just one,' she said. She turned back to the barman. 'A bottle of wine, please?'

'That's your idea?' said Jack. 'Alcohol?'

'It looks like we're going to have to wait for your friend, and if you can think of a better way to pass the time...?'

'I can think of one, but we'd need somewhere a bit more private.'

Jennifer gave him a disapproving glance as the barman placed an ornate green bottle on the counter, followed by two glasses. Jack pulled out his purse and plucked a coin at random from within. He held it up to the barman unsurely. The barman gave him a look of satisfaction and took the coin. 'Keep the change,' added Jack, uncertain as to how generous he was being.

Jennifer picked up the bottle and poured the wine into their glasses. It was a deep ruby red in colour with a rich fruity bouquet when she held it to her nose. She hesitantly took a sip; it was good. She nodded for Jack to join her.

'Let's go get a table,' suggested Jennifer, picking up the bottle.

'If Randolph arrives, can you tell him we're looking for him?' Jack asked the barman, who nodded by way of reply.

They sat in the corner of the bar, nursing their drinks for a couple of hours, until they could see the daylight fading through the bar's grubby windows. The barman had sent no one over to their table.

Jack got up, and wandered back over to the bar, with Jennifer close behind him. 'Still no sign of him then?'

'Nope,' replied the barman.

'And you're sure you don't know how to find him?'

'Look,' said the barman. 'I really don't know him that well. He's just someone that comes in occasionally, keeps to himself.' He turned away to serve a swarthy-looking man standing along the bar.

'Well, what now?' asked Jennifer.

'Excuse me?' came a voice from along the bar. They both turned to look at a man sitting several seats down from them who was nursing a small glass of clear yellow liquid. He was old and wizened, with white stubble on a darkly tanned face. 'I couldn't help overhearing – are you looking for someone?'

'Yes,' said Jack. 'We're meant to meet someone here, but...' he looked around, to indicate that he wasn't there. 'I don't know whether we're too early or too late... or if something's happened to him.'

'I see,' said the man. 'It's possible I may be able to help you.' He had a thin smile on his face.

'I don't know if you know him?' asked Jack. 'His name's Randolph.' Jack thought he saw the man's smile momentarily waver. 'I'm Jack, and this is Jennifer,' he added.

The man said nothing for a moment, simply giving them a long stare, as if trying to decide if he could trust them. Finally, he shook his head in disbelief before picking up his drink and finishing it off in a single gulp. 'I'm Armindel,' he said. 'Come with me.' He stood up, shuffling over to a table in the corner of the room. It was dark and secluded, offering more privacy than the bar.

'Can I offer you another drink?' asked Jack as they all sat down.

Armindel slid his glass over the table to Jack. 'Why don't we have another round of these?'

Jack took the pouch of money from his pocket and turned to Jennifer. 'Would you mind?' he asked. Jennifer gave him a quizzical look but took the pouch anyway. For a second, she contemplated taking the whole pouch, but then she reached inside and took just a few coins, handing the purse back to Jack. She stood up, walking back over to the bar.

'So, you're looking for a man called Randolph,' said Armindel quietly.

'Yes. I was expecting to find him here, but I suppose he could be anywhere. The barman said he hasn't seen him for several weeks.'

Armindel nodded. 'Just how well do you know this man?'

'Not well,' Jack admitted.

'You should be careful,' Armindel whispered to him. He took a glance at Jennifer, who was still standing at the bar, and then back to Jack. 'Is this your first time in these lands?' Jack nodded. 'Well, I'm sure you're aware that these lands are *different*, as are the inhabitants, but Randolph... Well, he's *more* different than most.'

'What do you mean, exactly?'

Armindel bit his lip. 'Rumours, mostly. Talk of strange rituals held for ancient gods – dark stuff. I've only met the guy a couple of times, but he gave me the creeps.'

Jack nodded. 'That's about what I guessed.'

'Just so you know. You should keep your wits about you when you're with him. Don't trust him an inch.'

'I appreciate the warning,' said Jack.

Jennifer had returned and sat down at the table again. 'Another round's coming,' she said. 'So... can you help us?'

Armindel nodded slowly. 'Yes. If he could be anywhere in these lands, I can fashion you something that can locate him. A talisman, if you like, that would lead you to him.'

'That sounds perfect, if you can–' started Jack, but Armindel held up a hand to silence him.

'My services are well regarded in these parts, but they do not come cheap.'

'We're kind of in a rush,' said Jack. 'How much do you want? I have money.'

'No,' said Armindel, shaking his head. 'I don't need your money. There is a task I need you to do for me.'

'How do we know we can trust you?' asked Jennifer.

At that moment, the barman arrived at their table, putting three more glasses of the clear yellow liquid on the table.

'Hey, Curtis,' said Armindel, looking up at the barman. 'These two want to know if I'm trustworthy.'

The barman gave a brief mirthless laugh. 'You two must be desperate if you're talking to him already. He's not cheap but he *is* a man of his word. If you ask me, you can trust him.' With that, he turned round and headed back to the bar.

Jack looked at the drinks on the table in front of him. He picked one up and sniffed it tentatively; it had a sickly sweet smell to it.

'It's not going to bite you,' said Armindel, mockingly. Jack took a sip; it was strong and raw, burning the back of his throat, but not entirely unpleasant.

Jennifer picked hers up, taking a brief look at it. 'Bottom's up,' she said, lifting it to her lips and downing it in one. Armindel smiled and gave her a nod of approval.

'Okay, what's it going to cost?' asked Jennifer, fearing the worst.

Armindel took a sip of his own drink, and then continued. 'Several years ago, there was a lady called Ilian Galandell, a client of mine who absconded without paying for my services. She died soon afterwards, but her debt still remains. I recently discovered that when she was buried, she was wearing some family jewellery. I need you to retrieve that jewellery for me, as payment for services rendered.'

'Grave robbing?' queried Jennifer.

'How?' asked Jack, ignoring her. 'Where?'

'Half a day's trek due west of here is an abandoned temple atop a hill. That is where you will find her tomb. I am not up to such tasks myself any more, and the trip may not be without hazard.'

'What do you mean?'

'There's a reason the temple is abandoned. The graveyard is rumoured to be inhabited by ghouls; you will need to be careful not to attract their attention. Her coffin will be in the family crypt, somewhere in the catacombs beneath the temple. The necklace I am after is silver, with three large green gemstones – it is of significant personal interest to me. If you can find her tomb and return to me this jewellery.... then I will prepare the means for you to find this man you seek. You can think of it as a compass which will always point towards his location.'

'I can see how that could be useful,' said Jennifer.

'There is one other thing,' said Armindel. 'In order to prepare the enchantment needed for this talisman, I will need the leaves of a rare plant.'

Jack sighed. 'And where would we find this plant?'

Armindel smiled. 'If you head north from the temple, you will come across a forest at the edge of the desert. Head towards the centre of the forest, and you should find a clearing containing this plant. It will be a tall bush with red leaves and yellow berries, quite unlike the plants that surrounded it. Bring me four or five of the leaves, but do not disturb the plant any more than you have to.'

'Red leaves, yellow berries. Got it.'

Armindel looked out of the window at the darkening skies. 'You should leave in the morning. I wouldn't venture too far from civilization during the night.'

'Why?' asked Jack. 'What's out there?'

Armindel ignored his question. 'Do you have somewhere to stay the night?' he asked.

Jack shook his head.

'There are rooms here that you can rent. That way you can still see whether your friend arrives tonight.'

Jennifer nodded. 'I'll go and ask Curtis,' she said, standing up and heading to intercept the barman, who was heading back towards the bar, his hands full of empty glasses.

'Do you think Randolph might arrive here tonight?' Jack asked Armindel. 'I mean, would he be okay with whatever's out there in the darkness?'

Armindel shook his head. 'They're more likely to be scared of him,' he replied in a conspiratorial whisper. Then he raised his voice again. 'When you're done, come meet me at my house – number fifteen on Rosewood Lane.' He looked at Jack and then over at Jennifer, who was talking to the barman. 'You should have something to eat. Curtis!' he called to the barman. 'Some food for us, my good man!'

Curtis brought them a large plate of bread and meat that they washed down with a carafe of weak wine, followed by a bowl of mixed fruits. Neither Armindel nor Curtis said what the meat was, and Jack and Jennifer both opted for ignorance; they were hungry and feared that if they knew it might ruin their appetite.

After they had eaten, Armindel fetched a pen and a sheet of paper, drawing them a rough map of the area. He sketched the surrounding geography and landmarks onto the page, before adding the route they ought to take. 'I wouldn't wander too far away from your path,' he advised them. 'Many strange creatures live out in the wilderness away from civilization.'

'Like what?' asked Jennifer.

'Just stick to your path, and you shouldn't need to find out.'

They spent the night in a cosy room that was furnished only with a four-poster bed, although there was an iron bath tub in a small adjoining chamber. Jennifer thought that back home it would have been advertised as *quaint*, but it was probably one of the better rooms on offer here.

'Do you think we should take up Armindel's offer, or just wait and see if Randolph arrives?' asked Jack as they both lay in bed. The night air was warm and still; he desperately missed the fan they had back in their bedroom.

'Let's just see if he turns up in the morning,' said Jennifer. She lay on her back, staring up at the ceiling and then closed her eyes, trying to get comfortable in the bed. 'Where do you think he is?' she asked after a few moments silence.

'I can only assume we're in the right place,' said Jack. 'If he's a frequent flyer to these lands, it's unlikely he's lost. Sebastian gave me the impression he spends more time here than in the real world, so... I don't know. Maybe he's delayed; maybe he's in trouble somewhere. Maybe we're just a bit early?'

'Regardless, there's nothing we can do until the morning,' muttered Jennifer. 'But personally, I'd rather *do* something than just sit around wondering if he'll ever turn up. If it's so important we meet this guy, let's make sure it actually happens.'

In the morning, they rose and checked out of the inn. They enquired with the barman as to whether there had been any sign of Randolph during the night, but unsurprisingly there hadn't been.

Resigned to their expedition for Armindel, they left the inn and headed for the market to equip themselves for what lay ahead. Jack started by buying a leather satchel and then filling it with food and drink from the other stalls: some bread and fruit, as well as several small glass bottles of water. Jennifer scoured through a nearby stall that was piled high with a vast array of oddities, most of which was ostensibly junk. Its owner was an elderly woman in a black robe, who sat behind the counter and gave Jennifer the occasional suspicious glance. Digging through the merchandise, she managed to find a small compass; it was primitive and battered, but it still appeared to be working. In addition, she uncovered two decent hunting knives in leather scabbards. She drew a couple of small shiny coins from Jack's purse to pay the woman, and in return was given a large collection of copper coins as change.

'Are we ready to go?' asked Jack.

'Hold on a minute...' muttered Jennifer as something on a nearby stall grabbed her attention. She wandered over to it, and Jack could see her haggling with the merchant. When she returned, she had her own leather bag hanging from her shoulder.

'What a surprise,' said Jack. 'Another handbag.'

'It's a practical purchase,' said Jennifer defensively. 'I need somewhere to store my knife.' She handed one to Jack. 'You never know. Given our past history, I thought we could do with something to defend ourselves.' Jack took it and undid his belt, threading it through the scabbard to attach it firmly to his hip. 'What do you think happens to us if we get hurt here... or die? Do you think we just wake up, or do we die in our sleep?'

'You know what?' said Jack. 'Let's just not put that to the test, eh?'

Jennifer chuckled. 'You've got a deal.' She looked at Jack. 'Have we got everything we need?'

Jack thought for a second. 'If we need to search through some catacombs, we'll probably want a light source.' Together, they combed through the market until they found someone selling a small oil lantern and tinderbox. Jack paid the seller and Jennifer stored them securely in her new bag.

Chapter 20.

They left the town through a smaller rear gate and marched west, Jennifer leading the way with the aid of her compass. As the town of Aladoth shrank in the distance behind them, the sun was already high in the sky above them, the day passing faster than they had expected.

The desert through which they walked was almost featureless, a flat and barren landscape with no landmarks to guide them, forcing Jennifer to make constant use of her map and compass. The wind was stronger out in the desert, constantly blowing sand into their faces. As with their previous journey, when their minds wandered they would find themselves jumping ahead through time. It was disorienting when it happened, but at least it did something to relieve the monotony.

Eventually though, they could make out a rocky set of hills before them. Jennifer checked her compass and nodded; that was where they were headed. Before long they could see that atop one of the hills was a tall thin building with a domed roof, silhouetted against a sun that was already descending in the afternoon sky. The ground here was also becoming harder than that of the desert, now just a thin layer of sand upon stone. Thankfully, this also meant there was less sand blowing through the air, and Jack and Jennifer were finally able to walk without covering their mouths.

As they drew closer, they could see that this building was surely the temple they were looking for. Dozens of headstones rose from the ground around it, like a field of stone growing from the desert floor. The building itself was circular and built from a smooth green stone with two stories of tall pillars rising up to support the hemispherical roof on top. The whole building looked ancient and dilapidated, with much of the stonework crumbling or missing. On the ground floor, the building had eight curved walls, each set between two huge stone pillars. Every other wall had a pair of huge wooden doors in them; the pair closest to Jack and Jennifer were lying on the floor half covered in sand, revealing a dark foreboding interior waiting for them inside.

They approached cautiously. They were about a hundred feet from the temple when they reached the first gravestones. They were all blank, their surfaces scoured clean of any writing by constant sand storms. Several gravestones had deep pits around them where the graves appeared to have been dug up. Jack could see long scratch marks in the hard earth around the holes; they looked worryingly like claw marks.

Jack signalled Jennifer to stop, and they paused, looking around for any sounds or signs of movement. They could detect nothing apart from the gentle whistle of the wind.

Jack drew his knife from its scabbard. 'Be on your lookout,' he said. 'Just because we can't see anyone doesn't mean we're alone here.'

Jennifer nodded in agreement and also drew her knife, holding it tight in her hand.

They approached the open temple doors nervously. As they drew closer, they could see that above each doorway was a faded inscription: a five-pointed star with what looked like some kind of eye in the centre.

'Any idea what that means?' asked Jennifer, pointing to the signs. 'Another five-pointed star.'

Jack frowned. 'I don't *think* that's our old friends.' He racked his mind, trying to recall where he had seen that sign before. 'I think that's something much older. Some kind of protection.'

Jack stepped closer. The shadowy interior was becoming more visible now and appeared to be a large chamber. By the dim interior light, they could just make out a plain altar on the far side of the room, made of the same green stone as the walls. Next to the altar, there was a dark opening in the floor: a stairway leading down. Jack took a few tentative steps inside, and then beckoned Jennifer to follow him. The inside of the building was indeed a single tall room. Once upon a time, maybe there had been decorations and trappings in here, but if there used to be anything of value, it was long gone now. Sand and debris littered the floor, and in one corner was a pile of bones. Jack crept over to it, picking one up and examining it. He wasn't sure, but he thought it might be a human tibia. As he inspected it more closely, he could see marks around the ends where it had been chewed and gnawed by sharp teeth. He dropped it in revulsion and took a couple of steps back.

'Let's just get this thing as quickly as possible, and then get the hell out of here,' he said.

'You'll get no argument from me,' agreed Jennifer. She retrieved the lamp from her bag and set about lighting it with the tinderbox. While she did that, Jack looked around the room. He managed to find a small wooden beam, which he picked up; it seemed quite sturdy and felt reassuring in his hand.

It took Jennifer a minute or two to get it lit, but they soon had a flickering lantern to see by. She held up the lantern to see Jack standing there, wielding a knife in his right hand and the beam in his left hand like a club. 'I guess I'll be taking the lantern then?' she asked rhetorically.

She led the way down the steps, holding the lantern in front of her to light their way. Jack followed closely behind, keeping a careful watch back over his shoulder.

When the steps levelled out, the passageway opened up into a long brick-lined corridor stretching off into the darkness. There were doors on either side, spaced irregularly every ten or twenty feet. The sturdier doors were still closed while some of the flimsier ones were hanging open or lying in pieces on the floor.

Jennifer stepped to the first doorway, one with a door still in place. A small metal plaque on it read *Bloodoak Crypt*. She looked at the other doors lying in tatters on the floor. 'What if the Galandell family crypt has already been gutted?' she asked.

'Well, let's just be optimistic and assume it hasn't,' replied Jack. 'If we get to the end without finding it... well, we'll have to take a different approach.'

Cautiously, they progressed down the corridor, checking each of the doors for any hint that they might be the vault that they sought. They reached the end of the corridor without success, and nervously descended another flight of steps to the floor below.

'How many levels do you think this place has?' asked Jennifer.

Jack simply shrugged in the flickering light, advancing to the first door on the right to check the name written on it. Together they silently crept down the corridor, Jennifer on the left and Jack on the right, until Jennifer suddenly broke the silence. 'Jack! Over here!' she called.

Jack turned to face her, and as he did so, they both heard a loud crash from further down the corridor. Lifting the lantern out in front of her, Jennifer gave a gasp as she saw a humanoid creature step through one of the doorways at the far end, barely visible in the shadows.

It was tall, hunched over in the doorway, and as it turned its canine head towards them, they could see large yellow eyes and glistening fangs reflecting the light. Its muscular body was covered in grey leathery flesh, half-caked in brown mould. In one hand, it was carrying a large bone, one half still covered in pale flesh, which it dropped as it turned to face them; it had found a fresher source of food. It stepped into the corridor, stretching to its full height and raising its head high, bellowing a nightmarish scream.

'Shit!' cursed Jennifer. 'In here!' she called to Jack, shouldering the door next to her open and stumbling into the tomb within. Jack sprinted in after her without a second thought, slamming the door shut behind him just before something heavy crashed into it with a dull thud that shook the frame.

They were standing in a small stone room, approximately twenty feet wide by thirty feet long. The walls to their left and right were lined with shelves on which sat a dozen stone coffins. Other coffins were lying on the floor, most with their lids removed and their contents missing. Jennifer had already put down the lamp and had started to drag a coffin across the floor towards the door. Jack held the handle to keep the door shut, bracing the door with his shoulder as the creature on the other side slammed against it again. Dust fell from the ceiling of the room as the thud reverberated through his body, but it was holding for now.

'Help me barricade the door with this,' cried Jennifer, as she tried to push the coffin along the floor towards Jack. He looked at the coffin and hesitated for a moment, before stepping forward to pull it towards the door. He struggled to pull the heavy stone, heaving with all his might to draw it closer, but between them they managed to slide it the last couple of feet up to the door, just before another loud thud struck the door, echoing through the small room.

'Help me with another one,' called Jennifer, and together they slid another coffin across the floor. Jack put every ounce of effort he had into lifting up the end and placing it on top of the first before they slid it across and up to the door. Another thump slammed against the door, but the weight of the coffins seemed to be holding the creature back, at least for now.

'Okay, I think we're safe for a moment,' said Jack, 'But there's one slight drawback. How the hell are we supposed to get out of here?' He looked around and saw his knife lying on the floor; he had dropped it when he was struggling with the coffins. He knelt down and picked it up, returning it to its scabbard. 'I sure as hell don't want to try fighting it off with this.'

'One thing at a time,' said Jennifer. 'According to the plaque outside, this is the Galandell family tomb. Maybe if we can just find what we want in here, then we can just outwait it. If it can't break in, maybe it'll eventually get bored and leave.'

Jack laughed and shook his head. He wasn't feeling too optimistic about her plan but was struggling to come up with a better one himself. He took a moment to get a better look around their surroundings. At the back of the room, there was a large pile of debris – what looked like the remains of shelves and wooden coffins. There were no bodies visible in here, just a few small bones lying in the corner of the room, the rest presumably having been a meal for the creature or one of its brethren.

Jack started sifting through the remains in search of ideas. As he lifted up the remains of a coffin lid that lay against the rear wall, it revealed a rough hole about two feet across. Jennifer noticed too and came over, raising the lamp up to look through the opening. A rough tunnel was visible, crudely dug out of the dirt and stone; she could only see a few feet before it twisted away into darkness.

'Was this used to get in or out?' she wondered aloud.

'And where does it go?' added Jack.

'The bodies that were in these wooden coffins are gone. I'm guessing something dug their way in and took them away for... well, that doesn't really matter now, does it.'

'We can't stay here,' said Jack. 'I don't know what's at the other end of the tunnel, but I do know what's on the other side of that door.'

As if on cue, another large blow struck the door, causing the stone coffins to shake. They could hear screams from the other side of the door – several screams, from more than one creature.

'If we climb down that tunnel and it's a dead end, or it collapses… we're dead,' said Jennifer.

Jack looked at the door. 'If we stay here, we'll be just as dead. I'd rather try *something* than just sit here waiting for the inevitable. Help me find Ilian's Coffin, and then we can get out of here.'

It only took a few moments to find the coffin bearing her name, which they slid from the shelf with a heave. It fell to the floor, the lid tumbling off, raising a cloud of dry dust into the air. Jack peered inside, coughing from the dust; he could see a desiccated female corpse within. Covering his mouth with an arm, he leant over the body. Around its neck was an old necklace, tarnished but intact; from it hung a pendant containing three large green gemstones, just as Armindel had described. He yanked at it, the catch snapping from the force, and stuffed the jewellery into his bag.

'Come on, let's get the hell out of here,' he urged, hurrying back to the tunnel opening.

'After you,' said Jennifer, passing him the lamp. He grumbled something inaudible under his breath but grudgingly took the lamp and poked his head into the tunnel. 'What do you reckon?' called Jennifer.

'It's just about wide enough to get through,' he replied, and started to climb in. 'If I can make it, you should be fine.' The tunnel was tight, the walls made of hard dry soil and stone that twisted and turned every few feet. He was forced to crawl on his belly, shuffling along at an agonisingly slow pace.

Jack wasn't normally claustrophobic, but these tunnels were oppressively tight, the air hot and stale. He tried not to think about reaching a dead end or meeting anything coming the other way; he'd have no way of turning and an uneasy path backwards.

He stopped as the tunnel split into a crossroads and paused to consider his options.

'What is it?' called Jennifer from behind him. 'Why have you stopped?'

'There's a junction,' he called back. 'I'm not sure which way to go.' He looked both ways by the light of the lamp, but neither tunnel gave any indication of what lay ahead. The only sounds he could hear were Jennifer's breathing and the distant screams of the creatures behind them, still trying to break down the door. He licked a finger and held his hand up in front of him; he thought he could just feel the faintest breeze from the passage to the left. He started crawling again, heading towards what he desperately hoped would be fresh air.

Jack could hear Jennifer following behind him as he dragged himself further and further through the tunnels. As their distance down the tunnels increased, so did his nerves. He could feel his pulse beating faster and his heart pounding louder with every passing minute. As they carried on down the tunnels, still with no sign of an exit, he felt like the passage was growing smaller and tighter every time it twisted and turned, but he was unsure whether it was the space that was shrinking or his claustrophobia that was growing. He could feel his level of panic steadily rising, almost threatening to overwhelm him, when at last he clambered round a corner and saw an opening. Breathing a little slower, the level of panic subsiding, he pulled himself out of the end and found himself on the floor of a stone cave.

He set the lamp down on the floor next to him and turned to help Jennifer out of the tunnel. She looked as relieved to be out of there as he was.

They both shared a few smiles of relief, and then Jack picked up the lamp again, turning around to inspect their surroundings. By the flickering light, they could make out two different passageways leading out of the cavern. The only things in here with them were several large piles of bones scattered around the floor.

'This isn't a tomb,' whispered Jennifer.

'No. More like a lair,' replied Jack in a worried tone. 'Should we...' He stopped as they both heard a sepulchral cry from down one of the corridors. They both stood there, frozen in silence for a moment, before Jack grabbed the lamp and frantically turned it out. As the wick went out, they were instantly cast into near-perfect darkness.

'Jack...' whispered Jennifer, the fear obvious in her voice.

'Quiet,' whispered Jack in reply, and took her hand in his. 'I think something's coming'.

They stood motionless in the darkness, blind but not deaf to the sounds of a creature shuffling towards them. As they waited in anticipation, their eyes were gradually becoming accustomed to the tiny amount of light in the room; they apparently weren't in complete darkness, a small amount of light must be leaking in from somewhere.

They could hear footsteps more clearly now, soft feet shuffling along the floor and then a humanoid shape lumbered in through one of the passageways. They could only make out a vague silhouette against the passageway behind it, but it was large and muscular like the creature that had chased them into the tomb. It stopped as it entered, glancing around the room, sniffing the air with its canine nose.

Jack was rooted to the floor with fear. He could feel Jennifer's grip on his hand tightening as he tried desperately not to move, not to make any sound.

The creature took a couple of steps closer, dragging one foot behind it before stopping and squatting down next to a pile of bones. It started digging through them, burrowing down until it found one it liked. It pulled out one of the larger specimens and started to chew on the end, its teeth making a horrible grinding noise as it gnawed on it. Maybe it was just his imagination, but even in the darkness Jack thought he could recognize the bone as a human femur. He started to feel nauseous and closed his eyes, but that just made it worse, the abrasive scraping noise of tooth on bone seemingly growing in volume.

He jerked his eyes open again as the sound of the bone hitting the floor echoed through the cave. The creature had stood up again and was looking in their direction. It sniffed the air, taking another step closer towards them.

Jack racked his mind for some options. Their chance of outrunning it was slim, even though it did appear to have a limp. In the near darkness, they would barely be able to find their way. He had his knife, but it was currently in its scabbard and Jennifer's was in her bag. With painstaking care, he moved his hand ever so slowly towards his belt, until his hand was resting on the butt of the dagger's handle. If he made a noise, maybe could he get the knife out before the creature was upon them.

The creature took another curious step closer and then stopped, turning around. From one of the other corridors behind it came an infernal howl, followed by several deep grunts. The creature turned, bellowing a cry of its own in reply, and then scampered off towards the source of the noise, any interest in their corner of the room forgotten.

'C'mon, let's go before it comes back,' urged Jack, when he was sure it had gone.

'Which way?' said Jennifer, looking towards the corridor that the creature had just disappeared down.

'I'm thinking we go the *other* way,' replied Jack, picking up the lamp from the floor.

They stumbled quietly across the cavern, leaving their lamp extinguished. When they reached the first passageway, they took it, moving as quickly as they dared. They shuffled down it for about fifty feet before it narrowed, ascending as it continued. Jack clambered upwards on his hands and knees, taking the rising floor as a good sign. Jennifer followed right behind him. He could feel a light breeze of fresh air in front of him now, giving him the faith to continue even as the corridor grew tighter and tighter.

He found himself emerging into cool, refreshing air as he crawled out of the tunnel and into a rectangular pit. He stood up, looking up to the sky above, and then his heart skipped a beat as he suddenly realized where he was standing – in a grave. At least it no longer contained its original occupant, he tried to reassure himself. Not needing any further encouragement, he clambered up the rough dirt wall up to ground level, then reached down to give Jennifer a hand, pulling her up to join him.

'Let's get out of here, before they find out where we went,' said Jack. 'Which way?'

Jennifer pulled the compass from her bag and gave it a quick glance. 'That way,' she said, pointing to their right. 'Let's put some ground between us and them.'

Chapter 21.

From the temple, they headed north, the screams of the ghouls diminishing as they went.

The sun was sinking low over the horizon as they walked, growing darker and darker until it was deep red in colour, giving the desert sand a brick-red colour as twilight approached. As the light grew dimmer, the wind grew stronger, blowing the sand higher into the air. Even though they were only at the edge of the desert, it still forced Jack and Jennifer to cover their mouths and shield their eyes as they walked.

They stayed at the desert's periphery as the sun disappeared below the horizon, a cool night breeze blowing in from the hills to the west. The sky was dark and clear, a large crescent moon hanging high in the sky, surrounded by a network of unfamiliar stars.

It was fully dark when they reached the edge of a thick and sombre forest, stretching back before them as far as they could see in the pale moonlight.

'I don't know about you,' said Jennifer, 'but I'd prefer to wait until daylight before heading in.'

Jack nodded. 'Let's make camp here and get some rest. I'll go get some wood and we can try to build a camp fire.'

Jennifer made a small clearing in the sand and dirt, while Jack went foraging for wood along the tree line. It didn't take him long before he returned with his arms full of sticks and branches. Together, they built a primitive fire, and Jennifer set about lighting it with her tinderbox. Ten minutes later, it was burning brightly, providing ample warmth against the cold night air.

'With the terrain so flat and open, you'll be able to see this for miles around,' Jennifer pointed out.

'It'll die down before long,' he countered. 'Why don't you get some rest first, and I'll keep watch. I'll wake you when it's time to swap.'

Jennifer lay down near the fire, using her bag as a pillow. She didn't expect to sleep well, but she underestimated just how physically exhausted she was; it took only a few minutes before she was fast asleep.

Jack sat by the glowing embers of the fire, watching her sleep under the moonlight. Her skin was a radiant white under the light of this foreign moon, and he still couldn't believe how much younger she looked here; she looked in the prime of her life, how he remembered her from when they first met. It only strengthened his determination that he was doing the right thing here; he couldn't bear the thought of losing her again. He leant over her, brushing a lock of hair from her forehead, before kissing her gently.

'Sleep well, my darling,' he whispered gently.

✳ ✳ ✳

Jennifer awoke the next morning with a yawn. The red sun was low in the sky, just edging up above the horizon, and all that remained of the fire was a pile of black ash.

'I thought you were going to wake me,' she said with a yawn. 'Did you fall asleep too?'

Jack shook his head. 'You looked so peaceful,' he said. 'I just couldn't bear to wake you.'

'Well, that was stupid,' she said. 'I mean... I appreciate the intention and everything, but now you'll be exhausted. Especially at your age.'

'And what age is that?' he asked. 'I know I'm meant to be old, but here...' He looked around at the clear blue sky above him and lush green forest before him. 'I feel decades younger. Honestly, I don't feel too bad.' Jack reached into his bag and drew out half a loaf of bread and a bottle of water. He ripped the bread in two, passing one half to Jennifer. 'Have something to eat,' he suggested.

She took the bread with a nod of thanks and started to break small chunks off, nibbling them slowly and washing them down with gulps of water. 'Have you looked around? Are there any paths into the forest?'

'None that I can see,' he replied. 'But it's not very dense. We shouldn't have too much trouble getting through.'

They finished their food and then packed their things away, burying the camp fire under a thin layer of earth and sand. Jennifer approached the tree line and examined what lay before them, getting her first clear look by the light of day.

Close to the desert, the vegetation was sparse and coarse, but as they strode into the forest, it wasn't long before they were surrounded by lush green plants. The temperature here was also comfortable for the first time since they had arrived; the air was cool, the trees and bushes exuding a powerful yet calming scent into the air. As they strayed deeper into the forest, animals started to become noticeable. At first, it was brightly col-oured birds high in the trees, merrily tweeting songs to one another. Fur-ther in, they started to spot the occasional small furry creature hiding behind a bush, nervously looking at them with large round eyes. Jack tried to get a good look at one, but they were too nervous to come close, and too fast and nimble to remain visible for long if Jack or Jennifer ap-proached them.

As the morning drew on, the forest became denser and their progress slower. They both found large branches to use as walking sticks, doubling up as clubs to break their way through the foliage where necessary. With the canopy of trees blocking out the sun in the sky, it was hard to estimate the passage of time, but Jack guessed they had been walking through the forest for at least three hours now; he had no idea how close they were to the centre, and they still hadn't found any of the plants they were looking for.

'This is useless,' said Jack, taking a seat on the trunk of a fallen tree. 'It's like looking for a needle in a haystack. How are we ever going to find the middle of this forest?'

Jennifer stopped and took a seat next to him. 'Well... if we hit desert again, we know we've gone too far.' She reached into her pocket and drew out her compass. 'We're still going in the right direction. It's a good thing we've got one of these, or we could end up walking round and round in circles for days.'

Jack reached into his bag, drawing out some more food – a couple of small apples this time. He passed one to Jennifer and took a bite of one himself. It was odd. Not unpleasant, but a different taste from what he was used to – sharper, more like a citrus fruit. He was too hungry to complain though, and wolfed it down. The trip was taking longer than expected, and he was starting to get concerned about running out of food and water. Jennifer wasn't saying anything, but he was sure she must be hungry too; their rations were becoming worrying low. There were some unrecognizable berries in the forest with them, but he wasn't about to risk foraging for food unless their situation grew truly desperate.

As they continued, the undergrowth grew even denser. Dark green vines were now becoming all too common; it felt almost like a jungle or rainforest in here now. Their speed was slowing to a crawl, their progress halted every time they came across dense clumps of creepers blocking the way.

Jack stopped and looked around. 'Do you notice anything different around here?' he asked Jennifer.

She stopped too and leant against a tree, taking a deep breath and mopping the sweat from her brow. She stood silently, looking all around. 'Now that you mention it, I do,' she said. 'Everything is darker here.' Jack nodded; she was right. Gone were the bright greens and sandy browns of the forest that had accompanied them for so much of their trip. The colour of the vegetation here was significantly more sombre – deep, dark browns and greens.

'That's not all,' said Jack. 'Listen.'

Jennifer stood silently. 'Just what am I meant to be hearing?'

'That's the point. Where's the bird song? I can't hear any animals here at all.'

Jennifer stood, straining her ears to pick up any signs of life. It didn't take her long to realize he was right. 'I can think of several reasons for that,' she said. 'And none of them are good.'

Jack nodded. 'Let's just go slowly and cautiously, okay?'

'Okay.'

They set off again, moving carefully now, but it wasn't long before they stopped once more. This time it was Jennifer who stopped, holding up a hand to Jack.

'What is it?' he whispered.

'Over there,' she said, gesturing ahead of them and to their right. 'Is that what we're after?'

Jack looked. In the distance, behind some thick brambles, he could make out what looked like a clearing. Even at this distance, he could make out spots of red through the foliage.

'Come on,' he said. He was relieved that maybe they had finally found what they were looking for but also cautious. 'Let's go take a look.'

They beat their way through a final set of brambles and stepped out into a small glade. It was roughly twenty feet across and clear of any trees, the grass thick and green. In the centre was a bush, about five feet high and the same size across. Its leaves were a dull cherry-red and scattered across them was a smattering of yellow berries.

Jack approached cautiously, kneeling down in front of the plant. He reached out his hand towards the berries.

'Careful,' called Jennifer quietly. She was looking all around, keeping watch for anything that might approach.

Jack leant forwards, looking more closely at the plant. Now that he was paying more attention, he could see that intertwined within the red leaves of the bush were thick brambles with dark matt-black thorns, almost invisible in the shadows. He pulled a small leather pouch out of his bag, loosening the drawstring to open it. Then he reached forwards again, carefully grabbing a red leaf, plucking it from the bush and dropping it into the bag.

Jennifer stood dead still, looking all around to check for signs of life. The unnatural silence in the glade was unnerving and made her flesh creep. As she stood there, straining her ears to detect any movement in the undergrowth, she heard Jack swear under his breath.

'What is it?' called Jennifer.

'Nothing.' He looked at down his finger where he had caught it on one of the brambles; there was a small drop of blood on the fingertip. He sucked the tip of the finger and shook his hand before dropping the final leaf into the pouch.

'Are you done?' asked Jennifer. 'There's something about this place that gives me the creeps.'

'You bet,' replied Jack as he placed the pouch into his bag.

✳ ✳ ✳

125

They trekked back through the forest, Jennifer trying to plot a more direct route with the aid of the map and compass so they could head back to the town without detouring via the temple. The journey felt faster on the way out; maybe it was just because they were no longer searching as they went and could relax slightly. The plants were starting to grow lighter and birds were audible again in the distance when Jack suddenly felt light-headed and stumbled, falling to his hands and knees.

Jennifer, who had been taking the lead, stopped and turned. 'Are you okay?' she called.

'I'm fine,' reassured Jack. 'I just didn't notice a tree root,' he lied as he climbed back to his feet again. 'You keep going. I'll just grab a quick drink of water.' He reached into his bag, withdrawing a bottle and removing the cork. Jennifer turned around and started walking again.

With Jennifer's attention diverted, Jack looked down at his hand where it held the bottle. There were violet lines under his skin, stretching from the fingertip where he had pricked himself on the thorn, up along his finger and then down to his wrist.

'Shit,' he cursed. He tentatively squeezed his finger; it didn't feel sore or painful, which he hoped was a good sign. He took a swig of water and then put the bottle back in his bag, trying to put his finger to the back of his mind. He jogged after Jennifer for a minute until he had caught up with her.

'Okay?' she asked again.

'Uh-huh,' he grunted non-committally.

It was half an hour later when Jack collapsed again, more clumsily this time. Jennifer turned around and came back over; she was slightly more wary this time.

'Need a hand, old-timer?' she asked, offering him a hand.

Jack shook his head and moved his hand behind his back, out of her sight; it was a clumsy gesture.

'What is it?' she said. 'Show me.'

'It's nothing,' said Jack, but Jennifer could see there was sweat on his forehead now.

'Show me,' she repeated, more forcefully this time.

Jack brought his hand out from behind his back. What had previously been a thin violet line along his finger was now a thick dark vein stretching from his finger to halfway up his forearm, thinner lines splintering off along it like branches on a tree.

'Shit!' she cursed loudly. 'Why didn't you say anything?'

'I didn't want to panic you, and I thought it might get better,' he said unconvincingly.

'You bloody idiot,' she said reproachfully. 'You may be older, but you're not much wiser, are you?' She looked him in the face. 'Look at me,' she told him, taking his chin in her hand and twisting his head to face her.

Jack looked her in the eyes. She could that see his pupils were dilated and he obviously had trouble focusing on her. 'How bad is it?' she asked.

Jack chuckled. 'I've had worse.'

'Enough with the macho bullshit.' She took her bag off her shoulder and started to detach the strap. 'Roll your sleeve up,' she ordered. He did so, and she could see fine lines stretching all the way to his elbow. She wrapped the leather strap around his upper arm, pulling it tight and tying a knot to make a crude tourniquet. 'Hopefully this will slow it down, whatever it is.'

She helped him to his feet, and he leant an arm across her shoulders. 'We need to go quickly, but let me know if you need a rest,' she said. 'We need to get you back to whatever passes for civilization around here.'

'I suppose we'll find out before too long what happens if you die here,' chuckled Jack with a groan.

Jennifer held him by the chin with one hand and turned his face to look at hers. 'We'll have none of that,' she said. 'We're getting out of here, and we're doing it together.'

Together, they staggered through the forest like a pair of drunken lovers, weaving through the undergrowth to take the flattest, easiest route.

'Jenn?' croaked Jack ten long minutes later.

'Yes?' she replied.

'Is it evening already?'

Jennifer looked up at the top of the trees. She couldn't see the sun directly but could still see its light poking through the canopy; the sun was still high in the sky. 'No,' she said, fearing the worst. 'Why?'

'Everything's getting darker,' he muttered. Even his speech was growing slow and slurred now.

Jennifer led him to a fallen tree trunk where she sat him down. She squatted in front of him, looking up at his face. His forehead was covered in sweat, his eyes wild and his pupils large. 'Look at my finger,' she said, holding her index finger up in front of his face. His eyes strained to focus on it and couldn't keep up as she moved it back and forth.

She grabbed a bottle of water from her bag. 'Here, have some of this,' she offered, holding it to his lips. Jack took a couple of swigs; it looked like he was having trouble swallowing. Jennifer placed the empty bottle on the floor. Normally, she'd be the last person to drop litter, but she needed to lighten their load as much as she could.

'Jenn?' whispered Jack.

'Yes?' she said, bringing her face close to his, cradling his head in her hands.

'Leave me here,' he said, his eyes closed. 'You can do this yourself. I know you can, just—'

'—No,' interrupted Jennifer. 'We're doing this together.'

'Please, just—'

Jennifer slapped him hard across the face. His eyes opened wide in shock and he looked back up at her. 'No, Jack. We're doing this together. Stand!'

'I'm too tired,' whimpered Jack.

'Stand, God damn it!' shouted Jennifer. With her help, Jack struggled to bring himself to his feet again and slowly they stumbled forwards. Jennifer could just make out the edge of the forest now through the sparse greenery, and the hot desert sand that lay beyond it. 'Only another hundred feet,' she reassured him. 'You can do this.' All her attention was on getting him to the edge of the forest. What she would do next, she had no idea.

She almost had to drag him the last twenty feet, but at last they emerged from the tree line, the pale red sand of the desert stretching off into the distance ahead of them. She sat Jack down on the ground and fetched the compass from her pocket, desperately judging what direction they needed to travel in.

When she turned around again, Jack was lying face down on the sandy floor. She rolled him over; he was unconscious but still breathing and had a steady heartbeat.

'What the hell are we going to do now?' she muttered to herself.

Chapter 22.

December 28th, 2012. Exeter Police Station, England.

Detective Inspector Cross opened the door and stepped into the interrogation room. Facing her from a chair on the other side of the room was the man she had arrested at Lamarre's house. He looked older and frailer now that he was sitting in the bright indoor lights. His black trousers and top were gone, taken away for forensic examination, and had been replaced by a blue boiler suit. A dark red tattoo of a five-pointed star was visible now on the back of one hand.

He sat calmly in the metal chair, holding his hands in his lap and quietly looking back at her. 'Well, hello,' he said cordially. 'We meet again.'

Cross pulled out a chair from under the table and sat down opposite him.

'Mike Barnes, is it?' she asked. He replied with an almost imperceptible nod. 'Why don't you tell me what happened tonight,' she asked slowly.

He looked back at her and shrugged. 'I've got no idea. I'm as much in the dark as you are.'

'Why were you there?'

'The owner of the house is an old acquaintance of mine,' he replied. 'He'd invited me over for the evening, for a chat and a glass of wine.'

'How did you get there? Was that your car out front?'

'My car? No, I don't know of any car,' he answered smoothly. 'I took a taxi. Wouldn't do to drink and drive, would it?'

'Can you tell me which taxi company it was?'

He shook his head. 'I hailed the car as it passed by in the city centre. I couldn't tell you who it belonged to.'

Cross scribbled something in her notebook; they would have to talk to all the taxi companies, try to establish if any of them had taken him. She looked up again. 'So what happened after you arrived?'

'It was all quiet when I walked up the driveway, and no one answered when I knocked on the front door. I was just about to leave when I thought I heard a noise from the rear of the house so I went around to the back garden. Something startled me in the darkness and knocked me over... I banged my head and had only just come to when you arrived.'

'So why did you run?'

'It was dark. I'd already been attacked. A stranger was pointing a gun at me. I was scared for my life. Who wouldn't run in that scenario?'

'I had informed you that I was a police officer.'

He smiled a thin smile. 'I certainly didn't hear that. Maybe it was lost in the wind. Maybe it was the blow to my head. My hearing isn't what it used to be, you know.'

'Why did you do it?'

'Do what?' he said, feigning ignorance.

'Kill all those people.'

He held out his palms towards Cross. 'My dear detective,' he said. 'Whatever happened at that house has nothing to do with me.'

'I find that very hard to believe,' said Cross, staring into his eyes. 'From what we know so far, at least eight people were brutally – no, *savagely* – murdered there this evening. I don't know why or how you did it yet, but I'll prove you were behind it.'

He looked back at her, matching her stare, and then leant closer. 'Oh, I think you'll have a hard time doing that,' he replied in a low cold voice. 'Your techs have run tests on me, taken my clothes for analysis. Tell me, what have they found?'

'I don't know,' said Cross, momentarily flustered. 'I haven't had the reports–'

'–I'll tell you what they won't find,' he continued. 'Any evidence of wrong doing. No blood spatter, even on the soles of my shoes. No gunshot residue. No trace DNA from any of the victims. None of my fingerprints on any of the weapons. Tell me, Inspector. Did you see me attack anyone?'

'No, but–'

'So you have no witnesses. By your own admission, you have no motive, and before long I'm sure you'll be informed that you have no physical evidence to tie me to anything. Look at me – I'm an old man. How am I meant to have physically attacked and killed eight men? Any half-decent solicitor would have this thrown out in a heartbeat – and my solicitor is much more than that.' He looked at his watch; it was 23:17. 'He should be here in a few hours.' He leant back in his chair, crossing his arms. 'I'll be out of here by dawn.'

Cross looked at the smug smile on his face. She guessed he was probably right about the lack of evidence, but she was also damned sure he was behind whatever had gone down tonight. 'I may not have seen you kill anyone, but I know what I *did* see in that garden,' she said.

'Be careful, Inspector,' he replied coldly.

'What were those creatures?' she whispered at him. 'What was it they had? Were they the ones behind the massacre?'

'I don't know what you *think* you saw,' he said. 'Didn't you also have a nasty bump to the head?'

'I know what I saw,' she replied grimly. 'And those monsters could easily–'

'–Monsters!' he laughed. 'Oh my dear, you're going to have to do a lot better than that.' He shook his head at her, smirking.

Cross leant forward and stared him in the eye. She decided to take a leap.

'I know about the Necropolis,' she said.

There was a momentary look of surprise in his eyes, only for a split second but long enough. She knew he was lying now, knew he was involved in it all.

'I don't know what you're talking about,' he said calmly. He took another glance at his watch. 'I'm not saying another word until my solicitor arrives. Take me back to my cell.'

Chapter 23.

The Dreamlands

Jack slowly opened his eyes. All he could see were blurred and indistinct shapes and his head was throbbing. Wherever he was though, it looked like a room. It was dark but at the same time still too bright for him to open his eyes fully. He closed them again, resting them for a moment before opening them very slowly and squinting through them. For a moment, he wondered if it was their bedroom back home but then decided not – he still had trouble making out any shapes, but he could see the colours and they were all wrong.

'I think he's waking,' came a man's voice from somewhere in the shadows. He could hear talking in the distance and sense movement coming closer to him.

He tried to sit up but found he couldn't move. In fact, he felt far too weak to do anything. He strained, trying to lift his right hand and only just managed to lift it off the bed. He let it flop back down onto the sheets.

'Whoa,' came a familiar voice. It was Jennifer's. 'Just relax – you're safe here. You had us worried for a while.'

Jack took a moment to reply. He was having trouble stringing the words together into sentences.

'Who's *us*?'

'Me and Armindel. You're in his house.'

'How?' he croaked. He was having trouble remembering what had happened. 'The last thing I remember, we were in the woods...'

'That's quite a woman you've got there,' said Armindel. 'She saved your life.'

'Not for the first time,' she chuckled.

'She managed to make a travois with some branches from the forest,' said Armindel. 'Dragged your unconscious body for nearly three hours through the desert before she managed to find a caravan.'

Jennifer picked up a cold damp cloth and wiped it across Jack's brow. 'We were worried about you for while. We didn't think you'd make it. You've been out for three days.'

'But...' started Jack.

'Shh!' urged Jennifer. 'Rest now. We'll talk when you're feeling stronger.'

Jennifer walked into the room to find Jack sitting at the table eating a bowl of soup.

'Feeling better?'

'Much better. I think we should head off in the morning.'

'Do you think you're up to it?'

'Definitely. I'm feeling pretty good now, and getting better by the hour.'

Jennifer came and sat down next to him, pulling something from her pocket. It was a metal locket on the end of a fine silver chain. The locket was made from an unusual-looking metal with a blue hue to it, constructed in the shape of an isosceles triangle.

'What is it?'

'This is what you wanted from Armindel.' She picked up the chain and let the locket dangle. It was perfectly balanced, so that as she held the chain up in the air, the metal triangle lay perfectly flat and horizontal below it. It span gently in the air until it drew to a stop, pointing off to the west. 'Whoever this Randolph actually is, this should always point us in his direction as long as he's still here in these lands. At first it didn't seem to work but then it kicked in a couple of days ago. I think he must have only arrived recently.'

Jack nodded, thinking to himself for a moment. 'Does it point directly to him, or to the best route to take?'

'As the crow flies, I'm afraid,' she replied. 'Which I suppose is better than nothing. Think of it like a compass with him as the North Pole.' She took the pendant and lifted the chain over her head, hanging it around her neck. 'You finish eating and recuperating, I'll go get some supplies. We're not short on money just yet.'

Jack returned to his soup. It was watery with lumps of unidentifiable meat and vegetables floating just beneath the surface. 'Do you know what's in this?' he asked.

Jennifer shook her head with a smile. 'You wouldn't want to know – but it's definitely having the right effect on you.'

She returned a couple of hours later, just as the sun was setting. She had been out shopping for supplies and placed her wares on the table to show Jack.

'I've tried to stock up a bit better this time,' she said. She was wearing a thin jacket and carrying another one, which she threw to Jack. This ought to keep the sun off in the day and the wind out at night.' Next, she pulled a couple of thin strips of white sheet out of her backpack. 'Turbans, to keep the sun off our heads and sand out of our mouths.'

'Very practical.'

'I tried to keep the foodstuffs light – dried meat and fruit, some bread, lots of water, that kind of thing.' Jack nodded. 'And I thought you might need this, old man.' She lifted up a wooden staff. 'It'll make a nice walking stick for you.'

Jack grinned humourlessly back at her. He stood up and picked up the jacket; it was made of a thin grey animal skin and felt light. He tried it on; it was a good fit, just slightly loose around the shoulders.

Just then, the door opened and Armindel walked in. 'Are you two off in the morning, then?' he asked, looking at the collection of goods on the table.

Jack nodded. 'We'll set off at first light.'

'Very good,' said Armindel. 'In that case, why don't you join me for a last meal; I've got a nice bottle of wine here somewhere.'

He had prepared a minor feast for them that night, the best they had had since they had arrived in these lands. Big legs of meat, roasted potatoes and bowls full of colourful fruit, as well as two bottles of a rich, deep-red wine. When they had finished, they retired to their rooms, swiftly falling asleep.

They rose early the next morning and set off just as the sun was rising in the east. As they were leaving, Armindel came to see them off. He grabbed Jack by the wrist as they stepped out through the door.

'Remember what I said,' he whispered to Jack. 'You can't trust Randolph.'

Jack nodded in reply. 'I'll bear that in mind.'

They headed west, Jennifer occasionally retrieving the locket from under her blouse and checking the direction in which it pointed; they were heading roughly in the direction of the temple they had visited on their previous expedition. Jack was finding the trek easier with the staff that Jennifer had purchased for him, but he was never going to admit that to her.

They walked for several hours through the featureless terrain of the desert, with only the occasional ragged plant or animal corpse to break up the monotony. In the far distance ahead of them, they could see a mountain range, the craggy peaks pointing high into the sky. At one point, they thought they could just make out the temple to their north, the tall building silhouetted against the horizon, but the pendant led them away from it, further off to the west, closer and closer to the mountains that were now growing larger before them.

They carried on across the featureless desert, their perception of time occasionally fracturing again as they walked, finding themselves suddenly closer to their target without experiencing any passage of time, although the sun had moved above them in the sky. Jack was almost starting to get used to it now.

The air grew colder as they approached the base of the mountains, the sand gradually turning from the pale red to a dull grey. The mountains stood imposingly in front of them, towering into the sky, which had changed from the perfect blue into a cloudy grey.

'So... around it, under it or over it?' asked Jack as they grew nearer.

Jennifer stopped and checked the pendant again. 'It's pointing straight to the base, but it doesn't really seem to do up and down.'

Jack looked left and right. The mountain range stretched off in either direction. He sighed. 'I can't see any obvious path around them – we might as well keep going in this direction for now.'

Jennifer nodded in agreement and started walking again, Jack following in her footsteps.

As they drew closer, all they could see before them was a vertical cliff, a sheer face rising up into the sky, where the mountain range started in earnest.

'Well, it doesn't look like we're going over it,' said Jennifer.

Jack, though, had thought he had spotted something. 'No – wait. What's that over there,' he said, pointing into the distance.

Jennifer lifted her hand to shield her eyes from the sun and stared in the direction he was indicating. 'Is that a path up?' she asked suspiciously.

'Could be. Let's take a look.'

It took them almost half an hour to reach it, but they could tell long before they arrived that it was indeed a path. Steep and rocky, it wound its way up the sheer mountainside. They started their ascent, climbing slowly, occasionally having to get on their hands and knees when the gradient proved too steep.

It was a long arduous ascent, but eventually they crested the top to reach a small plateau. To the east, they could see the desert disappearing into the distance. To the west, the rocky mountain range continued. In front of them, at the end of the path, lay a dark cave entrance.

'I think our way forward is clear,' said Jack.

'We don't have a lot of choice, do we?' sighed Jennifer.

Chapter 24.

The cave entrance was narrow, leading into a tight space about twenty feet deep and with a low ceiling, but as they stepped further inside they could make out a slim passageway leading away from the rear of the cave. The dark tunnel appeared to lead deeper into the mountain, descending as it led away from them.

Jennifer lit her lamp, and together they started their descent into the mountain. The passageway began as rough-hewn steps carved out of the rock but it rapidly became just a rough dirt and stone corridor. The rugged stone walls twisted back and forth but always on a gentle incline downwards, taking them deeper and deeper under the mountain. The only light was from Jennifer's torch, and the only sounds were those of their breathing and foot-steps. They walked for what felt like a long while, the passage of time impossible to gauge in this total isolation.

After what felt like at least an hour, the narrow stone tunnel finally grew wider and then opened up into an enormous cavern. By the light of their lamp, they could barely make out the far side, but what they could see looked like an enormous stone building standing in the darkness.

They were cautiously advancing across the cavern when Jack jumped as something flitted through the air in the darkness above them. Jennifer stopped and held her lamp up above her head. In the faint light, they could just catch occasional glimpses of a bat, or something *like* a bat, flying through the air high above them. It remained always on the periphery of the light, never coming close enough for them to get a good view.

Even more wary now, they resumed their silent journey across the cavern until they could see that there was indeed a colossal building front, built into the far wall of the cavern. It appeared to be constructed from smooth black and green stone, which reflected the light of their lamp, the front adorned with huge pillars six feet wide and easily thirty feet high. In the centre of the building between two of the pillars was an open doorway, twenty feet tall. The space inside was pitch black, the light from their lamp giving no indication of what might lie within.

Jack approached the building and ran his hand over one of the pillars; it felt as smooth as it looked, the stone cold under his fingertips.

'What does that mean?' asked Jennifer. She was pointing to the top of the door.

Jack stepped back to get a better look. Carved into the stone above the door was writing in letters a foot high: *Palatio Insomnia.* His Latin was a little rusty and he had to think for a second before hazarding a guess. 'The Palace of Dreams,' he said.

'Who the hell builds something like that in a place like this?' asked Jennifer.

'Who knows what used to happen in here,' said Jack, looking around the cavern. 'This place could be hundreds of years old. Hell, it could be thousands. Maybe this place used to be some kind of settlement. A safe refuge away from predators or the weather.'

Jennifer shrugged. 'Still, not somewhere I'd build a palace,' she muttered. She took out her pendant and let it hang for a moment until it steadied itself.

'Let, me guess...' said Jack.

Jennifer nodded. 'It's pointing in that general direction all right.' She lifted the lamp up high, peering into the darkness either side of the building. 'I don't see any other way out of here.'

Jack took her by the hand. 'Shall we?' he asked. Together, they walked through the doorway.

❋ ❋ ❋

The hall inside the building was immense, stretching out away from them in the darkness. The walls, floor and ceiling were all built from a jet-black stone embedded with tiny flecks of white. The black stone absorbed most of the light from their lamp, but the white flecks shone in the flickering light, giving the impression that they were standing in a vast field of stars. It had a calming effect on Jennifer, reminding her of standing in a country field at the dead of night and looking up at the heavens. Still holding hands, they started across the room, the tapping of their shoes on the floor the only sound they could hear. As they walked through the darkness, the walls and floor seemed to bend around them unnervingly, the sounds of their footprints growing softer and less distinct.

Jack turned around to look over his shoulder, only to realize that he could no longer see the doorway where they had entered. Neither could he hear his footsteps. He looked down and saw not a stone floor but an endless void stretching away beneath his feet, the infinite depths of space. 'Jesus!' he exclaimed, grabbing hold of Jennifer and turning to face her.

'What?' she asked, and then suddenly it hit her. She too was floating in the depths of space, all alone except for Jack. 'What the hell?' she uttered, as she was struck by an overwhelming sense of loneliness and isolation.

'Is this for real?' muttered Jack.

Jennifer shook her head in disbelief. 'If we were really in space, how would we be breathing?' she replied. 'Or be able to hear each other?'

'Okay... So where are we?' said Jack, his voice shaky. He tried taking a step forwards. His legs moved, but he had no sensation of movement and could hear no sound from his feet on the floor. He stopped, turning to face Jennifer again and taking both of her hands in his.

'Let's think about this logically,' said Jennifer. 'Either we're still in that vast hall, or else we're lost in the infinite vastness of space somewhere. If it's the latter, we're screwed whatever we do, so let's assume we're still in the hall and this is all some kind of shared illusion.'

'I like the way you think,' replied Jack. 'So what now?'

Jennifer shrugged. 'We keep walking,' she said simply. 'What else can we do?'

Jack released one of her hands but kept hold of the other, gripping it tightly for reassurance. 'Do we know which way to go?'

'I think so,' she replied. 'Follow my lead.'

Together, they walked. They could feel no sense of movement, but they kept going through the motions until the illusion suddenly vanished as quickly as it had appeared; they were standing in the hallway again, the white dots merely specks of stone once more.

Jack gave a nervous laugh and looked over his shoulder. He could see the doorway they had entered through again now, a plain black shadow barely visible compared with the walls around it. It looked quite a distance away. In front of them, they could see what they hoped was another doorway – an indistinct black rectangle in the otherwise uniform stone. They hurried towards it, the sounds of their footsteps audible again.

As they neared the gap in the wall, they could see it was another enormous opening, at least as tall as the last. Darkness beckoned to them from beyond, the light from their lamp unable to pierce the threshold.

They looked at each other briefly for reassurance, Jack squeezing Jennifer's hand as they stepped through the doorway. Once again, they found themselves in another vast chamber. This one appeared to be made of pitch-black stone, and once more the dark tiles beneath their feet barely reflected any light; they couldn't see the far side of the hall through the darkness before them.

Jennifer took another step forwards and then dropped straight through the floor as if it wasn't there; there was no visible pit, it was just as if the black floor suddenly wasn't there. The lamp hit the floor and rolled away, the light flickering but somehow still alight. She managed to keep hold of Jack's hand, pulling him to the floor as she fell. His body smashed into the inky stone, knocking the wind from him, but he just managed to keep hold of her. His arms were hanging over the edge and he peered over it, looking down to see Jennifer dangling beneath him, holding onto his outstretched arm with a single hand.

'JACK!' she screamed.

'Hold on!' he urged. He tried desperately to pull her up but couldn't; she was too heavy and the stone too smooth. *Please, God, don't let it end like this*, he prayed to himself. The light from the lantern was growing dimmer, threatening to cast them into total darkness.

'JACK!' she screamed again. 'I'm slipping!' Jack could feel her fingers starting to slide through his. She kicked her feet, desperately trying to get purchase on some surface, but everything was as smooth as polished marble; all it did was make it harder for Jack to hold on.

Jack watched in slow motion as his grip gave out and her fingers slid free. He saw the look of fear on her face, her eyes wide in panic as she fell slowly away from him, her arms and legs flailing wildly as she fell into the darkness. Her screams subsided and then she was gone.

The lamp went out.

'No!' he screamed into the darkness.

Chapter 25.

Ash House, Dartmoor, England

Jennifer awoke with a scream, sitting bolt upright in bed. Her heart was pounding, her throat raw. She felt hot and sticky, her clothes damp with sweat.

The room swam before her eyes, and she closed them, trying to expel the giddy feeling in her head. When she opened them again, her vision was steady. It was dark in the bedroom, the only light coming from the small LEDs on a few appliances and the light from the landing seeping in between the door and frame. She looked next to her and saw Jack lying asleep on the bed. His brow was furrowed, a look of concentration on his face as he slept. She wondered if she should wake him; if she did, then presumably he would return too and maybe this would all have been for nothing. Instead, she decided to let him sleep; he deserved a shot at this on his own.

She swung her legs over the side of the bed and sat up. Her legs were still unsteady and her whole body shook gently from the shock and adrenaline. Slowly, as if she were drunk, she pulled her shoes off and then carefully shuffled over to the window to look outside. It was pitch black, the moon hiding behind the dark storm clouds, but she could hear the wind and see the rain falling on the windows. She turned to glance at the bedside clock; it was a little after one in the morning.

It was still the middle of the night, but she knew she wouldn't be getting back to sleep anytime soon. She was feeling anxious and skittish, but there was also a deep pang of hunger in her stomach. Heading for the kitchen to make herself something to eat, she stepped over to the bedroom door, opening it and wincing at the brightness of the landing before she headed downstairs.

She left the kitchen light off, her eyes still not totally adjusted from the darkness. Shuffling into the room by the light of the hallway, she squatted down in front of the fridge, already having decided to make herself a sandwich. As she opened the fridge door, the light from inside lit up the room, making her squint again. *We need to go shopping*, she told herself; the shelves were almost empty. They did contain some butter and ham though, and she grabbed these, as well as a carton of orange juice.

Standing up again, she wandered over to the bread bin to find a loaf of bread. She stood at the kitchen counter in the dim light, looking out of the rear window as she prepared the food. The weather was getting worse outside. The wind was gusting harder and the rain was hammering on the windows; the noise of the drops impacting against the glass was growing in both frequency and volume.

She finished making the sandwich while still half in a daze, thinking of Jack. *Would he be okay on his own?* she wondered. As she cut the sandwich into two and dropped the knife into the sink, there was a flash of lightning outside, briefly lighting up the room and immediately followed by a deep rumble of thunder. Just moments later, it was followed by two more flashes of lightning, and then everything went black as the electricity cut out. It wasn't just dark but eerily silent too. There was no sound apart from the storm outside, not even the low hum of the refrigerator.

Was it their fuse box or had the power gone out for the whole area? she wondered. She cursed to herself and thought for a moment, running her hand through her hair as she tried to think of what to do next. It didn't take long before an idea came to her; there was a torch in one of the kitchen cupboards. She shuffled over to it, holding her hands out in front of her in the darkness. Feeling for the cupboard door, she fumbled around until she found the handle, pulling it open. She carefully explored around inside with her fingertips and found the torch sitting in the middle of the shelf, just where she had imagined it would be. She picked it up and turned it on. The narrow beam of light lit up the room and managed to calm her nerves slightly. With a deep breath, she tried to relax; there should be an emergency number for the electricity company around here somewhere.

As she stood in the middle of the kitchen, wondering just where that number would be, there was another flash of lightning. It lit up the garden momentarily, illuminating a man standing outside, standing right next to the back door. She only saw him for an instant, but the image of him was burned into her mind – a pale face surrounded by long dark hair and covered by a dark hood. She stood and watched, frozen to the spot with shock as the glass in the door exploded, shards of glass flying all over the floor. *We've only just replaced that,* said a small voice at the back of her mind. A hand came in through the space where the broken pane had been, reaching for the key in the lock and turning it.

Jennifer's mind snapped back into place, and she turned and bolted for the hallway. As she stepped through the doorway, she slid to a stop on the wooden floor. The front door was standing open and three men were standing in the hallway, rainwater dripping from their black robes to pool on the floor by their feet. Their hoods were down, and when another flash of lightning illuminated the room, she could see their faces clearly for an instant; these were some of the same men who had brought her to the Well of the Worlds in order to sacrifice her. The man in the centre smiled an evil grin and withdrew his hand from his robe, revealing a long curved blade, which shimmered in the light of her torch.

Jennifer ran for the stairs as the men slowly advanced, all three of them now holding knives. She ran desperately up the stairs, the socks on her feet slipping on the polished wood of the steps as she went. She clambered upwards on her hands and feet, sprinting as she reached the landing and throwing herself into their bedroom. She slammed the door shut behind her and turned the key in the lock, before turning to face Jack in the bed.

He was gone.

'What the hell?' she screamed. 'Jack! Where are you?'

There was a thundering crash against the bedroom door. She span around just in time to see it burst inwards, the door frame splintering. One of the men advanced through the doorway, holding his curved knife out in front of him. Jennifer stepped backwards and stopped as her legs hit the bed; she had nowhere left to go.

'You're going to pay for what you did to us,' came the man's voice; it was deep and husky. 'This time there's no escape, and there's no one here to save you.'

Another of the men stepped through the broken doorway into the room and stood next to him. 'You're going to die before the night is through, and we're going to make sure you suffer.' There was a cruel smile on his face.

The third man stepped to the other side. 'You're going to die alone and in pain, screaming for mercy. But there will be none here tonight.'

Together, they advanced towards the bed.

Chapter 26.

December 29th, 2012. Exeter Police Station, England.

'What the hell are you playing at?' the bellowing voice accused Detective Inspector Cross.

It was just after midnight and she was standing in the office of Chief Inspector Roberts, her boss. He was sitting behind his desk while she was standing to attention and facing him.

'Have you completely taken leave of your senses?' he shouted. 'What the hell were you doing? If his lawyers get hold of this conversation – and they will – we'll look like bloody idiots. With the blow to your head and your prattling on about monsters, no one's going to view you as a credible witness – and you're the only one we've got.'

'I just need five more minutes with him.'

'No,' he said simply.

'What?' she replied in surprise.

'You're done. I don't want you talking to him again.'

'What?' she replied again. 'He's guilty. I know he is.'

'Oh, I'm sure he's guilty of something, but he's right in that we've got no physical evidence. His clothes came back clean. It'll take longer for a proper DNA test, but there's no blood and no evidence of any struggles, nothing under any finger nails.'

'What are you telling me?'

'Apart from his presence *near* to the scene of the crime, we've got no evidence he had anything to do with it. If he had anything to do with what happened in that house, he ought to be covered in blood or at least show some signs of a fight.'

'But he's obviously–'

'No. We need evidence – or at the very least a motive. At the moment, you've got two things – Jack and Shit. We can hold him for twenty-four hours, and I think we could hold his lawyers off for that long, but after that we either have to charge him or let him go.'

'Couldn't we charge him with–'

'–Evidence, Cross. Without it, he walks.'

'What about the other crime scene earlier today. The two must be related. The first victim whispered the name of the house's owner to me just before he died. That can't just be a coincidence.'

Roberts shook his head. 'That's another thing I need to talk to you about. The medics who looked at the body said there's no way he could possibly have told you anything. With those wounds, he would have been dead for hours.'

Cross stared at him in disbelief. 'But he spoke to me,' was all she could say.

Roberts exhaled a long breath, his shoulders dropping. 'Look, you and I go back a long way, which is why we're having this chat – anyone else would probably be on administrative leave already. I know you're a seasoned detective, but everything you've been coming out with tonight... Tales of talking corpses and monsters... and what the hell is the Necropolis?'

'A separate case. I thought they might be related.'

'I think you need to go home and get some sleep.'

Cross shook her head in disbelief. 'You think I imagined it all? Made it up?'

'I don't know what to think. What would *you* think if a witness told you this story?'

Cross just stood there. She didn't know what to say.

'Go home. If there's any evidence at the scene, the techs will find it, and if there's anything even *hinting* at a connection, we'll look to charge him. But at the moment...' He let his words trail off.

'Where is he now?' she asked.

'He's in his cell, sleeping like a baby – something I wish I was doing at this exact moment. He doesn't seem particularly worried by any of this – and with the lawyers he's got coming down from London, I'm not surprised.' He shuffled some papers, opening a folder and stuffing them inside. 'You're dismissed, Cross. Go home. Get some sleep. It'll all look clearer in the morning.'

'Yes, sir,' she replied obediently, but she had no intention of giving up so easily. If it was evidence he wanted, then she would damn well find some.

Chapter 27.

The Palatio Insomnia

Jack lay in the darkness, unable to comprehend what he had just seen. She couldn't be gone, not like that. *Was she dead*, he wondered, *or had she simply woken up?* He prayed that it was the latter.

He jumped as a familiar voice came quietly out of the darkness. 'Now you've done it,' it said.

A small light flickered into life from the corner of his vision, Jennifer's lamp coming alight again somehow. He looked up to see the face of Jennifer looking back at him, but this wasn't Jennifer as he knew her; her skin was a bloodless white, her hair long and unkempt, and her eyes deep and sunk. She looked like a corpse, and not a fresh one. 'So you've finally killed me,' she whispered.

Jack jerked backwards, staggering to his feet. Jennifer just stood there, looking at him with a bleak look on her face. 'I trusted you one too many times and look where it's got me.'

'You're... You're not real,' he stammered.

'I'm as real as you are,' she whispered back. 'How does it feel to have killed the one person who truly loved you? The only person who will ever love you?'

'This isn't happening,' he muttered to himself.

Jennifer stepped closer to him. He could see the unnatural rigidity of her pallid skin and smell a faint odour of rotting meat. She stretched out an arm towards him, and he was powerless to move, frozen in fear and fascination. Her hand took hold of his and her flesh felt cold and clammy; a shiver of revulsion ran over him and he tried to step backwards.

Jennifer held his hand tight, not letting him pull away. 'That's no way to treat your lover,' she purred in a dry voice. If she was trying to be seductive, it wasn't working. 'Don't you think you should apologize to me?'

Jack tried to speak but his mouth was bone dry and his tongue felt too large for his mouth. 'For killing you?' he finally managed to say.

'For bringing me here in the first place,' she whispered. 'Risking everything on a foolhardy mission from a man who couldn't be trusted.'

'You... You wanted to come.'

'I wanted to keep you safe. You could only think of yourself, never putting the feelings of anyone else before yourself.'

'That's not true.'

Jennifer shook her head. 'Look inside yourself – you know that it is. And I've had to pay the ultimate price for your hubris.'

Jack just shook his head.

'Why did you do it, Jack?'

'I did it for you...' He looked her in the eyes, which were like small cold lumps of ebony.

'Well, I'm glad that's the case,' she hissed. 'You're going to stay here with me for a long time, Jack.' She grabbed his hands with hers and held them in a vice-like grip, the cold flesh sucking the heat from his own. 'You're going to stay here with me for all eternity.'

Chapter 28.

Ash House, Dartmoor, England

The man in the middle advanced towards Jennifer. As he did so she balled her fingers up into a fist and swung it at him; she connected with his chin, but his head barely moved. He swung his arm slowly back at her, hitting her in the face with the back of his hand and knocking her backwards onto the bed.

Two of the men grabbed her by the arms and pinned her down on the bed. She wrestled as hard as she could, her back arching off the bed as she tried to kick them away from her, but there were too many and they were just too strong – she couldn't escape.

The man she had hit stepped forwards and leant over her, his face close enough that she could smell his foul breath, the odour of decaying meat.

She had the coppery taste of blood in her mouth, and she spat at him, crimson saliva flecking his face. He ignored it and moved his knife in front of her head, moving its sharp point closer and closer until it wavered just above her eyeball. Jennifer lay as still as she could now, her eyes trying un-successfully to focus on the tip.

'I'm going to enjoy this,' he whispered in her ear, as he dragged the tip of the knife across her cheek. She could feel the stinging as the sharp metal ripped her flesh, but she refused to scream or beg. Even in her state of fear, a thought came to her: *Now I'll have a scar on both cheeks.* The man brought the knife up to his mouth and licked the scarlet blood from the blade. 'Sweet,' he muttered.

This couldn't be happening, thought Jennifer, panic rising in her. How the hell had this happened? Where the hell was Jack? It all made no sense, and for them to arrive right now was one hell of a coincidence.

And then a moment of clarity struck her. It *didn't* make any sense. The key for the back door shouldn't have been in the lock as they'd been careful about that ever since they'd broken in themselves. How could Jack literally vanish into thin air? And hadn't she gone shopping just yesterday and re-stocked the fridge?

She looked into the face of the man who stood leering above her. She knew he was one of the men who had abducted her and taken her to the Well of the Worlds... but wasn't he also one of the cultists that Jack had shot?

'You're... You're dead...' she whispered, almost too quietly to hear.

'No,' he replied, shaking his head. 'But you soon will be.'

Jennifer's conviction was growing; she refused to believe any of this. 'None of you are real,' she said. The expression on the man's face changed from a leering smile to a grimace of rage. He raised the knife up and brought it violently down into Jennifer's stomach; she could see spurts of ruby-red blood splash onto the man's arms but felt no pain. She closed her eyes and took a deep breath. When she opened them again, they were all gone; she was alone in her bedroom again. She ran her hand over her cheek — there was no cut, no blood.

'This is all just a dream,' she muttered to herself, as the walls of the room faded to black around her.

Jack looked into Jennifer's cold dead eyes. This wasn't the Jennifer he knew.

'If you were really Jennifer, you wouldn't be doing this,' he said. 'She'd never do this to me.'

'Hell hath no fury like a woman scorned,' she whispered with a cold smile.

'I don't know who you are–' he started.

'—I am your reckoning, a lover's vengeance from beyond the veil. I am the albatross that hangs about your neck,' she hissed at him. Her face was more skeletal than ever, the bone of her skull visible through almost translucent skin.

Jack stepped backwards, closing his eyes and ripping his hands from hers. 'You're not her.'

'Are you sure?' came a demure voice. He opened his eyes and found himself looking into the face of Jennifer, her normal face again, not the corpse-like visage he had been conversing with. 'I can prove it. Ask me anything.'

She smiled with a blink of her eyes and lifted her hand up to his face. She ran a hand along his cheek, but her touch was cold and impersonal.

A shiver ran up Jack's spine and he took another step backwards, shaking his head. 'None of this is real,' he said as he turned away, turning his back on her. From behind him he heard a momentary hiss of spite. The flickering light wavered for a moment and then winked out, leaving him in total darkness again.

Chapter 29.

Jack awoke in a dimly lit room. Jennifer was lying on the floor next to him, just starting to wake up herself. He was unsure how much time had passed.

'What happened?' he moaned, as he managed to sit up and then wished he hadn't. The room was gently spinning.

'I... I don't know,' she muttered. 'I think I had some kind of hallucination.'

'Or nightmare,' he suggested.

Jennifer swallowed, and then nodded. 'Yes.'

They looked around. They were sat on the floor of a stone cell. The walls were rough stone, the floor paved with flagstones. A door made of iron bars was before them, other bars stretching from floor to ceiling next to it. There was a corridor beyond, with more cells on the other side. A flickering light came from a burning torch at the end of the corridor, casting a dim light over their cell.

Jack stood up, taking the bars of the door in his hands and shaking them. 'This is solid, all right,' he said. 'What do you think happened?'

'Do you think someone captured us while we were unconscious?'

'A trap?' said Jack. 'Quite an effective one by the looks of it.'

'Hello?' he yelled through the bars. 'Is anyone there?' The only reply was a lonely echo.

'What now?' asked Jennifer.

'I don't know,' said Jack. 'I suppose all we can do is wait – wait until our captors return.' He looked around. The room was bare, except for a pile of golden straw on the floor in the corner of the room – not many opportunities for escape. 'What happened to you?' he asked. 'Before here?'

'Some kind of illusion. One of my worst nightmares, come to life.' Jack nodded back in agreement although he was staring into the distance, his mind obviously elsewhere. 'How about you?' she asked.

'The same,' he said with a shake of his head, bringing him back to the present. 'My worst fear, played out before me.'

Jennifer looked at Jack and could see he was shaking. Looking down, she could see that her hands were still trembling too. 'If you want to talk about it, that's fine. But if you don't...' She let her words trail off.

Jack looked her in the eyes and she smiled back at him, reminding him of happier times, times before all this insanity had taken over their lives. 'I don't think I tell you often enough how much I love you,' he said.

'You don't need to,' she replied, with a smile and a shake of her head.

'No. But I still should,' he said. 'And I know I haven't fully explained why we're here... But it's in your best interests, I promise you.'

Jennifer moved in closer and could see that there was a tear in the corner of his eye. She reached out, wrapping her arms around him. 'That's okay,' she said. 'I understand.'

'The quicker we can get this over with, the quicker we can get on with the rest of our lives together. If you'll still want me that is, now that I'm an old man.'

Jennifer gave a little chuckle. 'I've always known I'd grow old with you,' she whispered. 'I just didn't expect you to get such a head start.'

Jack squeezed her in his arms. He could feel the warmth of her body through their clothes, dispelling the remaining fears still lurking at the back of his mind. Gently, he kissed her on the forehead, and when he withdrew she moved back in, kissing him more forcefully on the lips. Her mouth opened to accept his tongue, which probed within her mouth, intertwining with her own.

His hands ran down her back and then moved to the front to undo the buttons on her blouse; it slipped from her shoulders, falling to the floor. His mouth moved to her neck, then her breasts, his lips gently kissing and caressing her skin. Her hands were holding his head, running her fingers through his hair.

While his lips caressed her, his hands moved down to her buttocks, sliding inside her pants and pushing them down over her hips. They fell to the floor and she stepped out of them, kneeling down, undoing the buttons on his shirt and then unfastening his belt.

She slowly lay backwards on the straw, pulling him down with her, the warmth of his body hot against her bare flesh. Jennifer moaned loudly as their bodies combined. Her nails raked down his back as their legs intertwined, their bodies merging until she no longer knew where her flesh ended and his began.

As their passion intensified, Jack continued to kiss her, her tongue caressing his own. He gently bit her lips, her neck, her ears. He pulled back and gazed upon her face, her eyes closed in ecstasy. As he watched, her face suddenly changed, growing older before his eyes. Lines appeared on her face and her hair was turning grey, before she was suddenly much younger, a Jennifer of ten years ago again, as she was when he had first met her. He was unable to stop as he felt his skin merging into hers, their two bodies now one inseparable whole. He could feel her fingers on his back, scratching deep and drawing blood, her teeth sinking into his shoulder, the pain a distant sensation.

They both looked into each other's eyes and saw not each other but the eyes of wild animals looking back at them. The room around them seemed to fade away, first becoming the bedroom where their mortal bodies lay before fading into the deep blackness of the night sky, the stars all around them the only illumination. Her hips moved in perfect synchronization with his, and he could feel her hands pulling him closer, until they sank into his flesh, fusing into his body. They floated, alone in the eternal void of space, as they both finally came together, their bodies contorting with ecstasy as they finally merged into one single being among the stars.

Chapter 30.

Jack awoke to find Jennifer standing by the door of the cell, looking out.

'Have you been awake long?' he asked as he sat up.

'About an hour.'

'Have you seen anything?' Jennifer came back and squatted down next to him, running a hand through his hair. 'No,' she said. 'Nothing. No movement, not even a sound.'

'Are you just going to leave us in here to rot?' Jack called out to no one in particular.

They sat on the floor together, both deep in thought, when Jennifer broke the silence. 'I've been thinking,' she said.

'Yes?'

'Since we entered this place – *The Palace of Dreams* – nothing we've experienced was actually real, was it?'

Jack thought back to the hall with the stars, and the alternative Jennifer. 'Right,' he said with a lump in his throat.

'So what makes this cell any different?' she proposed.

'You think we're still dreaming?' said Jack, as he climbed to his feet.

'Could be. How would we know?'

Jack took a few steps over to the bars and shook them with both hands. 'They feel pretty real to me.'

'So did my last nightmare here,' she said. 'It was only the tiny details that gave me a clue.' Jack nodded, thinking back to his own experience, but saying nothing. 'I've tried just walking through the bars, but...' She took a step forwards, before pressing gently against them. 'They feel pretty solid.'

Jack looked at her and thought for a second. 'You're flinching and stopping before you hit the bars. You're trying to tell yourself that they're not real, but your body's revealing your true feelings.'

'Then what do you suggest?'

Jack thought for a moment. 'Come here,' he said, beckoning her to come closer. He bent down to pick up their bags from the floor, putting his over his shoulder and passing the other to her. Then he took her hand and walked her to the back of the cell; it was a journey of only a few steps. He turned to face the bars and motioned for her to do the same. When they were both standing there, holding hands, he took a deep breath.

'Now close your eyes and don't open them again until I tell you.'

'Okay,' she said hesitantly.

'Imagine we're at home, standing on our rear porch. Can you do that?'

'Okay.'

'Just walk with me. We're just walking from our porch over to the orchard at the rear of the property. Whatever you do, just keep walking.'

Jack took a step forwards, pulling Jennifer along with him. They took another step and then another, until they were walking at a fluid pace. After about twenty steps, he stopped.

'Do we open our eyes now?' asked Jennifer.

Jack cautiously opened one eye. They were no longer in the cell – it was no longer anywhere to be seen. Instead, they were standing in another huge dark hall. In front of them stood an open doorway, a clear blue sky visible through it.

'Yes,' he said. 'Let's get the hell out of here.'

They broke hands and ran for the exit, not stopping until they were both outside. They found themselves emerging from a cave entrance onto the side of a mountain. Before them, they could see a rocky path winding its way down the side of the cliff to the valley floor below.

'Is that it?' he asked. 'Are we finally out of there?'

'I... I don't know,' replied Jennifer. 'How would we tell?'

Jack shrugged. 'Does this feel like a nightmare to you?'

Jennifer stood on the side of the mountain, the sun warm on her face and the wind blowing gently through her hair. 'No,' she said. 'At least no more than any other part of this journey.'

'Agreed. Let's assume the best and just get as far away from here as we can.'

'I don't have my lamp any more. We must have left it behind somewhere in there.'

'Well, I'm not going back for it.' He started jogging down the path. 'Come on,' he called. 'I'll race you to the bottom.'

As they worked their way down the mountainside, they could see a dense forest lying in the valley before them, the lush green vegetation a welcome change from the bleak deserts and mountains. On the far side of the forest, they could make out a wide river stretching away towards the horizon where it connected to a vast green sea. A collection of tall stone buildings were just visible on the distant ocean's edge.

Jennifer scanned the forest before them and spotted what looked like the top of a black stone tower poking through the tree-tops near the middle of the trees. She pulled the pendant from around her neck and checked it; it was pointing in the direction of the tower. 'That might finally be it,' she said, 'but it could also be that city on the horizon.'

'Okay, let's go,' said Jack.

They stumbled down the rocky path, their hearts lifted slightly by the hope that the end of this journey might now be in sight.

'Let's just be careful of the thorns this time, shall we?' said Jennifer as they arrived at the edge of the forest. The trees looked taller now that they were here; even the smallest trunks were at least three feet wide, with the tops of the tallest trees a hundred feet off the ground.

Jennifer checked the pendant again. 'That way,' she said, pointing off into the depths of the forest.

They made their way carefully through the undergrowth, but the plants at ground level were few and far between. It was cool and shady where they walked, most of the light being blocked out by the thick canopy of leaves overhead.

'Did you see that?' asked Jack, stopping suddenly.

'See what?'

'I'm sure there's something in here with us. Something following us,' said Jack. 'I keep seeing something moving out of the corner of my eye, but when I turn to look...' He shook his head. 'Nothing.'

Jennifer stood next to him and turned around, scanning the area around them. All she could see were the trees and plants. They stood still and listened but could hear nothing but quiet bird chatter from high above them.

'Are you sure you're not just imagining it?' she asked. 'I couldn't blame you after what we've just been through.'

'No,' he replied. 'It's a feeling as much as anything.'

'Well, if there is someone hiding out there–'

'–or *something*–'

'–and it's following us... Can we do much about it?'

'Not unless they reveal themselves,' he admitted.

'Then we go on. C'mon.' She checked the pendant and then strode off again. Jack took one last look around and then hastily followed after her.

They had been walking through the woods for almost an hour when Jennifer suddenly held up her hand to indicate to Jack that he should stop.

He drew to a halt next to her. 'What is it?' he whispered.

'There's some kind of building ahead,' she said.

Now that he was looking more closely, Jack could just about make out what looked like some white stone walls at the edge of his vision. 'You think that's where he is?'

Jennifer pulled the pendant out, checked it quickly and then dropped it back under her blouse. 'Looks like it to me. What now?'

'You stay here for a moment. I'll go ahead and get a closer look.'

'Jack?'

'Huh?'

'No heroics, okay?'

He nodded back. 'Okay,' he agreed with a grin.

Jack crept forwards slowly, moving from tree to tree for cover. As he approached the stone structures, it became obvious that they were all ruins. There were several piles of masonry, mostly covered in weeds and creepers, the remains of what must have once been some kind of habitation. He advanced to the first structure; all that remained were two low walls, the rest rubble or gone entirely. Anything that wasn't stone must have rotted away a long time ago. He stood there, observing quietly for a minute or two before he turned around and scampered back to Jennifer.

'Well?' she asked.

'Whatever civilization used to be here, it looks like it's been abandoned a long time ago. It certainly *appears* deserted. I couldn't see any signs of life or hear anything. Let's go take a look.'

Together, they approached the ruins, Jennifer leading, following the pendant. They walked between the remains of the stone buildings, the floor between their feet now an overgrown path, the weeds growing tall between the bricks. Jennifer was the first to spot where the pendant was leading them — a tall tower set apart from the other structures and built from rough black bricks, their coal-like colour a sharp contrast to the pale sandstone ruins all around. It had no windows at ground level; the first ones were at least thirty feet up. There was a small clearing around the base of the tower, and the top disappeared beyond the leaves of the trees, at least a hundred feet tall. Vines and creepers grew up the side of the tower, clinging tightly to the stone as they scaled their way up the walls.

There was a single wooden door in the side of the tower that looked at least ten feet tall. It was old and weather beaten, although the entire building was in significantly better shape than the others all around it. They took a final look around for any signs of life and then cautiously advanced. Jack headed for the door, while Jennifer slowly stepped to the side of the building.

She stopped several metres away from the tower. 'This seems to be the right area,' she said, concentrating as she tried to follow the pendant. 'It's started spinning about wildly.' She looked up and then all around her. 'The tower's the nearest structure. I reckon that's it.'

Jack stopped at the door and listened, placing his ear upon the rough wood, but there was nothing to hear. Carefully, as if expecting it to shock him, he took hold of the metal door handle; it felt cold and damp in the palm of his hand. He twisted it slowly and the handle turned, the door opening inwards with a low creak to reveal a dark and silent interior. He pushed the door open wider, swallowed, and stepped through.

The air inside was warm and musty, almost stale enough to make him choke. Mould was growing on the walls around the edge of the room, and weeds were poking their way through the large flagstones on the floor. Pieces of broken and rotting timber littered the floor – all that remained of what must have once been furniture or fittings. On the far side of the room were two sets of stairs curving along the outer wall, one leading up, one leading down. The room was dark, with most of the light coming in through the doorway behind him and only a small amount coming down the stairwell from the floor above.

'Up or down?' asked Jack as Jennifer came in and stood beside him.

Jennifer checked the pendant, but it just hung flat in the air, pointing in the same direction. 'I don't know how accurate this thing is,' she said, 'but this puts him somewhere just outside the tower. I'm guessing it's somewhere underneath.'

'Down it is,' he said with a sigh. 'Everything *always* seems to be down...' Together, they walked over to the stairs, the wide stone steps descending into an inky blackness.

'Are you sure?' asked Jennifer. 'I don't have my lamp anymore.'

Jack squatted down and squinted into the darkness. 'Hold on a second,' he said, and then took a few tentative steps downwards. Jennifer watched as he stepped briefly into the shadows and appeared to wrestle with something on the wall. When he returned, he was carrying a wooden torch. 'Have you still got your tinderbox?' he asked.

Jennifer rummaged through her bag and brought it out. The torch felt damp, but together they managed to find some kindling from outside and made a small fire. When that was ablaze, they started lighting the torch from that. It took a few attempts, but eventually they had it lit, its flames casting a flickering light around the room.

'After you,' said Jennifer.

Jack took the torch, grasping it in his right hand as he started down the steps.

❄ ❄ ❄

168

As they descended, the steps curved round, following the outer wall of the tower until they had made a complete revolution and were now well beneath ground level. As it levelled out, the stairwell turned into a paved stone corridor leading away from the tower, the walls and ceiling covered with hundreds of spider webs. Jack held the torch up to the thin strands hanging from the ceiling near him; they reluctantly caught fire, slowly disappearing in wisps of smoke.

Jack advanced slowly, ducking down under the larger webs. As they progressed along the corridor, he could see that the webs were clearly getting thicker and longer; some were like milky strands of string and, before long, like twine. Even the heat of the torch didn't seem to do much with these; it was like trying to light a wet tree branch.

Jack paused as he reached a T-junction. From the uneven light of the torch, Jack could see a mass of shimmering webs to the right; he couldn't see more than about twenty feet away. The passage to the left had its own webs, but it was definitely clearer. 'Which way?' he called back to Jennifer. She consulted the pendant, which was pointing to their left, and let Jack know. 'Okay,' he muttered under his breath before heading off in that direction, holding out the torch to burn the thinner webs away before him.

Jennifer followed closely behind. Like Jack, she dodged under the webbing that wasn't burned away, but it was impossible to avoid it all. It was tough and sticky, and she had to peel it from her clothes. As she stood behind Jack, pulling the webbing from her blouse, she turned her head as she heard muffled sounds of movement from behind them.

'*Jack*,' she whispered urgently.

Jack stopped walking. 'I hear it,' he replied. They turned and were peering into the darkness when a huge spider came scuttling out of the darkness. Its purple body was the size of a large rat, its spindly black legs tapping along the stone floor.

'Jesus!' exclaimed Jack, instinctively thrusting the torch towards the spider. It backed up, hissing, obviously afraid of the flames. It stood there for a moment considering them, before it turned and scurried back down the corridor away from them.

'Did you see the size of that thing?' asked Jennifer.

'Yeah. I don't want to know what kind of flies that thing catches. Let's get a move on before it comes back.' Jack sped up, giving up on the smaller strands of webbing, ducking and even crawling under them where he could. They turned a corner and drew to a stop as they found themselves standing at the end of a wider corridor, one that was blessedly free of cobwebs. Barred cells stood on both sides of the passageway and several unlit torches were attached to brackets on the walls between the cells. Jack stepped forwards until he was next to one and then held his torch to it; it reluctantly flickered into light, bringing more illumination to the corridor, as well as a thin haze of smoke to the air. Jack proceeded along the corridor, checking the cells in turn. As he reached the final cell, a body became visible in the far corner, lying curled up in the shadows.

Jennifer stopped next to him. 'Is that him?' she asked.

Jack knocked on the bars of the cell with the torch; it gave a dull thud. The man inside lifted his head from the floor where he had been sleeping. From the dark shadows, they could both recognize the face looking back at them from beneath his long black hair. It was one of the cultists from the Necropolis, one of the men who had kidnapped Jennifer and, along with Silas, had planned to sacrifice her. He appeared younger than when they had last seen each other just a few days ago, but it was definitely the same man.

'Him?' exclaimed Jennifer. 'What the hell? Did you know this was who we had to meet?'

Jack held up his palms towards Jennifer. 'I told you all I knew – that it was one of the Brotherhood. I never knew who – we weren't exactly on first-name terms before.'

'This is madness,' she replied. 'Tell me you're not planning on letting him out of there.'

'Look–' began Jack, deliberately keeping his voice low and calm.

'–You *know* you can't trust him,' said Jennifer, clearly exasperated. 'I don't know what he's promised you, but you can't believe a word of it. Have you forgotten that he wanted to kill me? To *sacrifice* me?'

'Look, I know this looks bad,' said Jack, 'but nothing's changed. We always knew it was going to be one of them, and this is something I have to do. I can't explain right now – I wish I could – but you're going to have to trust me for now. After all we've been through, can't you do that for me?'

'Oh Jack,' she moaned. 'I thought I knew you. You've changed… The old Jack would never have asked me to go along with this insanity.'

'And you can't tell me why?'

Jack looked her in the eyes. 'I think it's best if I don't. At least for now.'

Jennifer looked at him critically. She looked at the forlorn expression on his face and sighed. 'If it was anyone other than you…'

'I know,' said Jack. He took her hands in his. 'It'll be okay, I promise.'

There was a cough from within the cell. 'If you two have quite finished, you'll find the key to the door on a hook over there.' He pointed back along the corridor.

'Look, I'm obviously never going to trust him. But honestly… do you?' asked Jennifer.

Jack looked her squarely in the eyes. 'Yes. I think I do. At least until he gives me cause not to.'

She sighed. 'Then I guess that's going to have to do for now. Just don't make me regret this.'

'Look,' said Randolph. 'I *am* right here. If you've got a problem with me, you can talk to me to my face.'

Jennifer let go of Jack's hands and turned to face Randolph, taking hold of the bars instead. Jack wandered off back along the corridor, presumably to fetch the key.

'Okay,' she said. 'You wanted me dead before. What's changed?'

Randolph stepped forwards, out of the shadows and into the torchlight. 'To be fair, it was never about you personally. We needed a sacrifice and you were… well, *convenient.*' Jennifer snorted derisively. 'And that was before I understood who you are… who you *both* are.'

'Which is…?'

'I don't want to say just yet, not until I'm certain.'

'Does this joker ever give you a straight answer?' Jennifer called out to Jack.

'I've only ever dealt with one of his minions,' he replied as he arrived back next to her. 'But he was just as infuriating.' He was holding a metal ring with several large keys on it.

'It won't be much longer now, I promise,' said Randolph. 'Then everything will become clear.'

Jennifer stood there for a moment. 'How come you're imprisoned here?'

Randolph smiled. 'It wasn't my choice, obviously. There was a bit of a misunderstanding – I wasn't in a position to choose my place of arrival here.'

Jack turned to Jennifer. 'So… shall I let him out?'

'Do I have a say in this?'

'Of course you do.'

She sighed again and closed her eyes once more, her head dropping. 'Go on then. Just don't make me regret this, or else *you're* going to regret this.'

'Understood,' said Jack with a sheepish grin. He tried one of the keys in the lock. It turned with a loud click, and he pulled the door open.

Randolph walked out of the cell towards them. He held out a hand to Jack, who hesitated for a moment before shaking it. Then he turned to Jennifer, only to find her standing with her arms crossed in front of her chest. He put his hand back down by his side. He looked up and down the corridor they were standing in. 'Makes you appreciate more modern prisons, I suppose,' he muttered to himself. 'Shall we go then? I must say, you took longer to get here than I expected, but I suppose I should be glad that you managed to find me here at all.'

'There were… well, *complications*,' said Jack.

Randolph raised an eyebrow, giving him a curious glance, but didn't ask for an elaboration.

'So what's the plan?' asked Jennifer.

'First, I need to work out where we are.'

'We're in a forest just north of a place called *The Palace of Dreams*.'

Randolph thought for a second. 'You mean The Palace of *Nightmares*?'

Jack gave a small laugh. 'That does sound like a more accurate name, yes.'

'Yes, well, we'll find another way back then. I think we should be able to go east from here, around the mountain range. We need to head towards a town where I believe we will find the final legacy of Aloysius.'

'A legacy?' asked Jennifer.

'He really hasn't told you anything, has he?' said Randolph, chuckling slightly. 'Let's get out of here and then I'll explain on the way.'

Randolph and Jennifer both took torches of their own from the wall, and then they all headed back up the corridor, Jack and Jennifer in the front with Randolph following behind. As they reached the junction in the corridor, they stopped.

'What is it?' asked Randolph.

'This corridor,' said Jack, indicating the passage to his right. 'It was empty a minute ago.' The passageway they had come down was now blocked by a thick wall of webbing stretching from the ceiling almost to the floor.

'I'd be very careful if I were you,' warned Randolph. Jack reached into his bag and took out his knife. Holding the blade in his left hand and the torch in his right, he started to burn away the web. It was slow work; the thick strands were wet and reluctant to catch, but he gradually started to clear a hole near the floor.

'Here, let me help you,' said Jennifer, stepping forwards to his side and holding out her torch to join with his. As she started to burn the webbing, she caught movement out of the corner of her eye. She turned and screamed at what she saw, dropping the torch on the floor. An enormous spider was advancing down the other corridor towards them. Its purple body was three feet across and bloated, with large violet eyes reflecting their torchlight. Its long spindly legs were dark violet, turning almost black at the tips. The one they had seen earlier must have been just an infant.

The spider hissed, spitting two large strands of webbing towards them. They flew through the air; striking Jennifer and wrapping themselves around her like a whip, sticking to her face and clothes. She stumbled backwards, tangled in the thick fibres. The more she struggled, the more entangled she became and she tumbled backwards, falling to the floor.

Jack stepped backwards and turned, putting himself between the spider and Jennifer, waving the torch in front of him and thrusting it menacingly towards the spider. The spider shrank back slightly, not much but just enough to show that it was afraid – or unsure – of the flame.

'Jack! Your knife!' shouted Randolph.

'What?' he replied, not taking his eyes from the giant spider.

'Throw it to me!' ordered Randolph.

Jack hesitated for a moment and then threw it backwards along the corridor towards Randolph. He didn't take his gaze away from the spider, which was staring at him with a menacing look in its eyes. Its two front legs were moving up and down in a rhythmic manner, drawing his attention.

Randolph reached over to where the knife lay on the floor and picked it up, laying his torch down next to Jennifer.

'What the fuck, Jack!' screamed Jennifer as Randolph leant over her, holding the knife in his hand.

'Trust me,' said Randolph. 'We haven't got much time.' He brought the knife down, slicing through a thick strand of webbing.

The spider lifted one of its long legs towards Jack, and he thrust the torch towards it. As it made contact, a horrible chittering noise echoed from its mouth and it yanked its limb back violently. When it opened its mouth, Jack could see a terrifying array of sharp fangs within.

'Whatever you're doing, you'd better be quick,' uttered Jack through clenched teeth.

Randolph sliced through the strands in another couple of places; they were still stuck to her, but she could now move her arms and legs again. 'Go!' he shouted at Jennifer. She rolled over, scrambling on her hands and knees under the wall of webbing.

Randolph picked up the torch and followed her, crawling along the floor. Once through the webbing he passed the torch to Jennifer. 'Burn it,' he ordered, as he started to slice the webs between himself and Jack. Jennifer didn't argue, doing what she could with the torch.

'Don't turn around,' said Randolph in a low steady voice. 'We've almost got rid of the webs behind you. Whatever you do, don't turn your back on it.'

Jack took a tentative step away from the spider; it took a step too, matching him. From somewhere behind the spider, Jack could hear the noise of feet tapping on stone – lots of feet. There were more of these creatures approaching.

'Err, guys,' he urged. 'How's it looking? It's about to get real busy in here.'

'It'll have to do,' said Randolph. 'Duck down and go backwards – carefully.'

Jack took a step backwards, crouching down as he did so. He glanced momentarily to the side to check his position, and as he did so, the spider lurched forwards, its fangs glistening in the torchlight. Jack rolled to the side, falling to the floor, out of the way of the attack.

Jennifer thrust her own torch forwards towards the beast and it shied away again, hissing at them. Jack turned and bolted, grabbing Jennifer by the arm as he did so. The three of them sprinted away down the corridor, ignoring the myriad smaller webs that stuck to their faces and bodies as they ran.

They didn't look behind them until they were at the top of the steps, back on the ground floor of the tower again. As far as they could see, they hadn't been followed.

As they stood there panting, Jennifer held out her hand to Randolph. 'Knife,' she ordered.

'Don't I get a thank you?' he said, passing the knife to her, handle first, placing it gently in the palm of her hand.

'If it wasn't for you, we wouldn't even be here risking our lives. Here,' she said, passing the knife back to Jack, who was peeling the spider webs from his clothes.

'I don't know about you,' said Jack. 'But I'm about ready to get the hell out of this place.'

Chapter 31.

They set off rapidly, heading east through the forest and following Randolph now rather than the pendant. They only stopped when they reached a stream. Randolph knelt down at the water's edge and started to wash his arms in the water, using it to clean away the remains of the spider webs from his clothes and flesh.

Jack and Jennifer joined him at the water's edge, Jack kneeling next to him and Jennifer slightly further downstream. Large butterflies flapped around in the air above the water, flirting with each other in the warm sunlight.

'Let me guess,' said Jennifer, as she gazed at their reflections dancing across the water. 'They're deadly butterflies.'

'No,' chuckled Randolph. 'I think these ones are fine.'

'There are *some* things here that don't want to kill us then,' she laughed humourlessly. She stood up and took the pendant out from under her blouse. She span it around, amusing herself with how it continued to point towards Randolph, even as she paced in a circle around him.

'It's like having our very own GPS tracker, just for you,' she joked.

'Feel free to keep hold of it – a gesture of my good faith,' he said. 'You won't have to worry about me running off and abandoning you.'

'So,' she said to Randolph. 'Tell me about this Aloysius then.'

Randolph cupped his hands together and scooped a handful of water from the stream. He drank it carefully, then sat back down on the grass and looked up at Jennifer, who had remained standing. 'Aloysius was the founder of the Brotherhood,' he started. 'A very wise man.' Jennifer snorted, but Randolph continued. 'He was one of the first from our world to discover this place,' he said, indicating all around him with a show of his hands. 'The stories say there was another ancient society based in these lands who called themselves *The Thousand Young*. He was fascinated by their secrets and rituals and so he joined their number but soon became disillusioned with their ways. He infiltrated his way into their inner sanctum, learning much of their forbidden wisdom before he tried to lead an uprising, attempting to take with him some of the mysteries that they held for his own use. He failed and was banished from these lands, never to return, but he took with him a small cadre of followers – an inner circle of men who believed in him and were loyal only to him. They were the original members of my brotherhood.'

Randolph leant back out over the river again, taking another handful of water. 'After that, he never visited this world again, but was instead blessed with the gift of prophecy. According to legend, when he slept he didn't have what we would consider normal dreams. Instead, he would receive prophetic visions every once in a while.'

'And did he have much to say for himself?'

'Originally, yes. The visions died out in the later years of his life.'

'And he made prophecies about Jack?' she asked.

Randolph nodded to her. 'I believe you've already seen one for yourself.'

Jennifer thought back to the image of Jack painted beneath Bruadar Castle. 'And there are others?'

Randolph looked at Jack who was standing behind Jennifer, and smiled. 'That's why we're here – one big happy family.'

Jennifer shook her head in disbelief. 'My family outings were never like this.'

'No, I suppose your childhood was all rainbows and puppies.'

'And I suppose yours was spent torturing small animals and wetting the bed.'

'I'm sure you'd find my early childhood quite boring,' said Randolph with a small tilt of his head. 'I was the youngest of three brothers–' he started.

'—Well, that explains the overcompensation. Tell me, did your father beat you too?'

Randolph gave her an odd look of pleasure and nostalgia. 'My parents were both strict military types, not afraid of a little *discipline*. Well, until they had a nasty accident, anyway.'

'What do you mean?' asked Jennifer incredulously. 'Are you trying to tell me you killed your parents?' Jack turned around to face them too. His mind had started to wander, becoming bored of the incessant bickering between these two, but this had snapped him out of it.

'That's not what the courts said,' replied Randolph with a knowing smile. 'I wasn't to blame myself, apparently.'

'But...' was all that Jennifer could manage. She turned to face Jack who simply shrugged back at her. 'And you *trust* this man? You *believe* him?'

Jack stepped close to Jennifer, taking her gently by the arm. He leant forwards, whispering in her ear. 'Frankly, I'm not sure I believe any of this. I think he's just trying to rile you.' He let go of her again. 'He did make a convincing argument,' he said again in a normal voice.

Jennifer shook her head. 'I hope it was more than just that.' She looked at Randolph again. 'And what's to stop me killing you right here?'

'I'm not sure you're the type to kill a defenceless man in cold blood,' he replied, then looked at the expression on Jennifer's face. 'But apart from that, nothing really,' he added quickly. 'Except that without my help, you'd never find out the truth.'

'You mean the prophecies,' she corrected.

Randolph shrugged his shoulders and nodded.

'You said Aloysius was banished from here and never returned?' asked Jack.

'Yes.'

'Then why do you believe his final legacy is here of all places?'

Randolph smiled. '*He* was denied access here, but no so for all his followers. Many of the Brotherhood's ancient texts speak of something that he left behind, something of great importance to him – and now to me. I have spent many years researching this, tracking down rumours and searching through historical records. I could be wrong, but I believe I have located where this legacy may be, and I fear we do not have long.'

'Why?'

'If I understand correctly, we can only gain access to the location at particular moments in time. If we take too long, it will be several years until we can try again.'

'Well, I suppose we'd better get on with it then, hadn't we,' said Jack with a sigh. Jennifer just gave another derisive snort.

From the forest, they waded across the stream and then continued east, the terrain growing higher and the vegetation sparser. Before too long, they were struggling up steep hills. It was hard work, but Jack reckoned it was still better than going back through *The Palace of Nightmares*.

As the sun dipped below the horizon, they decided to stop for the evening in a cave mouth on the side of a rocky mountain. The cave was deep enough to provide good cover from the cold wind, which was strong up here; they expected it would only get colder and stronger at night. Jack wished they could make a camp fire again, but there was no more foliage around to use. Everything was rock and dirt as far as the eye could see, dull grey in colour. Some was light grey and some was dark grey, but it was all grey, drab and depressing.

'How about I take first watch this time,' said Jennifer to Jack. 'That way I know you'll get at least *some* sleep.'

'Would you like me to take second or third watch?' asked Randolph.

'I may have been stupid enough to come with you, but I haven't completely taken leave of my senses,' said Jennifer. 'If you think we're both going to go to sleep and leave you to watch over us—'

'—Okay, okay, I was only offering,' said Randolph. 'I'm certainly not going to turn down the offer of a good night's sleep.'

Jennifer reached into her bag and withdrew some dried meat and fruit, which she passed to Jack. She searched a little bit further down and pulled out some stale bread, which she passed to Randolph.

'Don't I—'

'Don't push your luck,' she said.

Randolph shrugged and took the bread, making an exaggerated show of gratitude. Jennifer did her best to ignore him.

When they had eaten, Jack and Randolph settled down for the night. Randolph removed his jacket and rolled it up to make a pillow. Jack emptied the contents of his satchel and used that.

Jennifer sat cross-legged in the mouth of the cave, looking outwards. It was cold, but it was also calm and peaceful. The moon hung large in the sky, illuminating the landscape. Like much of the world she now sat in, it seemed somehow unfamiliar and alien, although she couldn't describe exactly what the differences were; she had never been one for astronomy. The only sounds were the rush of the wind and the distant howling of some wild creature. She hoped that it would remain that way.

She decided to let Jack have a good rest before she woke him. He seemed okay, but she didn't know if his body was still recovering from the poison. He looked peaceful in his sleep; she wondered if he was dreaming. She tried to remember if she had dreamt at all since they had arrived here; she couldn't *remember* having any dreams, but then she rarely could.

It was the early hours of the morning when she finally woke him, allowing herself a few hours of sleep before they would have to leave. As she expected, she quickly fell into a deep, dreamless sleep.

Chapter 32.

They descended the other side of the mountain in the morning. The path was steep and winding, but not long after they had started the downward journey, they could see the remains of a settlement in front of them, several miles beyond the foot of the hills and across a grassy plain.

'Is that it?' asked Jack.

'Yes,' replied Randolph. 'The ancient city of Orlath – or what remains of it.'

They continued down the steep path, slipping and sliding their way down the side of the mountain, almost but never quite out of control. When they reached the bottom, they paused for a quick rest, and then set off along the flat plain, which was covered in long golden-yellow grass. It was uniformly knee-high, almost as if it had been deliberately cut that way, and when the wind blew it swayed back and forth in the breeze in an almost hypnotic rhythm.

As they approached the outskirts, they could see that this was now a mere shell of what must have once been a considerable city. Its towering walls lay in crumbling ruins, the huge sandstone blocks now weathered and broken. Further inside, the buildings were mere empty shells at best, the solid stone skeleton of a once-great civilization.

They circled around the walls until they found the main entrance, where gates must have once stood at least fifty feet tall. They walked through what was now just a large gap in the wall, and then down a wide paved street, heading towards the centre of the city.min

'Just how old is this place?' asked Jack as they passed the remains of a huge temple, its massive pillars now lying fractured and broken before it.

'Ageless,' said Randolph. 'By your terms, from the waking world, it was founded hundreds of years in the past, and fell maybe fifty years ago. With the difference in timescales, for someone living here it will have been sitting like this…' He sighed. 'Well, for millennia.'

They walked down the long street, the flagstones uneven and broken, with dead weeds poking up between the stone slabs. Their path was occasionally blocked by the rubble of fallen buildings, forcing them either to climb over the remains or to divert through smaller side streets. There were no sounds and no signs of movement apart from themselves and the occasional small bird on the roof of a building. They walked down the winding road for nearly half an hour, flanked by collapsed structures and piles of debris, slowly advancing towards the centre of the city.

'What can you hope to still find here?' asked Jennifer.

'Just wait and watch,' said Randolph. 'We're close now.' He drew to a stop as they neared a clearing in the centre of the town. An empty square stood before them, free from the rubble that littered the rest of the area. The wide main road split into two and circled around it before rejoining and continuing on the other side, eventually disappearing behind more ruins.

'Well?' said Jennifer. 'Is this it?'

'Appearances can be deceptive,' said Randolph simply.

He brushed a spot free of dust on the floor and then sat down and crossed his legs, closing his eyes and relaxing; he looked like he was meditating. He pulled a ring off his left hand and held it between his fingers, twirling it around a few times before giving it a brief kiss, as if for luck, and replacing it on his finger.

'What's that?' asked Jack, looking at the ring. The metal had an odd green hue and appeared to be entirely covered in some kind of markings.

'This ring is made out of a metal unique to the dreamlands,' said Randolph. 'It can allow you to take items from here back to the waking world —

without it, anything that didn't come with you to these lands won't return with you.'

'Useful,' admitted Jack with a raise of an eyebrow.

'In addition, it allows an experienced dreamer some degree of control over our environment,' he said. 'We can't change anything, but where something has been previously altered… or *hidden*…' His words faded out as he closed his eyes again, concentrating hard.

'Should we join you?' asked Jennifer.

'If you like,' murmured Randolph.

'Will it help?' she asked.

'No,' he replied simply. 'But it might make you feel more useful.'

Jennifer sighed in annoyance and stepped back, looking at the ruined buildings around her. From what remained of the architecture, she could tell this must have once been an incredible place.

Jack sidled up to her. 'Do you get the feeling we're not alone here?' he whispered.

'Have you seen something?'

'Not as such. It's more a feeling than anything. It's like – whoa!' He stopped, his jaw dropping open in amazement. Jennifer turned around. The empty square was no longer empty; a stone building was flickering in and out of existence before their eyes.

'What the…' began Jennifer before stopping, her eyes wide.

The flickering was slowing, the building remaining for longer and longer periods of time, until it finally finished phasing in and out of existence and merely stood there in front of them, as if it had always been there. Jack tentatively walked over to it and carefully touched it with his hand. It certainly felt solid.

'Is it…?'

'Real?' replied Randolph. 'As real as anything else here. It should remain here long enough.'

'Long enough for what?' asked Jennifer with an expression of concern.

Randolph ignored her. 'Come,' he said. 'Let's make haste before it wears off and the building returns.'

'Returns to where?'

'If I understand correctly… another dimension. A space between the stars.'

'And what happens if we're still in it when that happens?' asked Jack.

'Well… Let's just try not to let that happen, shall we?' sighed Randolph, like a teacher dealing with an incessantly curious child. He strode up to the large wooden door in the centre of the building. It looked pristine, as did the rest of the building, in complete contrast to the rest of the city. It was built from shining white marble and inlaid with other fine stones; Jack thought he could recognize onyx and jade among some others.

'You've never said what happens if we die here,' asked Jennifer.

'It's not as bad as you might think,' said Randolph with a shrug. 'You'll wake up back home, as if waking from a bad nightmare.'

'That doesn't sound too bad,' she replied.

'There is one drawback,' he said. 'Your physical body may be safe, but your dream body will be destroyed. For most people that means you'll never be able to return here. With more experienced dreamers, it can prove more of a challenge – difficult but not impossible. Still, better than the alternative, I suppose.'

'And if we end up in whatever it was you called it – another dimension?' she asked.

Randolph thought for a second. 'You know, I'm really not sure. As I said–'

'–Yeah, let's try not to let that happen. I get the picture.'

Randolph looked around and picked up a thick shaft of wood from a pile of debris lying nearby. He walked back to the door and rapped heavily on it with the end of the staff, making three loud slow knocks. A deep boom echoed within with each blow. He passed the shaft back to Jack, who hesitantly took it, and then he waited. Jack and Jennifer looked at each other, unsure of what was about to happen.

When nothing occurred, Randolph stepped forwards and twisted the handles on the doors, pushing on them as he did so. They swung inwards with a loud creak, revealing a dark hallway before them.

'Shall we?' he asked, and then stepped inside without waiting for a reply.

They walked into what must have once been a grand hallway, although it was now dark and oppressive, a layer of dust undisturbed on the floor.

Jack looked around them; the floor looked like it was made of obsidian, as did the walls around them, making memories of *The Palace of Nightmares* come flooding back to him. Above them stood a domed ceiling onto which the night sky was painted. Or at least he assumed it was a painting. As he looked up, out of the corner of his eye some of the stars seemed to twinkle. Near the centre sat a larger, red star that Jack recognized from his earlier encounters with the Brotherhood. 'What is this place?' he asked.

'According to my research, a shrine to the memory of Aloysius, built by persons unknown,' replied Randolph. 'From what I managed to discover, it was a sanctuary and a meeting place for his followers, until one day it just… disappeared. In one of his more enigmatic prophecies, Aloysius foretold that after his death we would find a legacy here, an inheritance left for his descendants and only accessible to them.'

'Well then… Why didn't you bring them instead of us,' said Jennifer. Then something clicked. 'Oh.'

'Are you telling me that we're descendants of Aloysius?' asked Jack incredulously. 'Descendants of the founder of your cult?'

'If the prophecies are to be believed, then yes. Well, technically I suppose only you are, Mr Knight. Why else would there be such a strong bond between us, such an ongoing connection between your family and the Brotherhood?'

'Coincidence?' said Jack.

'Bad karma?' added Jennifer.

Randolph shook his head, smiling. 'No, I believe you are a descendant of Aloysius, Mr Knight, and as such, you should be able to retrieve what he has left for you.'

'And what would that be?' asked Jack.

'An ancient relic of the Brotherhood, something I have hunted for many years. And with that will come knowledge and understanding for yourselves.'

'And we're just meant to let you take it?' asked Jennifer mockingly.

'Trust me…' started Randolph, making Jennifer laugh openly. Randolph started again. 'It is not dangerous. It will not bring about the end of the world. But it is highly symbolic to people such as myself.'

'Members of your cult, you mean?' asked Jack.

Randolph nodded with a wry smile. 'I told you before that there is a power struggle surging through the Brotherhood at the moment, caused by

Silas's death. Possession of the artefact will go a long way in convincing the rest of my brothers that the order belongs under my control – something for us to unify around.'

'I'm not sure we shouldn't just let the Brotherhood tear itself apart,' said Jennifer.

'Unlikely,' replied Randolph. 'More likely is that one of Silas's followers will rise in power to replace him. They belong to the faction who would love to take revenge against the two of you, and it would be well within their means to exact that revenge – as I believe you can bear witness to, Mr Knight. One of them might have already killed you if not for the help from one of my... well, in your words, one of my *minions*. No, whether you like it or not, if you give to me what belongs to the Brotherhood and leave us alone, then I can ensure that you two will have many peaceful years together.'

Jennifer frowned. 'And we're just meant to forget about you trying to summon your gods to rule the Earth and bring about the end of mankind?'

'I think you're being a little overdramatic,' said Randolph with an infuriating grin on his face. 'Besides which, you put an end to all that. The time won't be right again for, oh...' He looked at his watch in an attempt to inject a little levity into the conversation. 'Well, quite a long while now.'

'You seem very sure about all of this,' said Jack.

'All my life I have had faith in his prophecies. I'm not about to give up now... and I suppose we'll all find out soon enough, won't we?' He stepped towards a large pair of oak double doors on the far wall. 'Shall we?'

Randolph pulled open the doors, revealing another large room. In the centre stood a stone altar, ornately decorated in gold leaf, its sides engraved with a maze of interlocking shapes and patterns. Around the walls were a series of paintings. Most seemed to be scenes depicting the same man; Jack guessed he was probably Aloysius.

'Is this him?' asked Jennifer. She had moved over to stand in front of one of the paintings and was running her hand along the wooden frame.

'I believe so,' replied Randolph.

Jack was staring intently at the paintings on the wall. One showed a man standing before an altar, his hands held high in supplication. Another showed the same man holding some kind of metal orb high above his head. A third showed him in an alien landscape, standing atop a tall hill, the ominous red star large in the sky above him.

'So where's this inheritance?' asked Jennifer, bringing Jack back to the present. Apart from the paintings and altar, the room was bare.

Randolph walked over to the altar, kneeling down in front of it.

'Are you going to pray for inspiration?' asked Jennifer sarcastically.

Randolph started to run his hands over the engravings on the front of the altar. 'You forget,' he said. 'As well as a meeting place, this was also a sanctuary – somewhere where his followers could hide in safety.'

He gave a small smile as his fingers found something. 'It took me a long time to track down the secrets of the early Brotherhood,' he said as he rotated a small stone star and pushed it, the piece sinking slowly into the altar.

For a moment, nothing happened, and then a section of wall behind the altar started to slide to the side with a deep rumble, revealing a hidden corridor behind. Randolph stood up, wiped the dust from his legs and strode over to look through the newly revealed doorway. The corridor on the other side was constructed from red bricks with two white marble pillars at the far end. Above the pillars sat a triangular pediment, and between them was a set of stairs descending downwards. He strode off down the corridor, leaving Jack and Jennifer behind him.

As Jack started towards him, Jennifer gently grabbed him by the hand to stop him. 'Look. I know I've asked you this before, but do you trust him?' she asked. 'Really?'

'No. Not entirely. I trust him when he says he's not trying to harm us, and I don't think he's leading us into a trap, but we definitely can't trust him completely.'

'Do you believe all this crap about the Brotherhood and this artefact?'

'I'm not sure. Everything he's said has a ring of truth about it, but I'm also sure he's holding back on us.'

Jennifer nodded slowly. 'Agreed. We should keep a close eye on him. I don't want him running off without us.'

'You've still got the pendant,' Jack reminded her.

Jennifer put her hand on it, feeling its presence under her blouse. 'True,' she replied. 'But I can't help but feel that he's not being completely honest with us about that – or anything else for that matter.'

Jack looked back down the corridor again. Randolph was standing at the far end now, looking down the steps. 'Come on,' he said. 'Let's not let him get too far ahead of us.'

✳ ✳ ✳

At the bottom of the steps, they found themselves in a small circular room. Sconces hung from the walls to the left and right, their flickering flames illuminating the chamber although they gave off no noticeable heat or smoke. An arched doorway stood on the far side of the room, the space within it grey and hazy, like smoke trapped behind glass.

Jennifer walked over to the archway and ran her hand over the greyness. It felt cold and solid, shimmering under her fingers as she touched it.

'Any idea how to get through?' she asked.

'Let Jack try,' suggested Randolph. Jennifer noted that he was still standing near the stairs; he hadn't made any attempt to inspect it himself.

Jack stepped over next to Jennifer and put his hand next to hers. To his surprise, as he pressed his hand against the greyness his fingers sunk into it, disappearing from view. He yanked it back out again violently.

'Are you okay?' asked Jennifer.

'Yeah... I just wasn't expecting that, that's all.'

'I was expecting something that would allow only the descendants of Aloysius to gain access,' said Randolph. 'This would seem to be it. It would appear that I was correct about you; the prophecy was true.'

Jack looked nervously at Jennifer and then to Randolph. 'So what now?'

'You go in, you find whatever he left behind, and you bring it out.'

'And I suppose I'm on my own for this one?' he said, with a humourless smile on his face.

Randolph nodded. Jennifer turned to face him, taking both his hands in hers and giving them a gentle squeeze. She leant in towards him, kissing him gently on the lips. 'Good luck,' she whispered.

Jack stepped back and removed his satchel. 'Look after this for me,' he said, handing it to Jennifer. 'And keep an eye on him,' he whispered, nodding towards Randolph. He turned to face the doorway, took a deep breath, closed his eyes and stepped in. The grey air swirled around him for a moment, and then he was gone.

Randolph took a step backwards and then sat down on the bottom step. 'Nothing to do now but wait,' he said.

Chapter 33.

December 29th, 2012. Exmoor, England.

Cross pulled up outside Lamarre's country house and stepped out of her car. The place was swarming with police and paramedics now, the grounds ablaze from the blue lights sitting atop all the vehicles.

She wandered towards the main house, looking for someone she recognized. When she spied her partner, Dave Brooks, sitting on the floor by the front door, she headed over and sat down next to him.

'It's at times like this I wish I smoked,' she said.

Brooks said nothing, but pulled a small hip flask from a pocket and offered it to her.

She politely refused with a wave of her hand. 'How's it going in there?' she asked.

'It's an absolute blood bath,' he replied. 'They're up to twelve bodies so far.'

'Do they have any idea about exactly what happened yet?'

Brooks shook his head. 'The place is like a war zone in there. It's not your usual gangland stuff either – the closest comparison is that they were savaged by wild animals. The other significant news is that they've found a secret room in there – or at least it used to be secret. It was off the library behind the built-in bookshelves – the whole wall's been knocked in now. God only knows what did it.'

'What was in there?'

'Don't know – the crime scene guys are working on it at the moment. But by the sounds of it, it's looking like another shrine. Similar trappings and decorations to the basement last night – the same goat's head logo, the same goat-woman statue on the altar.'

'Then I'm not mad – the two are definitely related.'

'It would be one hell of a coincidence.'

'We've just got no idea what any of it means.'

They sat there in silence for a moment, sucking in the cold night air. Any initial panic was over now; the various members of the emergency services were now strolling quietly across the grounds, on their way to or from the various crime scenes.

Cross was just about to ask about the other bodies that had been found when the calm was broken by a paramedic rushing out of the front door pulling a wheeled stretcher, another pushing on the other end. They were obviously in a hurry.

Cross jumped to her feet. 'Wait!' she shouted after them. 'Is that man alive?'

'Barely,' replied the first paramedic.

'Is he going to make it?'

'I think so, but we need to get going.'

Cross nodded, and they resumed their journey down the driveway, loading the man into the back of a waiting ambulance.

'Dave,' said Cross. 'Go with them. If he comes to, I want to know anything he can tell us. We haven't got long until they let that son of a bitch go. If he can give a description of anyone looking even vaguely like him...'

'Got it, boss,' said Brooks standing up.

Chapter 34.

Beneath the shrine to Aloysius.

Jack found himself standing in a dark tunnel. The walls were made of dark grey brick with an arched ceiling and at the far end he could see a doorway opening into a dimly lit room. He looked over his shoulder to see the doorway behind him, still grey and hazy.

He hesitantly took a step forwards. The floor was smooth but covered with a thick layer of grey dust. The space near the ceiling was thick with spider webs, making him shudder with the recollection of the giant spiders they had only just escaped from. He ducked down to avoid them as he walked, but these all seemed to be of a much more mundane variety; he swatted at them with his hands as he passed, brushing them out of the way.

As he approached the far doorway, he could see what appeared to be a crude laboratory on the other side. He stopped at the threshold and peered in; there were benches around the walls as well as shelves covered with dusty glassware. Many of the bottles and jars were empty, but others contained a variety of materials; multicoloured liquids, powders and several small strange creatures.

In the centre of the room was a large stone table. Metal chains hung from each leg, manacles attached to the ends, which rested on the stone floor. Everything in the room was covered in a thin layer of dust and cobwebs, seemingly untouched for a long time. Again, flickering flames from sconces on the walls illuminated the area.

There were two solid wooden doors in the walls to his left and right, and an open archway in the centre of the wall opposite. Cautiously, he approached the archway and looked through.

It opened into a large room. The ivory-coloured marble of the floors and walls must have once looked majestic, but now it was covered in dull grey dust like everything else in here. It made Jack feel like an archaeologist, the first to discover an ancient tomb, hidden for hundreds of years. Four white stone pillars stood around the centre of the room, but it was what he saw on the far side that took his breath away.

A large marble throne was positioned against the far wall, an almost-skeletal figure sitting upright in it. The corpse's head was slumped forwards on its chest, its grey skin tight and dry. It was dressed in tattered black robes, and a small silver crown sat on top of the long black hair, which hung lifeless from the scalp. At its feet, Jack could see a small metal chest.

Jack started across the room, heading towards the chest; surely that was what he was after. He moved carefully, his eyes peeled for anything out of the ordinary, but he still wasn't prepared for what happened. As he approached the throne, the corpse's head raised up from its chest without warning, a scraping sound of bone against bone echoing through the silent chamber. It turned to look his way, its cold black eyes staring at him, burrowing into his soul.

'So... Finally a successor comes to seek their inheritance,' wheezed the voice, as dry as the dust on the floor. Jack stood in disbelief as the deathly figure slowly stood, long bony fingers emerging from the robe. 'You do not know how long I have waited.' Judging by the state of him, Jack reckoned it had been quite a while.

'Are you... Aloysius?' whispered a stunned Jack.

'Yesss...' the skeletal figure wheezed back. 'Come kneel before me, so I may judge whether you are worthy.'

Jack took a step forwards with trepidation. The black eyes that stared back at him were almost hypnotic, drawing him towards them. Jack glanced down at the chest that lay at the foot of the throne, in front of the spectral being.

'Yesss…' it wheezed again. 'You seek my treasures? They await you, if you are worthy.'

Jack quietly considered his options. He could flee, but then this would have all been for nothing. He could fight, but he had no idea how strong this opponent was – he knew almost nothing about him. By the looks of him, he might crumble with one good blow, but he could also be immortal. Alternatively, he could try and use his cunning and intelligence. *First time for everything*, he told himself. He took another step closer. 'What if I'm not worthy?'

'You would not be here if you truly believed that. Only an heir of mine should have been able to enter this sanctuary. You have nothing to fear.'

Jack edged slightly nearer. The chest was tantalizingly close now, just out of reach.

'My treasures are yours for the taking,' hissed the skeletal figure. 'I do not have much longer left in this world. I live only to see my gifts passed on to another generation.' It took a step forwards and then stopped. 'Use them well,' it rasped and then stopped, motionless.

Jack took another step forwards and waved a hand back and forth through the air; it remained motionless. He inched slowly forwards, checking for any sign of movement as he approached the chest. None was visible; it now appeared completely inanimate. He knelt down slowly, still looking upwards as he did so, keeping a watchful eye on the bony figure. Then, finally, he placed his hands on the lid of the chest, lifting it slowly. As he did so, he looked down to see what lay within.

At that instant, a skeletal hand shot forwards, grabbing the top of his head. Bony fingers squeezed his skull, their icy coldness sucking the warmth from him. He just had time to look up into the depths of those black eyes again to see a spark of a burning red fire within before he collapsed unconscious on the floor.

Jennifer was pacing back and forth in the small room while Randolph sat silently on the stairs. She looked at her wrist before remembering that her watch hadn't come with them; still, it felt like it had been at least twenty minutes since Jack left and there was still no sign of him.

As Jennifer turned once more, she saw the opaqueness in the doorway shimmer and then fade into nothingness. A long dark tunnel was visible now, a set of footprints visible on the dusty floor.

'Were you expecting that?' she asked Randolph.

'No,' he said, shaking his head and standing up.

'What do you think it means?'

'I don't know. Probably either something very good or something very bad.'

'Let's go,' she said, starting down the corridor without waiting for him.

As she reached the doorway, she stopped in surprise. The room in front of her looked like an ancient alchemical laboratory, untouched for decades. What grabbed her attention, however, was the stone table in the centre of the room, with Jack sitting on one edge, leaning forwards with his head in his hands. 'Are you okay?' she called.

'I think so,' he said, carefully sitting upright and then climbing off the table. He looked shaky as he took a couple of unsteady steps towards them.

'What happened?' asked Randolph, entering the room and walking cautiously towards him. Jennifer was right behind him. Lying on the floor next to Jack was a tattered pile of black cloth. Randolph pushed it with his foot and an arm revealed itself, a skeletal hand now visible. He knelt down next to the pile of cloth and lifted the hood off the robes. Underneath it, they could all see a small metal crown, sitting on top of an emaciated face, the skin so thin and grey it was almost a skull.

'It was Aloysius,' groaned Jack.

'You're kidding me?' spluttered Randolph.

Jack leant against the table in the middle of the room and shook his head. 'No. I think he's been here a *long* time, and he's showing his age. He was dressed in those black robes... He was practically a skeleton.'

'This was Aloysius?' said Randolph, still not quite able to believe it.

Jack nodded. 'I guess so,' he replied. 'I thought he wasn't able to come back here?'

Randolph shook his head. 'Maybe he worked out a way... or maybe it wasn't really him.'

'What the hell happened?' asked Jennifer.

'Well, whoever it was, he was waiting for me... attacked me,' said Jack. 'God knows how long he's waited here for someone to come. He did something to me, knocked me out. When I came around, I was lying on that table...' He took a deep breath and wiped the sweat from his brow. 'I don't think he expected me to come around so soon. I tried to get away, he tried to restrain me... there was a struggle, and I struck him. As soon as he went down, it was like all the energy left him. He just collapsed into that pile of bones.'

Randolph stood in silent contemplation for a moment, rubbing his chin. 'Back in the town, I told you that this place has been hiding in another dimension – maybe he's been living outside of time and space as we know it. That's the only reason I can think of for him to have lived so long.'

Jack looked at the body on the floor before him. 'If you can call that living.'

'So when he returned, time caught up with him... or he was on his last legs,' said Jennifer. Jack shrugged in response. 'And when he died, whatever that barrier was he'd put up to keep us out – that died too.'

'I guess so. I don't suppose we'll ever know what he intended to do to me.'

'Well, whatever it was, I'm glad he didn't get the chance,' said Jennifer.

Jack turned to face Randolph, but he had already stepped into the throne room beyond. Jack followed him through the doorway, the strength returning to his legs now. Randolph was bent over, running his hands over the small chest at the foot of the throne. 'That's mine,' growled Jack.

'Is this his legacy?' asked Randolph, not bothering to turn and look at Jack.

'His inheritance,' said Jack. 'That's what he called it. He said it was meant for me.'

'Don't forget our agreement,' said Randolph. 'This isn't why you came.'

Jack scowled for a moment, but then he let a smile form on his face. 'As we agreed then,' he said. 'Let's get out of here. I've spent long enough in this place.' He turned, and took Jennifer by the hand.

'Wait!' called Randolph. He was still kneeling in front of the chest.

'Bring it with you,' called Jack. He was heading out of the door with Jennifer. 'But be quick. With Aloysius gone, I don't know how long this place will stay.'

Randolph picked up the chest, holding it close in his arms. He hurried after Jack and Jennifer, but the chest was heavy and cumbersome, slowing him down. As he reached the bottom of the stairs, they were already out of sight, well ahead of him. The walls and steps started shimmering before his eyes, appearing slightly translucent before returning to solidity again.

'Fuck,' he cursed, bounding up the steps two at a time. As he reached the hallway at the top, the walls and floor were becoming glassy and ethereal. He thought he could almost make out the ruins of the city through them.

He sprinted along the corridor, the chapel and final chamber visible at the end of it. He could see the large outer doors through the walls of the building, which were now becoming translucent. Jack and Jennifer were running through them, out into the safety of the city square. As he made it into the entrance hall, the walls were just shimmering glass. He threw himself through the doorway, sliding to a halt in the dirt, the chest flying to the floor and bursting open, an ornate metal ball bouncing out and rolling along the ground.

Randolph peered back over his shoulder. The temple was gone; the square was empty again.

He looked forwards again, at the sphere that had rolled from the chest. It had stopped at Jack's feet, and he was bending down and picking it up. He held it in his hand, running his fingers over it; the sphere was about three inches in diameter and completely covered in minute engravings of signs and sigils.

Randolph drew himself to his feet. He held out his hand towards Jack. 'Give it to me,' he said calmly.

Jack looked at him coldly. 'And suppose I don't?'

'That's not why you're here, remember,' said Randolph, taking a step closer. 'You have more important matters.'

'This was left to me,' said Jack. 'Aloysius wanted me to have it.'

'You don't even know what it is,' said Randolph.

'Maybe...' said Jack. 'But I know that *you* want it.'

'Jack?' said Jennifer, unsure as to how this was playing out.

'Don't worry,' whispered Jack in return.

Randolph shook his head in a show of disapproval. 'I thought you were a man of your word. Never mind – there are other alternatives.' He raised a hand, motioning with his forefinger.

From the ruined buildings behind him stepped two people, a man and a woman dressed all in black. Both of them were holding loaded crossbows, which they now aimed at Jack. They walked slowly forwards until they were standing either side of Randolph, but never taking their sights from Jack.

'Now then,' said Randolph. 'The orb, please.'

Jack stood motionless, looking at each of Randolph's assistants in turn.

'*Jack!*' whispered Jennifer. 'Give it to him!'

Jack hesitated for a second and then threw it gently towards him. 'Here, catch!' he called as it left his hands.

Panic gripped Randolph's face as the orb flew in a slow arc through the air. He stepped forwards, cupping both his hands together and it landed gently within them. The expression of relief on his face was unmistakable.

'Please, Mr Knight!' he cried. 'You don't realize how valuable this is.'

Jack merely snorted.

Jennifer sighed. 'Is our business together completed now?'

'Not yet,' said Randolph. 'Unlike your partner, I am a man of my word.' He turned to his left, to face the woman holding the crossbow. She had long black hair, piercing blue eyes and an olive complexion. He moved in close, giving her a passionate kiss on the lips. Her crossbow remained resolutely focused on Jack, not even wavering. Randolph reached inside her jacket, pulling out a small black book. It was a tatty leather notebook, about four inches long and tied shut with black string.

He stepped forwards, holding it out at arm's length towards Jack.

'These are the prophecies of Aloysius, as promised,' he said. Jack looked him in the eye and then stepped forwards away from Jennifer, taking hold of the book. 'What you are after is at the end,' added Randolph in a quiet whisper as he let go.

Randolph turned and walked back to the woman, who slipped her arm around his waist. Then he slipped the metal ring off his finger. 'Here!' he called, throwing it to Jennifer, who caught it gracefully. 'Whoever wears that should be able to return with items from these lands – such as that book.'

Jennifer looked at the ring and then slipped it onto her ring finger. She held out her hand to get a better look at it.

'It's not a fashion accessory,' said Randolph. The woman with her arm around him gave a small cold laugh. 'I think that concludes our business,' he said coldly.

'Wait!' called Jennifer. 'How do we get out of here? How do we wake up?'

'The easiest way is to go back to where you arrived. Was it a hall in a mountain, up a tall flight of stairs? Close to Aladoth?'

Jennifer nodded.

Randolph looked around as if trying to get his bearings. 'It's about half a day's trek that way,' he said, holding out his arm to indicate the direction.

'What about you?' she asked.

'Oh, don't worry about me,' replied Randolph. 'We won't be meeting again anytime soon.'

The woman wrapped both her arms tight around Randolph, dropping the aim of the crossbow for the first time. Jennifer could see that she was sporting a ring, just like the one Randolph had given her. Randolph and the woman both closed their eyes and with a small *crack* they were gone, along with the other armed man. All that remained were a couple of small wisps of dust kicked up from the floor.

Jennifer sighed. 'Well, I guess that's that then.' She sat down on a large slab of stone and took the pendant that Armindel had given them out from under her blouse. She let it hang from her fingers and waited as it span back and forth. She gave it thirty seconds, and when it hadn't stopped spinning, took hold of it and stuffed it into her bag. 'I guess that bastard isn't around here anymore. This'll be no more use to us.' She turned to Jack. 'So what now?'

'I think it's time to leave this place,' he muttered. He turned to look in the direction Randolph had pointed. 'Let's go.'

'Do you want this?' asked Jennifer, holding out the book to him.

'You can keep it for now,' said Jack.

Jennifer shrugged and squeezed it into her bag. 'After everything we've been through, I'd have thought you'd be a bit keener to know what's in it.'

'It'll wait. It might take me a while to go through it all.' He grabbed her hand, pulling her to her feet. 'Let's go.'

Chapter 35.

As Randolph had said, it took them half a day of walking to reach the mountain where they had arrived in these lands, a tedious but blissfully un-eventful journey. Eventually, they found the path up the hillside to the plateau where the doorway stood in the side of the mountain. They stepped in, and began their ascent back up the stairway.

They were without a light source this time; the torch Jennifer had left behind outside was no longer there. Once they had taken just a few steps up the stairs, the darkness descended again, and they were forced to inch their way up, holding on to each other tightly for balance. They had lost count of how many steps they had taken, when the white marble of the arrival room swam into focus again, just a few feet ahead of them. Torches still illumin-ated the room including, Jennifer noted, the torch they had taken with them when they had arrived.

'What now?' asked Jennifer.

'First, give me the ring,' said Jack.

'Why, don't you trust me?' asked Jennifer, only half joking.

'It's not that, I just have more experience with these kinds of things,' said Jack. 'Trust me,' he added, when she made no attempt to remove it.

'I wish you'd stop saying that,' said Jennifer, as she twisted the ring from her finger. 'It normally means you're about to do something incredibly stupid and reckless.' She handed him the ring and he slipped it over one of his fingers, before taking hold of her bag as well as his.

'Now what?' asked Jennifer.

'Now, we try to will ourselves awake,' said Jack.

'Close our eyes and click our heels together three times?'

Jack looked confused for a second and then smiled. 'If you like.' He stepped forwards and took her by the hand. Jennifer moved in close to him, wrapping her other arm around him, holding him tight. She closed her eyes and focused her mind on their bedroom, picturing it clearly in her mind. She took a deep breath.

When she opened her eyes again, she was lying on her bed with Jack next to her. Jack felt his arms and legs as if checking they were still attached and functional. 'I did it,' he grinned.

'We both did,' said Jennifer. Jack was still holding both of their bags. She sat up and picked hers up; opening it, she found the small leather book was still inside. 'I guess that ring works – Randolph wasn't *completely* untrustworthy after all.' She looked at the clock by the side of her bed. It was just past three in the morning. 'I guess time flies when you're having fun.'

She stood up and stretched, before slipping off her shoes and removing her jacket. 'I don't know about you, but I still feel exhausted. I could do with some more sleep.'

Jack nodded. 'Our bodies may have been asleep, but our minds have been awake for quite a while now.'

Jennifer reached under the pillow, removing the sheet of paper covered with the inscriptions, folding it gently and putting it into a drawer of her bedside cabinet. 'Time for some proper sleep this time.'

As she stood up, Jennifer noticed for the first time that they were still wearing the same clothes they had worn in their dreams, rather than what they had worn to bed. She took them off, stripping down to her underwear and then started rummaging through a drawer for a nightshirt. 'Are you going to join me?' she said.

Jack was standing at the foot of the bed, looking at her.

'I did say *sleep*,' she said, noticing that look in his eye.

Jack turned and looked out of the window, looking out over their grounds. It was dark outside, but the sky was clear and the moon shone down from up high. 'Maybe in a minute,' he said. 'I might find something to eat and drink first. It's a long time since I had a decent meal.'

Chapter 36.

December 29th, 2012. Exmoor, England.

Detective Inspector Cross was standing in the rear garden of the country house. She had been looking for any trace of footprints left by the creatures she had seen, but the ground was too solid, frozen by the frost. She jumped as her phone buzzed in her pocket; it was her partner, Detective Sergeant Brooks.

'Dave,' she said. 'Tell me you've got good news.'

'The best,' he said. 'He came round ten minutes ago.'

'And you managed to speak to him?'

'I couldn't stop him. He was babbling and gibbering like a lunatic. Got to tell you, boss, I don't know whether any of it would stand up in court – he was going on about huge winged monsters and all sorts. Sounds like he'd been hallucinating pretty badly.'

'But did he ID our suspect?'

'He certainly did. Even down to the tattoo on his hand. From what I could make out, he seems to think that some kind of creatures were causing all the carnage, and they seemed to be under the control of your man. He claims he was looking for something specific, but he didn't know what. He's even got a name for us, although it's not the same one your man gave you.'

'What is it?'

'Randolph.'

'First name or last?'

'I don't know. He just heard Lamarre calling him that... just before he died.'

Cross looked at her watch. The sun was just coming up over the horizon; there was still plenty of time left until they had to release their suspect. She started running back towards her car. At this time of day, she should be able to get back to the station in half an hour.

'Good work, Dave,' she said into the phone as she ran. 'I'll meet you back at the station.'

'Like I said, boss, I don't know how well any of this will stand up. It all sounds pretty insane.'

'That doesn't matter. We've got a suspect who's identified him. That'll be enough to satisfy Roberts and to keep him in custody until we can find something more concrete.'

Cross hung up the phone and climbed into her car, starting the engine. She gunned it down the driveway, sending chips of gravel flying in all directions. She couldn't wait to see the expression on his face.

As she pulled up outside the station, her phone rang again. It was a number she didn't recognize this time. It was presumably business, though, at this time of night.

'D.I. Cross,' she said, getting out of the car and setting its alarm. The car flashed its lights to indicate that it was locked.

'It's Campbell here from forensics. I hope I haven't woken you – you said you wanted to know the minute we found anything.'

'It's fine. I haven't managed to get to bed yet.'

'Well, it's the crime scene from yesterday. The one with the... well, the one underground where that guy was tortured.'

'I know the one. What have you found?'

'A partial fingerprint. Everything seemed to have been wiped clean, but we managed to find one he missed.'

Cross was walking in through the front door. She nodded to the duty sergeant and swiped her card for entry, typing in her PIN. 'Where did you find it?'

'On one of the teeth he'd removed.'

'Holy shit!' she said in surprise. 'That's got to be a first.'

'Quite. Well, anyway, we've managed to match it against a recent entry.'

Cross thought she knew where this was going; she asked anyway. 'Who?'

'The guy that you booked in last night, Mike Barnes. It's a partial match to his forefinger – but a good one.'

'I've got you, you bastard,' she muttered under her breath. She turned down a corridor, arriving at the holding cells. She put her hand over the phone. 'What cell's Barnes in?' she asked the officer on duty.

He consulted a clipboard, scanning down the list. 'Number six,' he replied. Cross nodded, advancing towards his cell.

'Thanks a lot,' she said back into the phone. 'Email me a copy of everything you've got.'

She stopped at cell six, where Mike Barnes's name was written on chalk next to the door. She pulled back the panel on the door and peered in. The cell was empty.

'Where is he?' she shouted back at the officer. 'They haven't released him already, have they?'

'What do you mean?' he replied, a look of confusion clear on his face.

'Has he been moved? Released?'

'No,' replied the officer. He walked over, getting his keys out. 'I checked a couple of hours ago – he was fast asleep on the bunk. I've been here the whole time – no one's gone in or out.' He fumbled for the correct key and placed it in the lock, twisting it and unlocking the door with a heavy click.

Cross yanked the door open and stepped inside. The cell was empty. He was nowhere to be seen.

Chapter 37.

December 29th, 2012. Dartmoor, England.

Jennifer rolled over and looked at the clock next to her bed. It was a little after ten in the morning. Jack's side of the bed was empty; it didn't look like it had been slept in. She staggered to the bathroom with a yawn, taking a quick shower to freshen up before she got dressed and went downstairs.

She found Jack in the living room, lying on the sofa. He was holding a half-empty bottle of wine in one hand; another lay empty on the floor.

'Isn't it a bit early in the morning for that?' she said, a touch reproachfully.

Jack turned to look at her, and then took another swig of wine direct from the bottle without saying a word.

Jennifer took a longer look around. Jack was still wearing the same clothes as last night. The leather notebook lay open on the table; she picked it up and skimmed through it, but it was incomprehensible to her. The spidery hand-writing was in another language which she thought was probably Latin.

'Put that down,' growled Jack. 'It's not for you.'

'Calm down,' she said. 'What's up with you?' She looked closely at Jack; he had a strange look on his face, but she wasn't sure if he was angry with her or just drunk. She put the book back on the table. 'If we're going to get married, what's yours is mine, remember?'

Jack shook his head slowly. 'That's not going to happen.'

'Okay,' she sighed. 'No need to get all moody. If there are some things you don't want to share, that's fine. Quite frankly, I'm sure you've got some things hidden away I'd rather not know about.'

Jack looked her in the eyes, shaking his head slowly again. 'No. There's not going to be any marriage.'

Jennifer stood there speechless, her mouth hanging open. 'What...?' was all she could eventually manage.

'It was a mistake to think this was ever a good idea.'

'*What?*'

'I can see things more clearly now.'

Jennifer looked at the book lying on the table. 'Did you read something in there? Something about me?'

Jack shook his head. 'No,' was all he said.

'Whatever it is, it's rubbish. You can't take the words of some medieval crackpot over me. You *know* me.'

'Do I? And how well do you know me, Jennifer?'

'Well, until about a minute ago, I'd have said very well.'

'You know less than you think.' He gave a quick shake of his head, and there was a sickening grin on his face. 'I don't love you, not really. It was just easier to stay together than to break up... But it's time this charade ended.' He took another large swig of wine from the bottle.

There were tears in her eyes now. 'What the fuck, Jack? I don't understand. Why are you saying this?'

'You need to know the truth. There's no future for us.'

Jennifer was having trouble seeing clearly. She wiped her eyes, but it didn't have much effect. The tears were coming faster now. 'Jack... I don't understand what's going on.'

'Just go. Get out of here,' he mumbled, draining the last of the wine from the bottle and turning his back on her.

'Jack. Whatever it is—'

Jack swung around and threw the bottle towards her. It missed by a large margin, hitting the wall and exploding into hundreds of pieces. 'Just get the hell out of here,' he shouted.

Jennifer backed away, shaking, and then turned and ran out of the room.

✳ ✳ ✳

She got into the car and left. She didn't know where she was going, and didn't really care; she just drove, putting distance between herself and Jack. However, as her rage subsided, it didn't take her long to acknowledge that she was in no fit state to drive; her hands were shaking and she was still weeping. She pulled over into a lay-by and turned off the engine.

Opening the door and getting out, the cold winter wind hit her – she hadn't been thinking clearly enough to bring a coat. She looked out over the desolate country fields around her, trying to take deep breaths and calm down. The bitter wind made the tears on her cheeks sting; she wiped them away with her sleeve, but others swiftly replaced them.

She still couldn't understand what was happening. They'd had their problems before – who hadn't – but nothing like this, and it was all so sudden. She needed to talk to someone – an old friend, a shoulder to cry on. Lauren immediately sprang to mind, her oldest friend who had agreed to be the maid of honour at her wedding; she'd have to tell her that was off too. She started to reach into her pocket for her phone, and then realized she'd left it back in the house. Too bad – she wasn't going back for it now.

She climbed back into the car and started the engine again, wiping the tears from her eyes. They had died down enough now that she thought she'd be okay to drive. She turned the car around, heading for Exeter.

An hour later, she pulled into a parking space just outside Lauren's house – a small terraced house a few miles north of the city centre. As she locked the car and walked up the driveway, she looked at her watch; it was late morning, almost noon. When she reached the porch, she rang the doorbell, hoping she'd be in. When there was no immediate response, she rang the doorbell again, for longer this time, and then peered through the window.

She could hear some sounds of movement from somewhere inside, and then through the glass in the front door she could see an internal door opening, followed by movement within. The front door opened; Lauren was standing in the doorway wearing old jeans and a baggy green jumper.

'My God, Jennifer, what is it?' she exclaimed. 'You look awful.'

'Can I come in?' asked Jennifer. 'I need someone to talk to.'

'Of course,' said Lauren, opening the door wide to let her in. 'Bill's out for the day, so it's just us.'

Jennifer stepped over the threshold and into their living room. It felt cosy in the house; Lauren always liked to keep the temperature nice and warm.

Lauren showed Jennifer into the living room, and she sat down on one end of the sofa, Lauren joining her on the other. 'What's happened?' asked Lauren. 'I've never seen you like this.'

'I think it's over,' said Jennifer with a slight sniff. She was managing to hold back the tears for now.

'What is?'

'Us. Me and Jack.'

'*What*? What happened? Surely it can't be that bad.'

Jennifer told her about the fight while Lauren listened patiently, although she had to omit the details of the adventures that preceded it. 'What do you think?' she asked when she had finished.

Lauren thought for a second. 'And you don't know what brought this on?'

Jennifer thought about the book of prophecies Randolph had given her. Now that she had retold what had happened and was thinking more clearly, she was more certain that must be the cause. Something in there must have caused him to act like that, but what? And how would she explain this to Lauren?

'No,' she replied simply. Then she added 'At least, I'm not sure. I think he may have had his fortune read, and got some bad news.'

Lauren looked shocked and then confused, and then finally shook her head, laughing despite herself. 'That must be one hell of a bad fortune. He really doesn't seem the type to believe in all that mumbo jumbo. I suppose you never can tell.' She stood up. 'Look, I've got a really nice bottle of wine in the fridge. Do you want a glass to soothe your nerves?'

Jennifer nodded, and Lauren disappeared. When she returned a minute later, she was holding two large glasses of white wine, one of which she handed to Jennifer.

'I suppose the most important question is this,' said Lauren. 'Do you still love him?'

'Yes,' said Jennifer, almost without any thought.

'And do you think this fortune thing is the reason? There isn't another woman or something else that he's hiding from you?'

Jennifer managed a weak smile. 'I'm fairly certain there isn't another woman.'

'Well then, you have to talk to him. Tell him he's being a bloody idiot.'

Jennifer took a large gulp of the wine. It really was rather good. 'I don't know... he seemed so different. He seemed so *sure*.'

'Was he angry?'

'Yes. And he had been drinking.'

'So he was a bit drunk?'

'*Very* drunk.'

'Well then, it's probably just the booze talking. You need to give him a while to sober up and think about this with a clear head. He'll soon realize what a mistake he's making.'

Jennifer sighed. It sounded reasonable enough, but Lauren hadn't been there; she hadn't seen him. She managed a weak smile again. 'You just want to keep the bridesmaid gig, don't you?'

Lauren smiled back at her. 'Don't worry about any of that for now. Just stay here for a bit and relax. I'll make you some lunch.'

'Thanks,' said Jennifer. 'I'm actually starving.' It had been quite a while since she had last eaten, and felt like a lot longer.

Together, they walked to the kitchen. Jennifer sipped on her wine while Lauren prepared a salad from what she could find in the fridge.

'What do you think he was told, to make him act this way?' asked Lauren, as they sat down and ate at the kitchen table.

Jennifer thought hard. She didn't think it would be anything that was particularly bad for Jack. He had already shown his willingness to put himself through almost unimaginable peril to fight for her. No, it had to be something else. Maybe their continued relationship would have an effect on someone else. Maybe it was to protect *her*?

'I don't know,' she muttered. 'Maybe he thinks he's doing this to protect me.'

'Huh?'

'Maybe he thinks he's going to hurt me. Maybe he thinks that splitting up now will be less painful for me in the long run.'

'There's a lot of *maybes* in there,' said Lauren. 'If that *is* the case, don't you think you've got a right to decide that for yourself?' Jennifer nodded in agreement. 'You're a grown woman – you can make your own decisions.'

'If you say so,' joked Jennifer.

'There you go – you're getting your sense of humour back again,' smiled Lauren.

'I ought to talk to him,' said Jennifer seriously.

Lauren nodded. 'If you still love him, you've got to tell him to stop all that macho bullshit and deal with it. You don't have to use those exact words, though.'

Jennifer smiled. 'You're right. Again.'

'Look... Stay here for a bit and calm yourself down – at least stay for dinner. You won't be in the way – I could do with the company. And if you want to stay overnight, you're more than welcome – the guest bedroom's all made up.'

Jennifer shook her head. 'I don't need that–'

'–It's really not a bother.'

'Dinner would be nice,' she said, and smiled at Lauren. 'Let me get my thoughts together, and I'll see how I feel after a nice meal.'

Jennifer stayed until the evening, mainly reminiscing about old times. She thought Lauren was probably just trying to distract her from her current problems, but it seemed to be working. They ordered a Chinese takeaway and watched trashy TV, Jennifer even managing the occasional laugh. She knew that eventually she'd have to get back though. If she was going to face Jack and have it out with him, then she ought to get on with it and not put it off any longer than she had to.

She thanked Lauren and then set off, heading back to Dartmoor. The weather had worsened again and it was raining heavily, with strong winds lashing the rain against the windshield as she drove.

Forked lightning was flashing through the sky in the distance as she pulled back into her driveway and parked the car in front of the house. For a brief moment, it brought back memories of the nightmare where her home was being invaded, but she put that to the back of her mind – she had real problems to deal with now. She turned the engine off and took out the keys. Without the headlights, the area around her was cast into darkness. All the house lights were off; it looked deserted.

She climbed out of the car, slamming the door behind her and running to the house, trying not to get too wet from the storm. She slipped her key into the front door, unlocking it and letting herself in.

From the inside, the house looked just as deserted. 'Jack?' she called into the darkness. There was no reply. She flicked some lights on and stepped into the living room; the book was still lying there on the table, and the broken glass of the wine bottle was still all over the floor. She sighed and went to the kitchen to fetch a dustpan and brush. *Somebody* still had to clean up this mess.

She swept up the fragments of glass, taking care not to cut herself, and wrapped them in some newspaper before throwing the whole lot in the bin. Then she looked at her watch; it was past eleven o'clock and God knows where Jack had got to. She might as well go to bed and sort this all out in the morning.

She dragged her weary body up the stairs to the bathroom, brushing her teeth before returning to the bedroom. It had been a long day and the bed looked awfully inviting. She stepped over to her chest of drawers and opened it, searching through to find some nightclothes, which she threw onto the bed behind her. As she turned around and leant over the bed, somebody grabbed her roughly from behind, restraining her by the arms.

'I thought I told you to leave,' growled the voice of Jack from behind her.

'Ow!' she cried. 'You're hurting me!'

Jack pushed her roughly onto the bed, pinning her there, face down. She could feel the weight of his body pressing her into the mattress, and had to turn her head to one side in order to be able to breathe.

'Ow!' she cried again as he grabbed her hair with one hand, yanking it violently up from the bed. He brought his face down close to hers as he held her by the hair. 'You should know your place,' he whispered in her ear. 'I think it's time I taught you a lesson.' He ran his tongue around her ear, a gesture that would normally have made her smile. This time, it only made her feel sick.

He let go of her hair, pushing her head forwards into the bed again. As he stood up, the pressure on her released slightly, and she twisted underneath him, rolling over to lie face up on the bed, looking him directly in the face.

'What the fuck, Jack!' she cried, pushing him away with both hands. She rolled over and climbed off the bed, standing up to face him. 'What the fuck do you—'

Her words were cut short as he slapped her violently across the face. She stepped backwards, almost falling back onto the bed, her cheek red and stinging.

'Don't you talk to me like that,' he hissed at her.

Jennifer saw red; she wasn't going to stand for this. Almost without thinking, she stepped forwards and swung at him. Her clenched fist came up fast, catching him by surprise. It made contact with his jaw, jerking his head to one side; he staggered backwards, stumbling to the floor.

'Don't. You. Dare,' she growled, her voice low and rough. She looked Jack in the face, and was horrified to see that there was a wide grin on his face. He stood up, rubbing his chin and laughing; a hollow mocking laugh.

They stood there, face to face like two vicious animals sizing each other up, each getting ready to pounce. He took a step towards her, and as Jennifer looked him in the eyes, she could see they were pitch black, a stygian abyss into the very depths of his soul. Then he blinked, and they were Jack's eyes again.

'You need to sort your shit out,' she said unsteadily, trembling as she turned and walked from the room. 'I'm going.'

'I'll be here when you return. I'll be waiting for you... *honey*,' he called, followed by a low deep laugh.

She stormed out of the room, down the stairs and into the hallway. As she paused in the hallway, she turned to see the leather book from Randolph still lying on the living room table. She strode into the room and picked it up, closing it and stuffing it under her arm, before storming out the front door, slamming it behind her.

She ran back to the car, climbing inside again. She was shaking, not out of fear, but from rage. She was afraid, not of Jack, but rather of what was going on. This was worse than she thought, and she needed to talk to someone who might understand. She could only come up with one person.

She drove north-east, heading past Exeter and towards the motorway; this time, she was heading for Cheltenham General Hospital where she could hopefully still find Peter White. It would be too late to visit tonight, but she would find a hotel for the night, and pay him a visit first thing in the morning.

Jennifer arrived at the hospital reception as soon as visiting hours started and asked to see Peter. He had been transferred out of intensive care into the high-dependency unit, and as she strode in she could clearly make him out, sitting in a bed in the corner of the long room.

'I was hoping you'd visit,' he said as she approached, 'although I was expecting Jack as well. Is he okay?'

'That's kind of why I'm here.'

'What is it? Is there a problem?'

'You could say that,' she said, pulling up a plastic chair and sitting down on it.

'What is it?' he asked again with a look of concern on his face. 'I'd been told that you'd both survived and got out okay.' He beckoned Jennifer closer. 'Is it the Brotherhood?' he asked in hushed tones. 'Are they back?'

'Not as such,' replied Jennifer. She briefly explained their expedition to the dream world, and how they had found Aloysius before they returned home.

'So what's the problem?' he asked, looking at her with genuine concern but also confusion.

Jennifer shook her head. 'I don't know who it was that we rescued from Aloysius's shrine and brought back with us,' she said. 'But I don't think it was Jack.'

Chapter 38.

December 30th, 2012. Cheltenham, England.

Peter looked back at Jennifer, a look of shock on his face. 'Tell me,' he said in a whisper, leaning closer to her. 'Why do you think that?'

Jennifer sighed deeply. 'He's... He's not the same. Oh, he looks the same, and sounds the same... but he's colder. Crueller. No – not just cruel – *sadistic*. He hid it well when we were still in the dreamlands, but now that we're here...' She let her words trail off.

A period of silence descended, as Peter considered the situation quietly.

'What do you think?' asked Jennifer.

'I'm not sure,' said Peter. 'It's not really my area of expertise, but from what little I do know... I suppose it's possible. Do you think this is some kind of doppelganger, impersonating Jack, or is he being controlled somehow? Or has he just been manipulated?'

'I don't know,' she said with a sigh. 'I suppose it could be any of them. I just don't know.'

'And you don't have any other clues?'

Jennifer picked up her bag, opening it and lifting out the small leather book that lay within. She showed it to Peter. 'This book is meant to contain the prophecies of Aloysius. We were told that some of the last ones are meant to refer to us – Jack and I, that is. Maybe there's some kind of clue in here as to what's going on.' She opened the book, flicking through the pages. 'I think it's in Latin – can you read that?'

'A little,' said Peter hesitantly. Jennifer passed it over to him.

'Let's see how it ends, shall we?' he said, turning to the final page. His brow furrowed as he squinted at the page in front of him. Then he looked back up at Jennifer. 'Have you got a pen and paper?' Jennifer dug through her bag before pulling out a tatty sheet of paper and a cheap black biro, which she handed to him.

'This may take a little while,' he said as he took them from her. 'You might want to go and get a coffee or something.'

Jennifer nodded and stood up to leave.

'One more thing – can I borrow your phone?' he added. 'I might need to look some stuff up.'

'Are you allowed to use it in here?' she asked, looking around at the medical equipment.

'Don't worry,' he said with a knowing smile. 'I'll keep it subtle.'

Jennifer drew her phone from her pocket, passing it quietly to Peter and telling him the PIN before heading to the hospital cafe.

❋ ❋ ❋

She returned fifteen minutes later, which was as long as she could force herself to wait. 'How goes the great translation?'

'Okay, I think. Take a seat.' Jennifer sat back down again, and Jack handed her back the sheet of paper. 'This is what I think it says – these are the final prophecies.'

Jennifer looked through the handwritten notes, reading them back to Peter quietly.

'*An adversary from the present will travel back, in order to save what lies ahead.* Okay, that'll be Jack returning to the past, to try to save me and... well, everyone.'

'Agreed,' nodded Peter.

'*This heir of the prophet will fall from the sky, returning to behead the Brotherhood,*' she continued. 'Jack again, presumably? Falling more from the air than the sky, when he returned to the present, but beheading the Brotherhood must refer to killing Silas, their leader.'

220

'I think so, but *heir of the prophet?*'

'Randolph told us he believed Jack to be a descendant of Aloysius.'

Peter looked surprised. 'Well, I guess that makes sense, then.'

'*The order will be divided, turning upon itself and pitting brother versus brother.* Okay, that's what Randolph told us about the power struggle going on within the Brotherhood. *A son of two soldiers will be raised by his brothers and take them forwards into greatness.*' She considered this for a second. 'That must refer to Randolph – he said his parents were military, and I suppose he'll be taking over the Brotherhood. Now that we've helped him,' she added with a deep sigh. '*When he comes of age, the child will return, destroying she that created him.* That's still sounds like Randolph alright – he told us that he killed both his parents when he was still a child.'

'Sounds like a great guy to be around...'

'*A sun will fall and the city shall rise.*'

Peter looked at Jennifer. 'Does that mean anything to you?'

'No.' She looked at the final line. '*The nightmare child will herald a new age for man.* Hmm.'

'Yeah, I wasn't sure about that one either,' said Peter. 'Could it be Randolph again?'

'Maybe,' shrugged Jennifer. 'Or someone else entirely. The other prophecies only make sense to us in hindsight – I suspect this will too.'

Jennifer sighed. She handed the sheet of paper back to Peter, who folded it neatly and placed it within the book. 'I can't see anything here which has any relevance to what's happened to Jack. I don't suppose you can think of anyone who might have a better idea of what might be going on?'

Peter grimaced. 'I've been thinking about that. I do, but you're not going to like it.'

'Who?'

'You're *really* not going to like it.'

'*Who?*' she asked again, more emphatically this time.

'Randolph.'

'You can't be serious?'

'I said you weren't going to like it,' said Peter. 'But from what you've told me, he knows more than anyone else about what goes on in the dreamlands and how it actually works. I've only really dabbled without any real understanding. I can drive the car, if you like, but you need a mechanic who knows what's going on under the hood.'

'But *Randolph*?' She couldn't believe it had come to this.

'You're going to have to decide how important this is to you. If you really think this isn't Jack, and he's... well, *elsewhere...*'

'Then I owe it to him to try and bring him back.'

Peter nodded.

'But how am I going to find Randolph? He lives a pretty secretive lifestyle. He's not going to be in the phone book.'

'Well, I don't know for sure, but you've got one thing you can try.'

'What?' she asked.

'The pendant you used to track him down in the dreamlands. Do you still have it?'

Jennifer couldn't believe she hadn't thought of it. She picked up her bag and looked inside. The necklace was still there, the pendant still attached to it and she pulled it out. She held up the chain and let the pendant hang; it swung back and forth a couple of times then rested, pointing to the northeast. She spun it again; it came to rest pointing in the same direction again.

'Well, what do you know,' she muttered quietly. 'It works here too.'

'I don't know for certain, but it's possible that its power will fade now that you're back in the real world again. If you're going to do this, you ought to do it sooner rather than later.'

Jennifer stood up and sighed deeply. 'You're right,' she said, nodding. 'I need to do this.' She leant forwards and kissed him gently on the forehead. 'Thanks, once again.'

'Hey, you just take care,' he said. 'You may need his help, but don't trust him.'

Jennifer smiled. 'Oh, there's no need to worry about that.'

'Just bring Jack back safe, okay? Tell him he needs to come visit me.'

'Will do.'

'And tell him to bring grapes.'

Chapter 39.

Jennifer returned to the hospital car park and climbed back into her car, hanging the pendant from the rear-view mirror. It swung back and forth for a moment before settling down and indicating the direction she needed to head in. She started the engine and set off.

She drove for several hours following the pendant; it was leading her north-east across the country towards Lincolnshire. She spent most of the day travelling across the country, alternating east and then north along the major roads. As the day was drawing to a close and the night was drawing in, she checked her phone to see where she was: a lay-by outside a small village just east of Lincoln. All around her were open fields. As she sat in the car looking at her phone, she thought she could just see the locket moving slightly, swivelling ever so gently on the chain. Randolph was presumably closer now, and moving.

She started the car again and set off, paying close attention to the direction of the locket; it was pointing almost straight ahead. It stayed pointing to the east as she twisted and turned on the narrow country roads, and then started to move to the left. As she carried on down the road, it turned further and further anti-clockwise. To her left, set a fair way back from the road, she spotted an old country farmhouse; the locket was pointing directly at it. As she continued down the road, the locket continued twisting until it was pointing backwards, back at the house that now lay behind her. She kept going until she found a place where the road widened and it was safe to stop. She pulled in and killed the engine.

Sitting in the car, she realized that she hadn't planned this at all. She had no idea what she was going to do now that she was actually here. She unhooked the pendant from the rear-view mirror and then leant over and opened the glove compartment; it was full of all the usual junk. She rummaged through it until she found a small torch, which she pocketed. Then she got out and checked in the boot; under the floor, she found a metal wrench used for changing tyres, and pulled it out. In an emergency, it might make a serviceable weapon, but she hoped it wouldn't have to come to that. She stuck it through her belt and pulled the boot shut.

She locked the car and set off back down the road on foot. It was a cloudy night and there were no street lights on this quiet country road. It took her eyes a couple of minutes to fully adjust to the darkness of her surroundings. Luckily, there seemed to be no other traffic down this narrow lane.

There was an old wooden gate by the side of the road, blocking access to the gravel pathway that led up to the house. She stopped in front of the gate, its white paint peeling away to reveal the wood underneath, and looked across at the house; at this distance, it looked dark and quiet, but there was at least one light on in an upstairs room. She clambered over the gate and started towards the house, walking on the grass to the side of the gravel path to minimize any noise.

As she approached, she tried to decide; should she knock at the door and announce her presence, or try to sneak in somehow? She might need his help, but she still wasn't sure how much she could trust him. She wasn't in fear of her life; when they had met in their dreams, he had insisted that he had no interest in killing her, and she grudgingly had to accept that he had even tried to save her. No, she didn't think he'd try to harm her, but she doubted he'd go so far as to help her, not unless it was also in his own best interests.

She decided she would try the back door. If it was unlocked, she'd take it as a sign. She crept around the side of the house, past some large bushes and a garage. As she rounded the rear of the house, she could clearly see one of the upstairs rooms lit up brightly; that must be where he was. As quietly as she could, she sneaked up to the rear door and looked in. Putting her hands to the glass, she peered through and saw a kitchen. With her pulse racing, she placed her hand on the door knob and very gently turned it. To her surprise, it twisted and the door opened with an almost inaudible squeak. She hesitated, half expecting an alarm to go off; when none did, she stepped inside.

Standing just beyond the threshold, she quietly closed the door behind her and looked around. If this was Randolph's house, it was surprisingly mundane; it could have been any kitchen in any house in the country. She didn't know what she expected – she knew there wasn't going to be a pile of skulls on the kitchen table or occult signs daubed on the walls in blood, but it did made her hesitate. Might she be in the wrong place? There was only one way to find out.

She walked across the room towards a door, which stood ajar, and pushed it open further. It led into a hallway, and she stepped through. There was a low bookcase along one side, with a set of stairs behind it leading up. She scanned the books quickly: history, anthropology, the occult, many of them quite old. It was starting to look more promising. She ascended the stairs, keeping to the side as she went. Her hands were shaking and it was altogether too quiet in here; she could hear her own breathing and her heart beating in her chest. Light was spilling from a doorway on the landing that was open just a crack. *It's too late to turn back now*, she thought to herself and took a couple of steps forwards. Taking a deep breath to try and calm her nerves, she stepped into the doorway and pushed the door open.

The light in the room was bright and made her squint. It was some kind of study and Randolph was sitting in a leather armchair, reading a book. He jerked upright as the door opened, but regained his composure almost instantly.

'If it isn't the lady of my dreams,' he said in his most eloquent voice. 'I must admit, I wasn't expecting to see you again so soon.'

When he made no attempt to stand up or indeed take any kind of provocative action, Jennifer stepped into the room. There was another chair to the side, facing him.

'Be my guest,' he said, gesturing towards the chair. 'I would tell you to make yourself at home, but it seems like you've started without me.'

Jennifer hesitated for a moment. She seemed to be losing control of the situation already.

'Come now,' he said. 'To what do I owe this pleasure? Tell me... Is your fiancé here too?'

'No, it's just me,' said Jennifer, finally taking the seat.

'*Really?* I can't comprehend what would make you come all this way without him. How did you find me?' he asked, and then thought for a second. 'It was the pendant, wasn't it?' Jennifer nodded, and he gave a little chuckle. 'The effect won't last forever. I'm surprised it lasted this long, to be honest.'

'Is this your house?' asked Jennifer.

Randolph nodded. 'Yes. But enough of the chit-chat. What has brought you to me of all people? Are you here to kill me? I can't help but notice that you don't seem to be armed...'

Jennifer drew the wrench out of her belt, laying it on a small table next to her.

Randolph shrugged. 'Crude, but it could be effective I suppose. Not the obvious choice for pre-meditated murder though. I suspect you've got something else on your mind.'

Jennifer thought for a second. 'I've got a problem,' she started. 'And as much as it pains me to say it, I think you may be the only one who can help me.'

Randolph nodded slowly, looking at her intently. 'I'm not sure I can imagine the level of desperation you must be in to come crawling to me for help... it must be serious. Judging by the fact that you're here alone – and I must congratulate you on your bravery by the way – if you're alone, it must be a problem with Jack. Am I right?' Jennifer nodded. 'Is he ill? *Dead?*'

Jennifer shook her head. 'I don't know where Jack is, or even what he is. Whoever came out of that temple, it wasn't the man I know and love.'

Randolph looked genuinely shocked. He stood up suddenly, making Jennifer jump, but he simply moved over to the window and stared out of it.

'Tell me,' he said. 'Why do you think that?'

'He looks the same, but he's a completely different personality. He's cruel. Sadistic. He seemed to take pleasure in tormenting me. I should introduce you – he seems like your kind of person.'

Randolph ignored the insult and continued to look out of the window. A period of silence descended, as Randolph considered the situation quietly.

'It's possible – no, probable – that what Jack told us when we found him in Aloysius's shrine was a lie. I suspect something happened down there, and it wasn't the real Jack we brought up with us.'

'Is this possible?' she asked him. 'Could it really be someone else?'

Randolph thought for a moment and then nodded. 'Yes. Or more likely, it's someone else – *something* else – within his body. Within his *mind*. Someone or something that's possessing him.'

Jennifer thought for a second. 'Do you think it's Aloysius?'

Randolph nodded. 'I was unsure at first, but now... yes, I think it is – some part of him, anyway. Whatever is left after all those millennia.'

'So what can we do about this?'

'Uh uh! Not so fast,' he said, with a shake of his head and an infuriating smile.

'What?' she said in exasperation.

'Maybe I can help you. I'm not quite sure. But tell me this... what would you be willing to do to get your fiancé back?'

'Do you want to see me beg, is that it?'

'No, no. I don't need to stroke my ego like that. I'm more interested in a little *quid pro quo*.'

'Exactly what is it you want?'

'Just how far would you be willing to go to rescue Jack?' he asked again.

Jennifer didn't have to think about it. 'I'd do anything,' she said.

'*Really*?' grinned Randolph. 'Would you be willing to die for him?'

'Yes,' she replied without even hesitating.

Randolph shrugged. 'It's easy to say, not always quite so easy to do – but I don't think it should come to that. As I said before, I have no interest in seeing you die. *Either* of you. But there *is* something I want from you.'

'What is it? You can have it.'

'My, you have changed, haven't you,' chuckled Randolph. 'Not so long ago, I'd have bet you would have ripped out my throat with your bare hands, given half a chance.'

'I may still do so,' she growled, 'if you don't get on with it and tell me what you want.'

Randolph held his hands up in mock defence. 'Okay, okay,' he said. 'You don't have it yet, but there is something you will have in the future. It may not be for months or even years, but at some point, I will come and demand that you return this favour. At that time, you must give me what you owe me.'

'But you won't tell me what it is?'

'No,' said Randolph with a smile. 'That would take the fun out of it. Think of it as a gamble.'

'How do you even know I'll ever get this thing, whatever it is?'

'It has been foretold.'

Jennifer let out a single laugh. 'Really? More prophecies?'

'I have faith,' replied Randolph. 'And if it doesn't come to pass... well, you've lost nothing, have you?'

'I don't know...' hesitated Jennifer.

'Come now. You've already said you'd give anything to get Jack back, even die to rescue him. What could I ask of you that would be worse than your own life?'

Jennifer knew deep down that she couldn't trust him, but she couldn't see any other alternative. 'And whatever it is you want... it won't hurt us?'

'Giving it to me will cause you no physical harm, I promise.'

'Fuck it. I agree,' she muttered. 'But only as long as you save Jack. The real Jack.'

Randolph nodded. 'I agree. That much is in both our interests.' He stepped forwards and held out a hand to Jennifer, who stood up to face him. She hesitated for a moment; she knew she was making a deal with the devil, but she also knew that if their positions were reversed, Jack would do any-thing to save her. Hell, he'd proved that already. She took his hand, and they shook.

'*Excellent,*' he grinned.

Randolph told her he would need to seek some advice. He left her in the house and disappeared into the night.

She went to the kitchen and made herself a light snack before she had a sneaky look around his house. It was all very underwhelming: a normal Eng-lish country house, with nothing to hint at his alter ego. Did he invite the neighbours round to dinner parties, she wondered? Was he on the parish council?

As the night drew on, she settled down on his sofa, covering herself with a blanket that she found in a cupboard. As she closed her eyes and drifted off to sleep, she could see the face of Jack in her mind. Those jet-black eyes were staring into hers, as if looking into the depths of her soul, almost hypnotically drawing her in.

She awoke with a start as she heard the front door open. She looked at her watch; it was eight thirty in the morning and a dull grey light was coming in through the windows. The hallway door opened and Randolph stepped into the room carrying a package wrapped in brown paper. He laid it gently on the table.

Jennifer yawned. 'Well?' she asked, as she stood up and stretched.

'I have some ideas,' he said. 'But it may not be easy.'

'Nothing to do with you ever is. What are they?'

'Firstly, you must take him back to the dreamlands.'

'Just how am I meant to do that?' she asked, flustered.

'Well, when you last went, did Jack create a sheet with incantations on it?'

'Yes.'

'And do you still have it?'

'Yes,' she replied again. 'Well, we should do. I put it away when we returned.'

'Use that again. You've already been there once before, and it should be significantly easier the second time. Your mind starts to get accustomed with repeated use.'

'And Jack?'

'I imagine he won't go willingly – you'll probably have to subdue him. You could try using physical violence to knock him out, but it might be easier to just drug him. I have some barbiturates upstairs that ought to be able to sedate a man of his size.'

'Well, I suppose you'd know.'

Randolph smirked back at her humourlessly. 'Try and rest his head on the sheet as well. It ought to work, but I'd also consider holding onto him tightly.'

Jennifer nodded. 'Okay,' she said.

'You'll want to restrain him, but use something natural and old-fashioned. Hemp rope, for example. Don't use anything plastic, or there's a possibility it won't go with you, and you wouldn't want that.'

'Okay. And once we get there, what then?'

'You're going to need to take him back to the shrine. If there's any part of Jack left behind, you're going to want to get back in there.'

'But that's not there anymore!' she exclaimed.

Randolph thought for a second. 'If Jack is truly possessed by Aloysius, then if anyone can bring that place back, it'll be him. If my calculations are correct you should still have a small time-window before it becomes unreachable again.'

'But how the hell am I meant to make him do that?'

'I'm sure you can be very persuasive,' he said with the same annoying grin on his face.

Jennifer laughed. She knew this wasn't going to be easy, but it was getting harder by the second. 'I'm never going to get him all the way from that mountain back to that city.'

Randolph shook his head. 'First-timers normally arrive in one of several easily reachable locations, but now you've come and gone, you should have more control next time. Focus hard on the city of Orlath – try and see it clearly in your mind when you go to sleep.'

'But what if that doesn't work?'

'Then you'll have a long walk in front of you.'

'Okay,' said Jennifer with a sigh. 'Then what?'

'You'll need to force the spirit out of Jack's body and back into his own.'

'An exorcism?'

'Not unless you're Catholic. But it's the same idea.'

Jennifer thought for a second. 'What if I get him back to the dream world and then wake him up. Won't just Jack return then?'

Randolph shrugged. 'Maybe, maybe not. Now that whoever has possessed Jack has returned here, he may be more grounded in our reality. Also, we don't know for sure that Jack – the real Jack – is still in that body. You may just get back an empty shell. Do you want to take that chance?'

'And if I get Jack's – what would it be... His mind? His *soul*? – back into his old body?'

'Then run,' he said. 'Get Jack and run like hell.'

Jennifer sighed. 'This isn't going to be easy, is it?'

'No.' The answer was brief, but honest.

'Okay,' said Jennifer. 'Talk to me about performing an exorcism. How am I meant to do that?'

'I have some ideas – but some of them you're not going to like.'

Jennifer swallowed. 'Okay, talk to me.'

'Firstly, the most important thing you can do is to convince the spirit to leave his body. Talk with him, bargain with him, convince him it's in his own best interest. If you can do that, you're laughing.'

'And how am I meant to do that?'

'Well, I'd look to either make Jack's body less hospitable, or give him a better option – a better body.'

'And by less hospitable you mean...?'

'You could break some limbs, amputate some even. Drug him... bleed him out. Imprison him somewhere where he can't escape – bury him alive.'

Jennifer shook her head in disbelief. 'That all sounds rather dangerous to Jack. If I do all this to him in the dreamlands, will it have a permanent effect on him when he wakes up again?'

Randolph shrugged. 'It's hard to say, but definitely possible. While physical effects in the dreamlands don't normally remain with you when you return, psychological effects definitely can. I did say you may not like it. It's always possible the threat itself may be good enough, it depends on how good you are at bluffing.'

'Okay, let's call that plan B. What else have you got?'

'Offer him another body – a better body.'

'So I have to sacrifice somebody else?'

Randolph looked her in the eyes. While he often had the manner of a charismatic and jovial politician, he looked colder and more ruthless now.

'You're going to have some difficult choices ahead of you, Jennifer. You are going to have to decide exactly what's important to you and just how far you're willing to go.'

Jennifer sighed. Did she have it within herself to sacrifice someone else, an innocent party, in order to save Jack? That would make her no better than Randolph.

'I'm not willing to put someone else in danger, to sacrifice their life for Jack's,' she decided.

Randolph shrugged, as if she had just told him she didn't fancy going out for a drink tonight. 'Then you're back to plan B.'

Jennifer sighed and nodded towards the bundle wrapped in brown paper on the table. 'So what's in the package?'

'That?' said Randolph. 'That's my lunch.'

Chapter 40.

December 31st, 2012. Dartmoor, England.

Jennifer was standing in the darkness behind their house, looking through the kitchen window. She cautiously grasped the handle of the back door and gave it a gentle twist. The handle turned in her hand, and she pushed the door ajar. With a deep breath, she opened the door wide enough to slip through, and then quietly pushed it shut behind her.

The house was deathly quiet; she could hear no signs of activity, although many of the lights were still on. The lights in the kitchen were off, although there was enough light spilling in through the open door to the hallway for her to see by. On the kitchen table sat a bottle of red wine, half drunk with the cork stuffed back in the end. She tiptoed over to it and picked it up, removing the cork. It smelled like a good wine and she checked the label; it was a good wine. It would be a perfect choice for giving Jack the drug.

From her pocket, she pulled a small plastic vial containing the sedatives that Randolph had given her. She unscrewed the lid of the vial, removed the cork from the wine and then hesitated. She considered saving some in case she needed a second attempt, but then remembered how Jack had acted before. *Better safe than sorry*, she thought to herself. She tipped all the white powder inside the bottle, before reinserting the cork and giving it a gentle shake to remove any trace of powder from the neck and to help it dissolve.

When all visible traces of the powder were gone, she headed for the hallway. Her next step was to find Jack, play nice and convince him to drink the wine. *One step at a time*, she told herself. First she checked downstairs, looking in the living room, games room and then the study; he wasn't there. Next, she headed up the stairs – maybe he had already gone to bed?

As she reached the top of the stairs, she hesitated, sensing movement from the master bedroom.

She swallowed. Her heart was racing and her palms sweaty; she wiped them on her hips. 'Jack?' she called quietly. 'I've come to apologize. I think I over-reacted.'

She pushed the door gently and stepped into the bedroom. It was dark, with the lights off and the curtains closed, but she was certain that there was no one in the bed. She stepped to her left, towards the light switch. As she did so, Jack silently emerged from the darkness behind the door.

Jennifer flicked the switch, bathing the room in a soft light. She turned back around, and jumped as she saw Jack standing in front of her. 'Jesus!' she cried.

'No, only me,' growled Jack. He stepped forwards, his fist swinging towards her. She instinctively tried to duck, but wasn't fast enough to dodge the blow; his fist made contact with the side of her head, sending her reeling. The wine bottle fell from her hands, hitting the floor and rolling away into a corner. She staggered backwards, the room spinning before her eyes. Her legs made contact with the bed, and she fell back onto it.

All she could see was the bright light on the ceiling, spinning before her eyes and making her feel queasy; she briefly closed her eyes to try and compose herself. She was desperately trying not to panic; she hadn't expected this to turn violent, at least not so suddenly.

Then she felt something grab both her wrists and pull them apart, pinning them to the bed. She opened her eyes to see Jack's face pressed up close to hers, a sick leering smile on his face. She looked into his eyes; they were wild and darting, the eyes of a maniac. She struggled as hard as she could, trying to wrest her hands free, but couldn't – he was just too strong.

'Oh, no, you're not getting away this time,' he whispered in her ear. 'Not until I've finished with you.' He started to run his tongue up the side of her cheek and then suddenly stopped, an expression of pain on his face; Jennifer had brought her knee up violently, striking him in the groin. The grip on her wrists lessened, and she ripped them free, rolling away from underneath him. She dropped onto the floor and was scrabbling towards the doorway on her hands and feet when she was grabbed by the ankle. She kicked out with her other foot, hitting only air. She kicked again, this time hitting some part of him. There was a grunt of pain and her foot was released; she crawled away, faster this time, making it through the doorway onto the landing.

She had only just clambered to her feet when Jack smashed into her, trying to grab her from behind. He snatched at her hair, and she twisted away, stumbling sideways. Her back foot came down and missed the top step; for what felt like a long moment, she wavered, trying desperately to regain her balance, but it was no good. She fell backwards, her back smashing against the wooden banister. She fell sideways, dragged downwards by gravity, and continued to fall, tumbling down the stairs uncontrollably until the back of her head slammed into a step. She just had time to see a hazy image of Jack standing at the top of the stairs, silhouetted against the light behind him, before she slipped into unconsciousness.

Jennifer opened her eyes to see a dim room all around her. Her head was throbbing with pain and her vision was blurry, but she could recognize the ceiling of her bedroom once more. The lights were turned off, but some light was still sneaking in around the frame of the closed door. Everything was silent.

She was groggy and in pain, but it didn't take her long to realize that she had been restrained, her hands and feet tied to the bed; she couldn't see with what. Then, out of the corner of her eye, she saw something in the corner of the room, movement from deep in the shadows.

'What have you done to me, you bitch?' came a low angry whisper.

She craned her head as much as she could to look at him. He was standing, but staggering from side to side as if drunk. In his right hand he held a long kitchen knife and in his left an open bottle of wine. It was hard to tell in the dim light, but it looked almost empty.

'You never could hold your drink,' she chuckled. She knew it wasn't wise to antagonize him when she was in this position, but she couldn't help herself.

He lifted the bottle up to look at it and then threw it at the wall, uttering a scream of almost primal rage. The bottle hit the wall above the bed, shattering into dozens of pieces, causing Jennifer to flinch as they rained down all around her.

'YOU BITCH!' he screamed again. He took a step towards the bed, the knife outstretched before him, but he staggered, dropping to one knee. 'I'll kill you for this,' he spat, on his knees now and leaning against the bed. It looked like he was struggling to keep his eyes open. 'I'll...' he repeated, and then he collapsed to the floor.

'Shit,' cursed Jennifer under her breath. She had taken care of Jack for now, but sooner or later he would wake. If she was still tied up here when he did... She didn't want to think about it.

She tried pulling on the restraints, but they were bound tight around her wrists. It looked like some kind of cloth strip, knotted around her wrists and the bedposts. As hard as she tried to twist and pull, it made no difference.

She frantically looked around the room, looking for something, anything that could help, when she spotted a shard of broken glass lying on the bed near her left hand. She twisted her wrist, desperately trying to get her fingers to it. She could just about touch it, the glass cold and sharp under her fingertips. She pulled hard on her restraints, edging slightly closer, but still not quite close enough to be able to grab it. She bit her lip, grimacing from the pain in her right wrist and shoulder as she stretched and pulled with all her might; she wondered whether she would dislocate her shoulder, and whether that might actually help. She twisted her hand as much as she could, and managed to get two fingers touching it. She slid them over the smooth glass, trying to slide it towards her until suddenly it caught and jumped towards her with a jerk.

She dropped it, but it didn't matter; it was closer now. She stretched again, and this time she could easily get two fingers to it, slipping one either side. Carefully, she lifted it up, dropping it onto the palm of her hand. She took a few deep breaths – she was making progress, but still had to cut her way out without losing it. She pushed the glass along her palm and managed to grab the glass between thumb and forefinger, holding it out towards the cloth. With some gentle strokes she tried to cut through the material; the glass was sharp and with the cloth pulled tight she found that she could rip the material. Slowly and carefully, desperate not to drop the glass, she began to saw through her bindings.

As she cut further, the remaining cloth became harder and harder to reach, but it was no matter; the damage was done now. With a sharp yank, she pulled at the restraint with all her strength and the remaining material snapped. She was free.

With one hand released, it didn't take her long to undo the other hand and then her feet. She still had a piercing headache and the side of her face was throbbing where Jack had punched her. She stood up, rubbing her wrists, and was overcome with dizziness; she sat straight back down again. Slowly, she tried again – she had to do this, no matter how bad she felt.

She looked down at the unconscious body of Jack on the floor and was overcome with a powerful urge to kick him while he was down. She knew better though; she'd only be hurting Jack, whereas her business was with Aloysius.

She left him lying on the floor while she went back to her car to fetch the rope she had brought with her. As she walked back up the stairs and approached the bedroom door, she momentarily hesitated. *What if he's come round?* she wondered, but he was still there, just as she had left him.

The knife was still lying on the floor next to him – that was stupid of her and she knew it. She picked it up, placing it on the small table next to the bed, and then set to restraining him, tying his hands tightly behind his back. She thought about stuffing one of Jack's socks into his mouth, but thought better of it – she didn't want to risk choking him; with the amount of alcohol he'd drunk, she didn't know if he might throw up.

Once she was certain that he wasn't going to be able to break free, she heaved him up onto the bed. She'd forgotten just how hard it is to move an unconscious body, but eventually she managed it. When she had his head on the pillow, she went over to the bedside cabinet where she had placed the sheet of incantations. She slipped it under the pillow and then lay down beside him. The thought of being so close gave her chills, but she put that to the back of her mind and shuffled up next to him, holding him close to try and ensure that they would both travel to the dream world together. She reached over and picked the knife up from the table, holding it in her hand, and then she closed her eyes and tried to relax.

Sleep came easier than she would have imagined.

Chapter 41.

The Dreamlands

Jennifer found herself in the desert once more, standing before the ruined city of Orlath. The knife was still in her hand and Jack lay at her feet, still unconscious. She checked the rope was still present and that his hands were firmly tied behind his back before she slapped him hard across the face.

He stirred slowly, shaking his head and sluggishly opening his eyes. All the colour from Jack's eyes was gone now – his irises were a deep uniform black. 'You...' he hissed, looking directly at her. He struggled with his bonds, screaming and heaving as he desperately tried to break free, but ultimately his struggles subsided, his shoulders slumping. 'Why are we back here?' he growled. 'What do you want?'

'I want my fiancé back.'

Jack smiled back at her and shook his head. 'You think I'm going back to what I was before? That's not going to happen.'

'We'll see.' She grabbed him by the arm, pulling him to his feet. 'Start walking.'

'Where are we going?'

'Back to the centre of town, back to where you came from.'

Jack gave a brief laugh, but started to walk. They walked in silence, back through city gates and then along the main road; she walked behind him, holding the knife out in front of her.

Jack stopped as they caught sight of the square where Aloysius's temple had been. 'Just what is it you hope to achieve?' he asked with his back still to Jennifer. 'You're no match for me.'

Jennifer chose to ignore him, instead poking him with the tip of the dagger to prompt him to resume. He started walking again, only stopping when they reached the clearing in the centre of the city.

'What now?' he asked.

'On your knees,' commanded Jennifer.

'Or what?'

Jennifer placed the knife against the small of his back, applying gentle pressure – enough to cause discomfort through his clothes but not enough to draw blood. 'I said, on your knees.'

Jack snorted in derision, but capitulated, slowly kneeling down on the floor. 'Now what?'

'Now, you wait,' she said. She sat down several feet behind him and took a few long breaths, steadying her nerves. She cautiously closed her eyes, focusing on the image of Aloysius's temple in her mind. She opened her eyes again; nothing had happened.

She tried to calm her mind, focusing on the temple as hard as she could. In her mind, she could see its shining marble walls and the pillars that stood either side of the large wooden doors. She remembered standing inside, looking up at the domed roof and painted ceiling within, standing on the black stone floor, and focused hard on those memories. She opened her eyes; before her in the middle of the square was the faintest glimmer of a building, a translucent ghostly image that swiftly disappeared before her eyes.

'Shit!' she cursed.

Jack merely laughed. Jennifer stood up and walked around to stand in front of him. She held the knife in her hand, pointing it towards him. 'You're going to help me bring it back,' she said, a grim expression on her face.

Jack smiled back at her. That damned grin was starting to get on her nerves. Jack – her Jack – had never looked so smug and arrogant. 'What makes you think I'm going to do that?' he asked.

'Because I'm the one with the knife,' she replied calmly. She squatted down in front of him, pressing the knife gently into his chest. 'Do it.'

Jack shook his head. 'You're not going to kill your beloved. Not when you think there's still a chance you can get him back.'

'Then there is a chance–'

'–I said that *you think* there's a chance. If you didn't, we wouldn't be here, would we?'

'I said *do it*,' said Jennifer, her voice trembling but more forceful than before. The point of the knife was pressing harder into his chest now, a thin crimson circle appearing in the centre of Jack's white shirt.

'And *I* said *no*,' he replied calmly. He looked down at the knife pressing into him. 'You won't hurt me, only your lover. He's still in here with me, you know. It amuses me how much pain this is causing him.'

'Stop it,' said Jennifer.

'I can hear him screaming when I hurt you, you know,' he whispered. 'Poor little Jack...'

'I said *stop it*.'

'I don't know how you could love such as person,' he sneered at her. 'So weak and pathetic, so– ' He stopped short as Jennifer slapped him hard across the face with the back of her hand.

'Don't you say that – he's twice the man you'll ever be,' she spat at him. She was shaking. The fear within her was growing as she realized that she was starting to lose control of the situation.

'I know him better than you think,' he said in a soft smooth voice. 'All his greatest fears. All his dirtiest secrets. Do you want to know who he secretly lusts after? All those things he thinks about you that he's never said out loud...'

Jennifer held out the knife towards his face. 'I'm warning you,' she snarled. Her hand was trembling.

'Or what?' he snapped back at her. 'You haven't got the guts. Just like your lover... I know all his darkest desires, all the things he wants to do but has never told you. All the women he would rather be with but thinks are out of his reach.' He threw his head back and laughed – a long maniacal laugh. Then his head snapped back and he looked her long in the eyes. 'There's no hope for him now. He is almost gone. You cannot save him, and if you want rid of me, you're going to have to kill us both.'

'No,' she insisted, 'I'm not going to give up on him.'

Jack shrugged his shoulders. 'Too bad for you. The longer you leave it, the stronger I will become. You can't save your lover, and you're not even strong enough to save yourself. Your love for him will be your downfall, and you're too blind to see it.'

Jennifer swallowed and stepped closer, holding the knife to his throat. 'I'll do it,' she said.

'Go on then,' he murmured softly. 'Do it.'

Jennifer gripped the knife harder and looked deep into his eyes.

'Do it,' he urged again, 'if you've got the guts, little woman. DO IT!'

Her hand was shaking with rage as she brought it back, about to strike. Then she stopped. *This is what he wants*, she told herself. He had been controlling the conversation, trying to enrage her. She didn't know why, but this was what he wanted.

'No,' she said softly, taking a step backwards, the rage subsiding. 'I won't do it. I'm better than that.'

'I thought as much,' sneered Jack. He hesitated for a moment and then smiled up at her. 'We should work together, you and I.'

'That's never going to happen.'

'Not long ago, you would have said that about Randolph,' teased Jack. 'You managed to put aside your differences there.'

'That was different. That was to help Jack, not to betray him.'

'Oh, how easy it is for you to rationalize your decisions after the fact.' He took a moment to look her up and down.

'You should be with me, not him,' said Jack. 'The places I could take you... The adventures I could give you... I could show you treasures beyond your wildest dreams and fulfil your most carnal desires. I could take you to worlds you can scarcely imagine.'

Jennifer didn't have to think twice. 'No,' she said calmly, although her hands were still shaking with rage and anxiety.

'Too bad,' said Jack, shrugging. With no warning, he thrust upwards, flying into Jennifer and knocking her backwards, the knife flying from her hands and skittering across the floor. She fell back onto the ground, banging her head against the rough dirt and then Jack landed on her, knocking the wind out of her.

She struggled to push him off as he straddled her waist, one leg to either side of her to stop her rolling away. Jennifer had her hands in front of her, her palms digging into his chest and her muscles straining, but even with his hands tied behind his back, the combination of his weight and strength was proving too much for her.

His face was pressing down close to hers, and she could feel his hot breath on her skin, so close she could smell the scent of wine on his breath. She continued to try and push him away, not giving up as he edged nearer, a sickening leering grin on his face, spit dripping from his mouth onto her face. His head drew closer, and she was half expecting him to kiss her when their foreheads touched; there was a spark and a shock leapt through her skin. A burning white light enveloped her, and then all she saw was blackness.

Chapter 42.

Jennifer opened her eyes to find herself standing in a room; an old English living room that felt vaguely familiar. There was an old green sofa sitting on top of a threadbare carpet. Faded wallpaper was peeling from the walls. A chunky old black and white television sat in the corner, some old show that she couldn't recognize playing in silence. Through the window, she could see a uniformly grey sky. With a gasp, she realized where she was: the living room of her parent's house from when she was an infant.

Standing in front of her was an old man, dressed in purple flowing robes, his thin grey hair cut short. Looking at his face, she could see the same black eyes she had seen in Jack. This was surely Aloysius.

'Where are we?' she asked.

'This is your subconscious.'

Jennifer looked around her. 'Why here? I haven't thought about this place in years... *decades*.'

Aloysius shrugged. 'It's probably somewhere you associate with feeling safe. Somewhere for you to run to, with your tail between your legs.'

'So... you're in my mind with me?'

Aloysius nodded. 'I thought we should talk on a more even footing. I must say, it's amazing how you can cope with something so small.'

Jennifer felt sick – she felt *violated*.

'Get out of here!' she shouted at him.

Aloysius shook his head. 'Not until we've dealt with the situation between us. You want me to leave Jack, but...' he chuckled to himself. 'That's not going to happen.'

'I'm giving you one last chance,' she said, sounding much braver than she felt.

'Or what? You're not going to get rid of me without killing Jack, and I know you're not going to risk hurting him.'

'Are you sure? Are you willing to risk your life on that?'

'You can't lie to me,' he said with a leery grin. 'In here with you, I can sense your feelings and emotions. I can even sense your future.'

'You can't be serious?'

'Oh, I can assure you, my powers of prophecy are real. Would you like to know your future, Jennifer? I can tell you so much, and all you have to do is to walk away, to leave me here. You can keep the house, the money, the possessions – all I need is this body.'

Jennifer shook her head. 'I don't want any of that – all I want is Jack.'

Aloysius shrugged. 'Then I will destroy you. Take your mind to pieces bit by bit from the inside.'

To his surprise, Jennifer smiled back at him. 'I don't think so. I think I'm slowly starting to understand what's going on here. If you could attack me here, you already would have, while you had the element of surprise. No – I don't think you can possess just anyone, I think there are only certain people you can control, probably just your relatives and descendants. That's why there was that barrier at your temple – you didn't want just anyone to find you, you needed it to be one of your heirs.'

'That's not true,' snarled Aloysius. 'I'll give you one last chance to surrender...'

'You have no power over me here,' she replied. 'In fact...' She stepped forwards so she was directly in front of him. 'Get out of here,' she whispered, and swung her right fist at him. The attack caught him by surprise, her fist connecting with his chin. He flew backwards, and as he hit the floor he just faded. Then the rest of the room faded too.

Jennifer found herself back in the city of Orlath again, lying on her back facing the sky. Jack was lying next to her. She clambered to her feet quickly, grabbing the knife from where it lay in the dirt.

She knew now what she had to do, or at least she hoped she did. If she was wrong, Jack would pay a terrible price. He was starting to come around too, climbing to his knees with a grunt. She stepped behind him, planting her foot into his back and kicking him back into the dirt. She knelt down, pushing her knee into the small of his back, pulling his bound hands upwards as far as they would go and receiving a cry of pain in return.

She took hold of his left hand and looked at it – he was still wearing the ring given to them by Randolph. She pulled his ring finger up, but when she tried to pull the ring from it, nothing happened; the ring was on tight. She bent forwards, looking closer; it wasn't just tight, it was actually fused into the skin.

Jack laughed. 'That ring isn't going anywhere,' he spat, saliva flying into the dirt.

Jennifer looked around her. She leant over and picked up a smooth flat stone, sliding it under his hands.

'What are you doing?' he barked, fear and uncertainty audible in his voice.

Jennifer took a deep breath. She really hoped she knew what she was doing. With her left hand, she pushed his hand down onto the stone and then with her right, she brought the knife down, just above the knuckle of his ring finger. She pushed with all her might and heard a sickening crack as the knife chopped through the finger, separating it from his hand. It rolled to the floor, the ring falling from the finger as it hit the dirt, no longer joined to the flesh.

'You crazy bitch!' screamed Jack in a fit of rage. 'I'll kill you, you stupid whore!' Blood was pumping from the severed joint on his hand, turning his back crimson.

Jennifer rolled him onto his back. Jack's blood was on her clothes, but she ignored it. 'I don't think so,' she whispered between clenched teeth. 'You won't be hurting anyone anymore.' She shut her eyes and took a deep breath. When she opened them, she leant right in to Jack, so their faces were almost touching. There was a look of panic in his eyes now. 'You need that ring. When we originally left this place, you insisted on wearing it – you *needed* it to return within him. Without that ring, you're powerless to stay in that body if Jack leaves here.'

With that, she thrust the knife into Jack's torso with all her might, piercing through his ribcage into his chest. His eyes opened wide in shock and horror and then he howled a guttural scream of rage and fury, fine droplets of blood flying from his mouth. His arms gave one final strain against his bonds and then he collapsed, his head slumping to the sandy floor.

Jennifer collapsed next to him. She turned and looked into Jack's lifeless eyes; they were no longer black but his natural blue again. She began to shake and then to weep uncontrollably. *Oh God*, she pleaded to herself, *please let me have done the right thing*. As she lay there, Jack's body slowly started to fade, until all that was left were some marks in the sand. Even the blood was gone.

Jennifer stood up, wiping the tears from her eyes with her sleeve. Then she saw something lying on the floor, glinting in the sunlight. She bent over and picked up the ring. She started to pull her arm back, about to throw it into the rubble of a great building, when she stopped. The ring had caused immense grief, but it could also be of great use here. She hoped she would never have to return to these lands again, but with their misfortune... who knew? She wasn't going to wear it anytime soon though; instead she slipped it into her pocket.

Her tears were still flowing freely as she walked over to a pile of rubble and sat down on a rock. She lay back and looked up at the clear sky above, waiting for the tears to stop.

Chapter 43.

December 31st, 2012. Dartmoor, England.

Jennifer awoke with a start to find Jack shaking her. Tears were streaming down his face.

'Are you okay?' he asked frantically.

'Never mind me, what about you?' she asked in return.

'I'm fine, I think,' he said. He held up his left hand; there was a red scar on his ring finger. 'It hurt like hell when I awoke a few moments ago, but it's just a dull throb now.'

Jennifer wrapped her arms around him and squeezed hard. 'My God, I'm so glad to have you back. The *real* you.'

Jack wrapped his arms around her too, nuzzling his face into her hair. 'How did you know what to do?' he whispered in her ear.

'I was fairly certain that he'd made it back here only by the power of that ring, the one that allowed you to bring things back from the dream world. When I had the knife to his – *your* – throat and he dared me to kill you.... It struck me that he *wanted* me to kill you. If you died there with the ring on, you'd both return here, but never be able to return. I'd never have been able to force him out. I wasn't one hundred per cent sure, but...'

'That's one hell of a gamble.'

She pulled away from him slightly and looked him in the face. 'If I wasn't able to get him out of you, then killing you both was probably the best I could have hoped for. I wasn't going to let him murder you and then walk around in your body, desecrating your memory.'

Jack nodded solemnly at her and his tears started to flow again. 'I'm so sorry for what I... he... *we* did to you Jennifer. All that time, I could see what was going on. It was like being in a dream where you have no control over your actions. I'm just...'

Jennifer took his head and held it against her chest to comfort him. 'I'd say I forgive you, but there's nothing to forgive,' she whispered to him. 'It wasn't you.'

'But it was. I can remember what I did to you. I can remember everything.'

'No,' she said simply. 'It wasn't. If I thought even for a second that it was, would I still be willing to marry you?'

'Then we're still...?'

'Of course.'

They sat there on the bed, silently cradling each other in their arms for several minutes. It was eventually Jennifer who broke the silence.

'Was it worth it?' she asked quietly. 'Did you find what you were after?'

'I'm not sure,' he said. 'That remains to be seen.'

Jennifer was lying in bed next to Jack the next morning, the sun streaming through the windows; it looked like it was going to be a nice day. It was the start of a new year, and she was ready to put the past behind them and concentrate on their future. That thought made her wonder for a moment. 'So, do you suppose he really could see the future?' she asked as she ran her fingers through Jack's hair.

'Aloysius? I think he could to some degree, or at least his dream self could.' He turned to face Jennifer. 'When he was in me, he could read my thoughts and emotions, but a bit of that went both ways.'

'You mean you could read his mind?'

'I wouldn't go that far. There were certain thoughts and memories that came to me, well, like dreams. I think those were *his* memories.'

'And he *could* see the future?'

'I don't think it's as simple as that. When he got inside my mind – and yours too, I suppose – I think he was able to see inside us. If he could see inside our minds, maybe he could extrapolate what may happen to us. Or he may have actually been psychic – I just don't know.'

'Okay... but that doesn't really explain the prophecies made hundreds of years ago.'

'Something happened to Aloysius all those years ago – the *real* Aloysius.' Jack scratched his head. 'It's all a bit hazy.'

'If it's something you'd rather not...'

'No – it's not that, it's just not all that clear.' Jack gave a brief chuckle. 'I suppose it's like waking from a dream that you can't properly recall – it all seemed so vivid just a short time ago, but now it's little more than fragmented visions and emotions.' He closed his eyes and took a deep breath, exhaling slowly. 'He came to the dreamlands to search for something – something of great power. He was captured and banished from those lands, never able to return – but something went wrong with the banishing. His real self and his dream self were split apart, living separate and independent lives from that point.'

'Okay...' said Jennifer, a bemused look on her face.

'I don't know for certain, but maybe there was a link between them all that time. Randolph said that Aloysius only started getting prophecies after he was banished – that fits with the two of them being separate but still interconnected somehow.'

'You think... what? He got the prophecies from his dream self?'

Jack nodded. 'The people he came into contact with, the experiences he had. If he could get into people's minds, maybe he *could* see their future. We know he lived – or survived anyway – until recently. Maybe some of his dream experiences filtered through to his real self.'

'That's a lot of maybes.'

'It does tie up with what we know, though,' said Jack. 'We were the last people to interact with his dream self, and we're among the last of the prophecies. It fits.'

'So... No more dream-Aloysius... No more prophecies.'

'We can only hope so.'

'And Aloysius's Legacy... the orb that Randolph took. Do you have any idea what that was?'

'I'm not sure, but it felt important to him – like he had some kind of connection with it. When he held it in his hand, it felt unusually heavy, even for metal – and warm too.'

'Warm?'

'But that wasn't the oddest thing. When he focussed on it, it was as if nothing else in the world was real. For a moment, everything around him seemed to slow down and become dull and muted – almost like watching a movie in slow motion. Whatever it was, I don't think he wanted to leave it to anyone but himself; he was angry as hell when he had to hand it over to Randolph.'

'Maybe we'll never know.'

'With any luck...' he said with a wry smile.

Chapter 44.

January 4th, 2013. Dartmoor, England.

Jack was just sitting down to dinner when the phone rang; it was Detective Inspector Cross.

'I hope I haven't caught you at a bad time,' she said.

'No, not at all,' said Jack, looking at his food on the table, which was already starting to grow cold. He held up his hand to Jennifer to indicate this could take a while and gave a little shrug. 'How can I help you?'

'I'm just ringing to update you. With your assault, running the prints, you know.'

'Oh that.' With everything else that had gone on, Jack had completely forgotten about that. 'What did you find?'

'A lot more than I bargained for,' said Cross.

'What do you mean?' asked Jack. 'Did you find him?' He picked up a glass of red wine from the table and took a sip.

'I didn't find the man who was in your car, or the man who assaulted you, but in the process, I did track down a whole heap of trouble.'

'Like what?'

'You may find this hard to believe...'

'Try me,' chuckled Jack. 'You'll find I'm surprisingly open-minded.'

Cross took a moment to gather her thoughts before she resumed. 'I went back to see Peter White in hospital, and saw someone who matched your description of the man who attacked you. He ran and I chased him. One thing led to another and I ended up at a scene of... well, it was a cross between a torture and a ritual sacrifice. Then *that* led to the scene of the biggest massacre I've ever seen in my professional career. I saw things that night that...' she sighed. 'I'm no longer exactly sure what I did see that night. We arrested a man who I thought was behind it. He managed to kill a dozen people to get to what he wanted, without getting a drop of blood on him.'

Jack felt a cold chill creep across his flesh. 'Who was this guy?'

'We still don't know for certain – the identity he originally gave us turned out to be fake. It's the damnedest thing – he disappeared out of his cell while sleeping, without leaving a trace. We wouldn't have a clue who he was if it wasn't for a survivor – someone he left for dead who managed to give us a name.'

'Who was he?' Jack asked again, but he feared he already knew the answer.

'We think his name might have been Randolph.'

Jack froze. 'Do you know what it was that he was after?'

Cross was silent for a moment. 'I don't know for certain,' she said in a distant voice. 'But I did see something being taken away. Some kind of metallic ball – about three inches across.'

Jack's wine glass slipped from his fingers, dropping to the floor and smashing into a thousand pieces. He didn't know what they were, but Randolph had at least two of them now. He had told them it wasn't dangerous, but you don't take the lives of a dozen men to get hold of something that's purely symbolic. He felt a deepening knot in the base of his stomach. Whatever these orbs were, they were important to him, and he and Jennifer had taken him straight to another one.

'No,' said Cross, carrying on. 'We don't really know the first thing about him, except for that name. We've got his photo and prints if we ever run into him again, but...'

Jack contemplated telling her that they knew where he had lived, but he didn't think it would be much use. He and Jennifer had returned there to find the place deserted, no indication that anyone had lived there in years.

Wherever he was now, Jack was sure he would remain hidden until such time as he was ready to reveal himself again. Besides which, it would be hard to explain just how they knew so much about him.

'What about the other man you arrested at the Necropolis? Have you managed to squeeze any information out of him?'

There was another long sigh from the other end of the line. 'Another dead end there too. He was found dead in his cell – some kind of brain embolism. As far as we can tell, it was natural causes, but well... with everything else, I just don't know any more.'

'So where does that leave your investigation?' asked Jack with a resigned shrug of his shoulders.

'It leaves us precisely nowhere. All I've got out of this is more questions – and a boss who's now questioning my sanity.'

'So what do I do now?'

'I suggest you try and put it behind you and get on with your lives. If you're looking for closure, I'm afraid I'm not going to be able to supply it.'

It was two days later, and Jack was sitting in the study, the book of Aloysius's prophecies lying open on his lap.

Several sheets of paper had been inserted between the pages of the book where Peter had translated the final prophecies for him, and he had been going through it again and again, trying to make some kind of sense of it all. He had looked at those pages and read through Peter's translations a dozen times and still had found nothing to make him any wiser about Jennifer's death.

He closed the book with a *snap* when the phone rang. He stood up, placing the book onto his desk. 'Jack Knight,' he said, picking up the phone and speaking into it.

'Hello, Mr Knight,' came the sound of Randolph's voice. In the background, Jack thought he could hear sounds of construction and far-away voices in a language he didn't recognize.

'You lied to me,' said Jack. 'There was nothing in that book about Jennifer's death.'

'You don't beat around the bush, do you?' replied Randolph. 'But you're wrong. On the final page, there was a prophecy referring to a child.'

Jack thought for a second. 'There was the prophecy about the son of two soldiers, but surely that refers to you?'

'No,' said Randolph simply. 'You need to brush up on your Latin. Not the child of two *soldiers*, but the child of two *Knights*; you, Mr Knight, and your wife to be. Your child will be raised by the Brotherhood. He is destined to lead us into a new era, and when he comes of age he will return to kill his own mother. You will not be able to save your wife, Mr Knight, unless you are willing to sacrifice your own child.'

Jack suddenly felt faint and his legs buckled, collapsing him back into his chair. Surely this couldn't be true. Then it struck him. 'Jennifer can't have children,' he blurted into the phone.

'What?'

'Children,' he said. 'We tried before. We even saw a specialist. She's not able to conceive.'

'But...' was all that Randolph could say. For the first time since Jack had met him, he seemed unsure of himself.

'This whole prophecy is a crock,' laughed Jack. 'Everything we went through, and it's all bullshit.'

'No...' said Randolph. 'No. The prophecy must be true. 'If Jennifer cannot have children, then you will marry again in the future. Your second wife, she must be the one–'

'–Admit it,' said Jack, cutting him off. 'You're wrong.'

'No!' exclaimed Randolph, with a force that surprised Jack. 'The prophecy cannot be wrong. It can't.'

'How does it feel to know that your entire life has been for nothing?' laughed Jack.

'At some point in the future, you *will* marry a woman who will bear your child,' said Randolph, regaining his composure slightly. 'It may not be Jennifer, but it *will* happen. It is your *destiny*. That child will belong to the Brotherhood, and we will raise him as one of our own.'

'That's just not going to happen, for so many reasons,' said Jack.

'We had an agreement,' said Randolph. 'You promised to give to the Brotherhood that which is ours – and that child is *ours*.'

'Goodbye, Randolph,' replied Jack simply. 'I trust I won't hear from you or your friends again.' And with that, he pressed the button on his phone to end the call. He shook his head in disbelief, putting the phone back on the desk.

He felt as if a large weight had been lifted from his shoulders. He was free. It may have all been for nothing, but Jennifer was not going to die prematurely after all. Things were looking up.

Epilogue.

Six weeks later. February 12th, 2013. Exeter, England.

It was the morning of the wedding and Jennifer was at Lauren's house getting ready for the ceremony. She had spent the night there with Lauren and was now going through the final preparations for her big day.

'Oh my God,' said Jennifer. 'I can't believe it's here already – it's come around so quickly.'

'Not that quickly,' said Lauren. 'You *have* been together for ten years.'

'Not that – it's only been a couple of months since we got engaged.'

'It's been a busy few weeks,' Lauren agreed. She looked closely at Jennifer; there was an odd expression on her face. 'How are you feeling?' she enquired.

'Nervous. *Really* nervous. I've got serious butterflies in my stomach.'

'You're not having second thoughts, are you?'

'Oh no,' she said. 'Nothing like that. I'm just feeling a bit queasy.'

Lauren looked her in the face. 'Are you okay? You do look a little pale.'

'No...' said Jennifer, standing up and running to the bathroom. 'I think I'm going to be sick.'

She made it into the bathroom just in time, bending over and throwing up in the toilet. 'At least I'm not in my wedding dress yet,' she muttered under her breath. 'Now wouldn't that be a pretty sight, vomit all down the front of my dress.'

She stood up and flushed the toilet, running the tap and filling the sink with cold water to wash her face. She opened the cabinet looking for something to wash her mouth out when she saw something else that made her stop. She stood looking at it for several long moments before she made a decision.

Three hours later, Jennifer and Lauren pulled up outside the registry office in a vintage chauffeur-driven Rolls Royce. It may have been a small wedding, but Jack had spared no expense on the details. Lauren opened her door, jumping out and running round to help Jennifer out with her dress.

Together, Lauren holding the trail of her dress off the floor, they walked into the building and through the large double doors to the hall; Jack was standing at the front of the room with the registrar. Neither of them had any parents any more, but all their close friends and family were here, smiling and looking at Jennifer as she entered; even Jennifer's sister had made the effort to come back over from America for the occasion.

A wide smile on her face and a glow in her cheeks, Jennifer walked up the aisle between the seats, stopping when she got to Jack.

She turned to the registrar and held up a finger. 'Can I just have *one moment*?' she asked. The registrar looked slightly confused, but nodded back in agreement. Jennifer turned to Jack, taking both of his hands in hers.

'You look beautiful,' he said to her.

Jennifer smiled. She moved in close to him, speaking in hushed tones. 'Before we do this, there's something you need to know.'

A worried expression spread across Jack's face. 'Oh God, what is it? What's wrong?'

'Nothing's wrong. Or at least I hope not. It's just...'

'What?'

'I'm pregnant.'

'What? Are you *sure*?' A look of shock had spread across Jack's face.

'I took a pregnancy test at Lauren's this morning.'

'They can be wrong...'

She shook her head. 'I don't think so, not this time.'

'But how did this happen? *How*? I thought you couldn't...'

'I think it was six weeks ago when we were in the dreamlands. I'm guessing you weren't the only one who brought someone else back with them.'

'But...' was all Jack could say. His face had turned as white as a ghost.

'Oh God,' said Jennifer, suddenly panicked. 'Tell me you're okay with this. I did do the right thing in telling you, didn't I?'

'Yes... Yes, of course you did,' he said, regaining his composure slightly. 'And I couldn't be happier – *honestly*.'

'Well, you've got a funny way of showing it,' she said. She took a step backwards, letting go of his hands.

'Shall we begin?' asked the registrar.

Jack looked at Jennifer. It was all going to come true. Aloysius had been right after all. His wife was destined to be killed by their own child. But Jack knew something else. If there was anyone who would be able to save her, anyone who would be willing to do whatever needed to be done, it would be him.

He turned to the registrar. 'Let's do this,' he said.